Expectations

A Novel

Expectations

TONI V. LEE

TRUSTED
BOOKS
A DIVISION OF DEEP RIVER BOOKS

© 2007 by Toni V. Lee. All rights reserved.
2nd Printing 2014.

Trusted Books is an imprint of Deep River Books. The views expressed or implied in this work are those of the author. To learn more about Deep River Books, go online to www.DeepRiverBooks.com.

Unless otherwise indicated, Bible quotations are taken from the New King James version of the Bible. Copyright © 1979, 1980, 1982 by Thomas Nelson, Inc. Used by permission. All rights reserved.

ISBN 13: 978-1-63269-135-4
Library of Congress Catalog Card Number: 2006910062

Dedication

I n loving memory of my mother, Ira Bell Ford, who was the inspiration
for the character Aunt Lenore.

Acknowledgments

Special thanks to my mentor, Louise Gouge, whose friendship and advice are priceless. I'll always be grateful that the Lord allowed our paths to cross.

Many thanks to Carolyn Carter, Gloria Martinez, and Arlene Rashy for volunteering their critiquing service. Thank you for the encouragement you gave me when you demanded to have the next chapter, so you could find out what was going to happen next!

Thank you, Laura Kittleson, for your help with the Festival of Nations, and for introducing me to Louise.

Thank you, Ronald L. Sims, P.A., for the crash course in Florida law as it pertains to living trusts and guardianships.

Thank you, Phylena McCall, R.N., for your invaluable medical advice.

Thanks, Brad Smith, for answering my numerous guy questions.

Thank you, Brandon Lee, Vera Bolden, Gwendolyn Floyd, Beatrice Jackson, Vanessa McCall, Faith Assembly CIC, and a host of others for believing in me.

Chapter One

Tired and feeling more than a little sorry for herself, Daria Simpson moaned her relief when she walked into her air-conditioned home. After walking from her office building to her car in Orlando, Florida's sweltering heat, her blouse stuck to her back.

The fifteen-minute drive home from her job at the university wasn't long enough for the car's air conditioner to do much good.

Daria flung her briefcase into the nearest leather armchair and dropped a printed copy of the computer program—which had given her fits all day—onto a mahogany end table.

She kicked off her pumps and unbuttoned her suit coat as she crossed the living room and headed down the hall toward the bedroom to undress.

When she entered the room, her favorite fragrance, *Morning Glory*, floated around her. The familiar scent gave her some comfort, but not nearly enough.

Okay, here we go again. It's Friday night, and all is the same—no date! One of these days, I'm going to have a life, she thought as she rummaged through her dresser drawers.

"Ah, there you are. You're just what I need right now." She buried her face in her favorite ratty old t-shirt before slipping it on. Pulling on a pair of baggy shorts, she stopped to look in the mirror that hung over her cherry wood dresser. She ran her fingers through her black, highlighted, shoulder-length hair, and then smirked at her reflection. *Girl, you look like you're having a serious bad hair day.*

She pursed her lips, making her high cheekbones—a much-appreciated gift from a Blackfoot ancestor—stand out. "I'm not all that, but I'm not exactly canine either. So what's the problem?" Dark brown eyes stared back at her quizzically.

Lord, why is it taking You so long to send me a man? I'm trying to wait patiently and contentedly for You to send me somebody, but it's just taking sooooooo long.

The doorbell rang, startling Daria.

"I wonder who that could be?" she muttered as she walked barefoot across the beige carpet in the hall.

The doorbell rang again, followed by rapid pounding. A quick peek through the security hole showed her neighbor from the other side of her entryway.

She jerked back. *What's he doing here?*

During the three months he'd lived in her condominium complex, they'd exchanged smiles and waves when their paths crossed, but he'd never sought her out before.

She snorted. Sought her out? He'd never stood still long enough for her to find out his name or any other important information such as marital status, current employment, number of dependents, soul status, church affiliation, and an approximate income range.

She peered through the security hole again.

A frown marred his dark, chocolate-brown face. He kept glancing back over his shoulder.

His strong, square jaw flexed as he knocked again.

She placed her hand on the doorknob, then snatched it back. *Oh no, why'd he have to come to my door now? He'll take one look at me and run for the hills.*

Daria quickly tried to smooth her mussed hair before opening the door. "Hi. May I—"

He pushed his way inside.

"Hey, what do you think you're doing?" Daria watched his every move as she backed up toward her kitchen.

He immediately closed the door, set his briefcase on the floor, and dashed to her living room window. He peered out at the sidewalk that led to their recessed entrance, and then turned to face her.

If he tries anything, he's going to be sorry. Thank you, Aunt Lenore, for dragging me to that self-defense class.

She started to rehearse self-defense moves in her head.

Knees spread slightly apart. Wait. No. Not that far apart—shoulder width to maintain balance.

Get centered.

Arms raised. Not high enough. There, at the hips.

Fists clenched. Turn them over. No, the other way.

Okay, finally she was ready for his next move.

When she looked at him, he laughed.

I'm ready to do him bodily harm, and he's standing there laughing at me!

Daria couldn't decide if anger or embarrassment heated her cheeks.

He walked slowly toward her with both hands raised, palms out. "Look, my name's Michael, and I'm not going to hurt you. Someone's following me. If you'll give me a few minutes, I'll explain."

Daria searched his face, trying to determine whether she could trust him. For some unaccountable reason, deep down, she felt she could—as much as she could trust any man.

Daria heard rapid footsteps outside on the sidewalk. Giving Michael a wide berth, she moved toward the window and looked out.

A woman scampered by in skintight black jeans and stiletto heels. She stopped at the door across the way, looked around, knocked on the door, and waited a few seconds.

She had long, black silky hair that probably came out of a cellophane wrapper. Her thick lipstick made her lips look too big, instead of just pouty.

"C'mon, boo, open the door. It's me, Shaniqua. We need to talk," the woman called as she knocked on the door again. She tossed her head, let out a big sigh, and placed her right hand on her hip just below the patch of bare skin flashing past the hem of her top.

Uh-oh, she's assuming the pose.

"Uh, boo, there's a very angry woman named Shaniqua knocking on your door," Daria informed her intruder.

Michael rubbed his distinctive round-tip, flared-nostril nose. "That would be the 'someone' who is following me." Frustration and a bit of sheepishness laced his answer.

Daria's jaw dropped. "Do you mean to tell me you barged in here because you're running from a woman?" Her eyes started at his neatly edged black hair, then traveled over his suit-clad form. "You're no light-weight. You've got to be over six feet, yet you're running away from *her*?" Daria pointed her thumb toward the window.

"I wanted to avoid a big scene. Shaniqua can be…" He grimaced. "I'll just say she can be rather vocal at times."

Shaniqua's voice distracted Daria, and she turned back to the window to see what would happen next.

"See, you ain't right. I know you're in there. I followed you here all the way from your job. Open this door right now!"

Each sentence was said with increased volume and neck movement.

"See, you don't know who you're messin' with. Nobody, and I mean *nobody*, kicks Shaniqua Brown to the curb. It ain't over until *I* say it's over. Just so you have the facts straight, I was about to write you off anyway. You know what Shaniqua can do for you, but don't even come running back to me when you start feeling your itch." Shaniqua walked away toward the parking lot, swinging her hips for all she was worth.

Daria looked back at Michael and lifted a brow. He winced and ran a hand across his forehead.

She turned back to the window and watched Shaniqua until she disappeared from view.

Feeling his itch? No, she didn't just yell that out in public. Honey, have a little bit of class. No wonder I don't have a man. Daria shook her head in disgust and shot Michael a disgruntled look. *They're out there hookin' up with women like Shaniqua.* At least now Daria knew Michael wasn't for her. The guy obviously wasn't a Christian.

And until I have a wedding band and a sizable rock sitting on my ring finger, I don't do itches!

Daria turned away from the window. "Unbelievable."

Irritation sparked in Michael's eyes. He ran a hand over his low-cut hair, and then stroked his beard-shadowed jaw. "As you can see, I had a good reason for coming here."

Daria could feel her anger begin to simmer.

He's lived in this complex for three months. Three months! And not once has he come here. Not even for a lousy cup of sugar. The only reason he's here now is because he didn't want to face another woman!

Her anger erupted into a full boil. "A good reason? Let me get this straight. You came here because you didn't want to deal with Shaniqua, right?" She continued before he could respond. "What if she'd seen you entering my place? While you were hatching this crazy plan of yours, did it ever occur to you that you could've put me in danger by bringing her drama to my door? What if she'd been carrying a weapon?"

"I didn't think—" Michael began.

"Yeah, I know you didn't," she retorted.

"Honestly, at the time I didn't think about that. I just wanted to avoid a scene. You're right, and I'm truly sorry. It will never happen again," Michael said.

His contrite look told her he was genuinely sorry.

Daria smiled. "Your apology is accepted, but you've got to answer just one question. Where in the world did you find that woman?"

"Don't go there." He chuckled. "You sound just like Moms and Sis."

She extended her hand. "After all of this, I guess we should introduce ourselves. My name is Daria Simpson."

A smile creased his even-toned face. He clasped her hand in both of his, searched her face, and then stared warmly into her eyes. "I'm pleased to have finally met you, Daria. My name is Michael Greer. I wish we'd met under different circumstances."

He dropped her hand and looked around her living room.

"It looks like the basic layout of your unit is the same as mine: a galley kitchen and breakfast bar—except the window in my living room faces the parking lot."

His eyes paused briefly on her small stereo system. She guessed it didn't have enough gadgets to hold his interest because his attention moved on.

She sensed a change in him and glanced at his face. He was staring at a picture of her and her friend Peaches with a puzzled look. She and Peaches were wearing floppy, oversized hats and mugging for the camera. Peaches' hat had tiny peaches dangling from it. The hats cast shadows over the upper half of their faces.

It really wasn't a very good picture, but it reminded her of the good times they'd shared before things had changed.

He walked over to her fireplace and lifted the picture from the mantle. "Who is she?" He turned slightly and pointed to Peaches.

"That's my best friend, Peaches. Why do you ask?"

"She looks vaguely familiar. I think I've met her somewhere before."

Daria smiled fondly. "Peaches is unforgettable. If you'd ever met her, you'd remember."

Michael replaced the picture and headed for the door.

Daria followed him with good-humored mischief. "You're sure that you can make it home alone? You're not afraid big bad Shaniqua is going to come back and pound you on your way home are you? If you are, let me know, and I'll escort you."

Michael laughed. "Not unless you have better moves than those you demonstrated earlier. By the time you got ready for her, she'd be all over you."

Daria chuckled. "That's what you think. I took a beginner's self-defense class with my aunt. But my girl, Peaches, has taught me how to incorporate some serious street fighting into what I learned. I can do some real damage if I have to."

"This Peaches sounds like a character." Michael picked up his briefcase.

Well, she used to be, Daria thought sadly.

After she closed and locked the door, Daria stepped over to her window and watched Michael as he walked to his door.

She smiled. "He's wearing that suit!" Her smile morphed into a grin. "He may not be for me, but that doesn't mean I can't appreciate the view. Mmm-hmm, he's fine! He looks good coming and going."

Tap. Tap. Tap.

Daria heard her before she saw her.

Michael stood frozen at his door with the key inserted in the lock. He was looking down the sidewalk that led to their entryway.

Daria laughed to herself. "She's baaaaaack."

Michael's shoulders slumped in defeat.

"Why you trippin'? I was sitting right there in my car waitin' for you." Shaniqua pointed in the direction of the parking lot. "I saw you come out of that apartment over there. You heard me out here callin' you." She turned slightly toward Daria's door and pointed. "Who lives over there anyway?"

Shaniqua turned back to Michael when he answered, "It doesn't matter who lives there."

"This is better than a soap opera," Daria said gleefully. "I've got a movie right outside my living room window. All I need now is the popcorn." Daria slowly widened the blinds to give herself a better view. "Humph, if they're going to put on a show in public, I'm definitely going to watch and listen."

"Look, Shaniqua, there's nothing here for you. Please leave," Michael said.

"I ain't goin' nowhere! You ain't the boss of me."

"I don't want to argue with you. We've said everything that we have to say to each other. Please, just go."

Shaniqua stared at Michael for a couple of heartbeats and then made a mercurial change.

"Boo, you know we're good together." Shaniqua ran a long fingertip down Michael's chest and licked her lips suggestively. "Why mess up a good thing?"

He captured her wandering finger and removed it from his chest. "Shaniqua, you're living in the past. When was the last time we were 'a good thing'?"

"'Bout six months ago. And?"

"Six months? She ain't been *doing* no itches either—at least not his," Daria commented from her vantage point.

"Doesn't that tell you something? I don't want that anymore. It just…it just feels wrong. That's all we had. I want more than that." Frustration filled Michael's voice.

"Yeah? Hmm…interesting," Daria said softly.

"But I thought things would change when you moved here from Atlanta. I thought we'd get closer…you know…maybe get married. C'mon, let's go to Jake's and talk over a long cold drink like we used to," Shaniqua cajoled.

Daria's stomach clenched as though she'd been punched. References to bars and drinking caused that reaction sometimes—but not so often anymore. "Breathe, girl. Let it go. Different man. Different circumstances. Just breathe," Daria told herself, as she took several deep breaths, and then refocused on Michael and his lady.

"Get married?!" The horrified look on Michael's face was almost comical. He took a step backward. "I never, *ever* said anything to you to make you think I wanted more from you than what we already had."

Shaniqua's hand flew to her hip. "Oh, so I'm not good enough for you?" she huffed.

"Be honest, Shaniqua. You don't love me. You love my wallet."

The hand made a slow trip down her hip until it dangled at her side. She studied the fingernails on her other hand and shrugged. "Ain't nothin' wrong with a man takin' care of his woman."

"Well, this bank is closed."

Daria chuckled softly. "Ooh, now that's cold."

Shaniqua's right hand flew to her hip and the left started flashing in Michael's face. "All right, be that way. You think you know me, but you don't know me. I'll cut you. You better watch your back." Shaniqua turned and stalked off.

"Whoa! If that girl ain't ghetto, I don't know what is," Daria exclaimed.

Michael shook his head as he watched Shaniqua walk away.

Just when Daria thought he was going to turn and enter his condo, his brown eyes swiveled to her window and pinned her to the spot.

Busted!

Instead of showing embarrassment at having been caught eavesdropping, Daria plastered a big grin on her face and wriggled her fingers at him in a little wave.

Chapter Two

Michael switched on the dishwasher, then wiped down the kitchen counter. He gave his kitchen a final look and grunted his satisfaction before putting the dishcloth away.

He flexed his muscles as he stretched to relieve the tension that had dogged him all day.

Man, what a day! First, I spend all day at work trying to figure out a computer-network glitch, and then Shaniqua stalks me. That girl's enough to stress anybody out!

The telephone rang. Michael dried his hands before going to answer the phone. He checked the caller ID, then lifted the receiver. "Whatsup, David?" With a smile on his face, he sat down in the nearest black, leather chair.

"Hey, man. How's it hangin'?" David Monroe asked with a smile in his voice.

"I'm not complainin'…well, not much anyway. What's goin' on with you?" *Not much with a new Christian, I bet,* Michael thought with a soft snort.

"Workin' hard and prayin' hard."

Michael chuckled. The pre-Christian David would've said, "Workin' hard and playin' hard." Playin' would've been an apt description for his activities, considering their history of drinking and chasing women.

"What do you want?" Michael asked with mock fierceness.

"Hey, don't handle a brother like that. You've been in Florida three months now, and I haven't heard a peep out of you. What's up with that?"

Guilt gnawed at Michael. "I know, man. I'm sorry. I'm just trying to get a handle on things here."

"Get a handle on what? You're living close to your family and an unlimited supply of home-cooked meals. You're making an obscene amount of money, and you had a honey waiting for you when you got there," David scoffed with the ease of a long-time friend. "Are you kiddin' me? I'd trade places with you any day." David paused minutely. "Wait. Wait. Hold up. Let me qualify that. You can keep your honey. Noooo, I don't want her," David finished with a laugh.

Michael made a rough, noisy sound. "Yeah, well, my honey turned out to be vinegar."

"Trouble in paradise?" David paused for a second. "Uh, Michael?"

"What?" Michael grunted.

"Is now a good time for me to tell you I told you so?"

Michael and Shaniqua had met in Atlanta last year while she'd been visiting family in the area. Shortly after they'd started seeing each other, Michael had introduced her to David, who'd been very expressive about the fact that he didn't think very highly of Shaniqua.

"No," Michael snapped jokingly.

"What happened?"

"I broke things off with her, and now she's stalkin' me," Michael said with exasperation.

"Stalkin' you?!" David howled.

"What's so funny? I don't see the comedy in the situation myself. You're not the one who's dealing with her drama."

Restlessness drove Michael into the kitchen. He opened the refrigerator door, and not pausing long enough to really study its contents, he closed the door and moved to the living room window where he stared unseeingly out at the parking lot.

"I'm sorry. I'm sorry." David chuckled without a hint of repentance in his voice. "It's just that you had to know she wouldn't calmly accept that you didn't want to kick it with her anymore. This is Shaniqua we're talking about here. Man, you were too free with your money. She knew she had a good thing."

"Yeah, well, it's over, and she'd better deal with it." Michael migrated to his aquarium.

"Why'd you break it off anyway?"

"It just wasn't happening for me."

"What do you mean, 'It just wasn't happening for me'? What kind of answer is that?"

Michael sprinkled fish food into the tank. "The relationship wasn't going anywhere."

"That didn't used to bother you. So *who* changed? *You* or Shaniqua?"

C'mon, man, don't go gettin' all deep on me.

David had a way of asking questions that caused you to look deeper than you really wanted to.

Michael returned to the chair he'd vacated earlier. "I guess I did. I'm not saying I'm ready to go out and get myself put in lock-down, but I want more than what I had with Shaniqua—partying, drinking, and sex."

David laughed. "Man, only you would describe marriage as being put in lock-down."

Michael snorted. "I don't see you sprintin' to the altar."

"Ah, but see, I'm just waiting to meet the right woman."

"Right."

David laughed. "Have you met any new ladies yet?"

"Funny you should ask. I met my neighbor today." Michael had no intention of telling David how that meeting had come about. David would never let him live it down.

"And? You wouldn't have mentioned the meeting if it didn't hold some kind of significance. What's going on?"

"Nothin'. We've only spoken one time since I've been here."

"Uh-huh. So, what does she look like?"

Michael settled into a comfortable spot in his chair and grinned. "Black female, five-nine, black hair, and brown eyes."

"Okay. I see. You've got jokes. Funny. Now, tell me what the sister *looks* like," David demanded with mock anger.

Michael laughed and rose from the chair. "Okay. Okay. Let's see. Daria—that's her name—looks to be about twenty-eight. She's ho... Uh..." Michael made a circuit around the oak coffee table that sat in the middle of his living room. "She's all that and some. She's not one of those stick ladies. She'd be a pleasing arm full. Just right if ya' know what I mean."

"Michael, saying she's *hot* won't offend me. I'm saved, man—not dead." David chuckled.

Michael laughed. "You caught that, huh?"

"Yep. Bro', that's a pretty detailed description for somebody you've only spoken to once," David remarked dryly.

Michael picked up a small, African statue from an end table. "I said I'd only spoken to her once. I didn't say our paths hadn't crossed before."

"All right. Fair enough. She's a knockout. What's she like? And please tell me she's not another Shaniqua."

Michael laughed and replaced the statue. "No. She's nothing like Shaniqua. I believe she's a business professional. I've seen her leaving every weekday morning around the same time dressed in a business suit and carrying a briefcase."

"Sounds good. Keep talking."

Michael sat on the couch. "She seems to be intelligent."

"Then she's definitely not another Shaniqua," David commented.

Michael chuckled and continued. "She has a good sense of humor. Shaniqua put on a show in front of my door earlier tonight, and Daria witnessed it."

"Man, I can just imagine what a spectacle that was. How did Daria react?"

"She stood at her window and watched. When I caught her, she grinned and waved at me." Michael chuckled appreciatively.

David laughed. "I like the sound of this one. You planning to get with her?"

"No. I've seen her walking to her car with her Bible on Friday nights and Sunday mornings. She's a church girl. You know I don't mess with them." Michael picked up the remote and turned on the stereo. Soft, soulful R&B music crooned from the speakers.

"You're sure about that? You said she's a church girl. I think I can get with her myself. When can I come for a visit?" David's voice held a note of seriousness.

The idea of David and Daria hookin' up didn't sit well with Michael, and he didn't particularly want to examine his reaction too closely to figure out why.

"I'll let you know." Michael's objection reverberated loud and clear through his short answer.

Silence.

"I thought so. Just don't take too long to figure out that you want her."

David knew Michael too well. It'd be a waste of time to try to argue with David. Michael knew his argument would lack conviction anyway.

He thought about the handshake he'd shared with Daria earlier that evening. The jolt of awareness had caught him off guard. To give himself time to recover, he'd started looking around her living room.

The picture of Daria and her friend flashed in his mind.

"Say, do you remember the night we met Fruit Lady?" Michael asked, changing the subject.

David gave a shout of laughter. "Yeah. Man, I haven't thought about that night in a long time. You got stinking drunk." David's laughter trailed off. "That wasn't like you. Something was eating at you. What was going on?"

For days leading up to that night, Michael had felt an overwhelming sense of listlessness and dissatisfaction. He'd started drinking, hoping that each glass would numb those feelings.

"Just trying to enjoy the moment," Michael answered. He hoped David wouldn't probe any further.

"I hear you. Looking back on that night, I'd say we were both struggling with some stuff. If you'll recall, shortly after that, I gave my life to Christ. And you, my brother, went off the deep end and hooked up with Shaniqua." David laughed softly.

Michael shook his head and chuckled. "That was one wild night. I can't even remember what Fruit Lady looked like. All I remember is that she had light skin, hazel colored eyes, and these crazy-looking, dangling peach earrings."

David snorted. "That was her all right. I remember that you got frustrated when she wouldn't tell you her real name. She kept saying, 'Just call me Fruit Lady.'"

Michael laughed softly. "When I asked her where she was from, she'd only tell me that she was from Florida."

"I couldn't figure out why she was being so secretive." David snorted. "She probably didn't know herself. She was as high as a kite. I got tired of her game and left. You never did tell me what happened after I split."

The smile slowly melted from Michael's face.

And I'm not going to tell you now, either. I'll keep my stupidity to myself.

"We talked," Michael answered shortly.

"Now, why do I feel like you're leaving something out?"

"We talked. That's all you need to know."

David chuckled. "Why'd you bring her up, anyway?"

"I saw someone in a picture earlier today that kind of reminded me of Fruit Lady."

"Ah," David said and dropped the subject. "Well, I don't own stock in my telephone company, so I'm going to end this call. But, before I go, I've got some things that I feel compelled to say to you."

Michael silently groaned and lifted his eyes to the ceiling. *He's feeling compelled. Here we go.*

It wasn't often David felt "compelled" but when he did, he made Michael squirm. Michael had been doing enough of that on his own lately and didn't particularly want to go down that road tonight.

"Man, how long are you going to fight to hold on to your discontent?" David asked intensely.

Michael flinched.

David continued. "When are you going to stop running from God and surrender to Him? Man, you're searching for fulfillment in all the wrong places."

Michael's muscles tensed, and he ran his hand over his face and neck.

"Michael, you know what I'm saying is true. You're going to be miserable until you surrender. I've walked in your shoes. I've been where you are. I know what I'm talking about.

Michael shifted in his seat and pinched the bridge of his nose.

"You think about what I've said," David went on. "I'm praying for you, bro'. Keep in touch." David ended the call.

After replacing the receiver, Michael sat with unshed tears burning his eyes. Was he ready to give up...*what?* He couldn't remember what he was struggling to hold onto.

Chapter Three

On Saturday morning, Daria woke up reluctantly to bright Florida sunshine streaming through her bedroom window. Her sleep-filled eyes focused on the alarm clock on the nightstand next to her bed.

Nine o'clock. Hmm, I'd better get a move on if I'm going to get to Aunt Lenore's house on time.

She stretched, yawned, and snuggled deeper in the bed.

Michael Greer.

His smiling face flashed in her mind and stayed there until she dropkicked it out. He wasn't for her, and she refused to waste her time thinking about him.

A sheepish grin put a curve in her cheeks.

But girl, shame the devil and tell the truth. Saved or not, that man looks good!

The telephone on the nightstand rang, interrupting Daria's thoughts. Before reaching for the telephone, she jumped out of the bed. "Hello?" she said, trying to sound alert.

Aunt Lenore's chiding tone flowed into her ear. "Good morning. Daria Alexis Simpson, are you up yet?"

"Yes, Aunt Lenore. I'm up, and how are you this fine morning?" Daria grinned to herself. *Score one for me.*

"As well as can be expected, but never mind all of that. We'll talk when you get here. Now get yourself in gear, because I know you're just getting yourself up out of that bed. If you don't get to Docks Landing early, you won't get any good crabs."

"Yes, I know, and I'll be leaving here soon. I know you like to start eating by one o'clock at the latest. I promise you I'll have the crabs ready by then." Daria laughed because they had this same conversation every Saturday they got together to eat crabs.

Daria's parents, Ralph and Evelyn, were tragically killed in a gun shooting incident when Daria was eight-years-old. Charles and Lenore had taken her in and raised her like she was their own child.

She couldn't wait to tell her aunt about Michael and Shaniqua. She had no idea what her eccentric aunt would say, but she had learned to expect the unexpected when it came to Aunt Lenore.

Two hours later, Daria stood before Lenore's door with a bag of scrabbling crabs at her feet. Before knocking on the door, Daria absorbed the peace and quiet of the little retirement community. Christmas was only 20 miles east of Orlando, but the rural surroundings made her feel like she'd taken a trip deep into the country.

"It's about time you got here," Lenore said after she opened the door for Daria. "What took you so long?"

Lenore Jackson was sixty-eight years old. She was small in stature, but her dignity and poise more than made up for her diminutive height. She had a heart of gold, but she had no qualms whatsoever about speaking her mind.

"Aunt Lenore, it's only eleven o'clock. I made good time." Daria gave her an indulgent smile.

"Yeah, I guess you did at that. But you know I've got to say something." Lenore smiled at Daria affectionately and kissed her on the cheek. "Were you able to get some nice-sized crabs?"

The familiar cinnamon potpourri her aunt favored tickled Daria's nose as she moved past Lenore into the living room. Overstuffed, fabric covered chairs and table tops covered in lacy doilies brought an instant feeling of home and comfort.

"Yes, they look pretty good to me, but you never know what you have until you open them up." Daria headed for the kitchen.

"To save you some time, I've started the smoked neck bones to cooking," Lenore called after her.

After putting the water on to boil and adding the seasoning, Daria dropped in four ears of corn, white potato chunks, smoked sausage, and the smoked neck bones.

Carrying two glasses of iced tea, she walked back into the living room where Lenore lounged on the sofa watching a Christian program on television.

"I finally got a chance to meet that guy who moved into my complex three months ago," Daria said, sitting down beside Lenore on the sofa.

"Oh, how did that come about?" Lenore tasted her drink.

"You're going to love this..." Daria recounted last night's events.

Concern wrinkled Lenore's brow. "Child, were you really afraid?" She shook her head and continued indignantly. "The nerve of that boy, barging in on you like that."

Anybody under the age of forty was a child to Lenore.

"I was afraid until I realized who he was hiding from, and then I got angry."

"Well, I'm glad it turned out to be harmless."

"Yeah, me too. It could've easily turned into something nasty." Daria sipped her tea.

"That girl sounds like a hoochie mama."

The tea spurted back into Daria's glass. "A hoochie mama? Auntie, what do you know about hoochie mamas?" Daria's laughter floated around the room.

Lenore sent her an indignant look. "I do have cable. I learn all kinds of interesting things looking at TV."

"I bet you do. Maybe I need to set the channel blocks," Daria teased.

"You said his name is Michael Greer. Who are his people?"

"I have no idea. We didn't get into all of that. All I know is that he moved here from Atlanta."

"I wonder if he's related to Amelia Greer," Lenore said, referring to one of their church members and good friends. "I seem to remember her telling me that her son recently moved back home from Atlanta. I believe she said his name was Michael. It could very well be her boy."

"Well, I don't know about that. But I do know that if last night's events are a true indication of his lifestyle, I won't need to buy any more movie tickets."

"What are you talking about?"

Daria chuckled. "I can watch him and his women go at it outside my living room window instead."

"Hopefully, he has enough sense to stay away from that kind of girl now. Sometimes, I don't know what to think about young men today." Lenore shook her head and waved her hand in the air. "Why would he even look at a girl like that when you're living right across the walkway from him?"

Now, why did she have to go down that road? She doesn't know anything about this man.

"Auntie, he's not for me. He's not a Christian. It wouldn't do him a bit of good to come over to my side of the walkway."

"The Lord can fix that. You never know why He causes people to cross your path. Did you invite him to come to church with you?"

"No."

"You should have." Lenore shot Daria a mischievous smile. "Maybe he's supposed to be my new nephew."

"Puh-leeeeeeease. Auntie, you can't be serious. The Lord wouldn't send me a man who's not a Christian."

Daria squirmed in her seat. *I'm going to derail this uncomfortable conversation train right now!*

"Aunt Lenore, have you found anyone in your retirement community to go with you on your European vacation yet?" Daria asked.

"Daria, I don't know what's wrong with these people." Disgust filled Lenore's voice. "They act like they're sitting around waiting to die.

"Yesterday, I asked Essie Polk—she lives over on the next street— if she'd consider going with me. You'd think I'd asked her to do herself bodily harm. She went on and on about who'd watch her cat? What would she do if her blood pressure went up? What would she do if she got ill? There's nothing wrong with Essie but a little arthritis. If she'd lay off of some of that salt and pork she likes so much, she wouldn't have a problem with her blood pressure either. You can't get her to eat any other kind of meat. Believe me, I've tried." Lenore sliced her hand through the air. "If meat doesn't come from a pig, she doesn't want any part of it."

Daria laughed. "You're too bad. I hope you didn't say that."

"I most certainly did, but she didn't pay me any attention. She's like everybody else around here. They think I have a few loose screws because I don't go around acting like I have one foot in the grave." Lenore placed her hand on her hip and rolled her neck. "Shoot! I may be old, but I'm not dead yet."

She's such a character, and I love her dearly, Daria thought fondly, as she walked back into the kitchen to put the crabs into the pot.

"I'm going outside to get the patio ready," Lenore called from the living room.

Fifteen minutes later, Daria heard the patio door slide open. "Aren't those crabs ready yet?" Lenore asked. "Girl, I'm ready to eat."

"Give me five more minutes," Daria answered from the kitchen. "I'm about to bring everything out now."

Daria poured the water off the crabs and transferred them to a large bowl. She put the corn, meat, and potatoes in smaller bowls, then loaded the food onto a rolling food cart. After adding a pitcher of iced tea, she pushed the cart out to the patio.

Lenore glanced at her watch. "One o'clock on the dot. Perfect." She rubbed her hands together. "Mmm-mmm, that looks good. Let's eat!"

They lapsed into silence as they enjoyed their feast.

"Ooh, I'm stuffed," Daria moaned as she got up from the table and began to clean up. "I can't believe I sat there and ate that much."

"I ate too much myself," Lenore admitted as she walked into the kitchen carrying the leftovers. "Don't leave this stuff here. Bag it up and take it home. You might want to eat it later on tonight."

They worked together to finish cleaning the patio and kitchen.

"I'm going home to relax," Daria said. "I'll see you in the morning when you pick me up for church." She kissed Lenore on the cheek and moved toward the door.

"Are you and Amelia's girl, Calyssa Mitchell, leading the praise and worship service tomorrow?"

"Yes." Daria opened the door. "Why do you ask?"

"I love it when you two lead the worship together. Folks at Prayer Tabernacle say that God has anointed your voices. The Lord's presence seems to flow through the place." Lenore shrugged. "I don't know. I just can't explain it."

"I understand what you're trying to say. It's hard to explain the way I feel when I'm singing praise to God. His presence becomes so real to me. It's like He's right there with me. Calyssa told me that she feels the same way."

"Don't forget we're supposed to go over to Amelia's for Sunday dinner tomorrow after church," Lenore said when they reached the door. "I've been looking forward to it ever since we received the invitation.

That Amelia can cook! I mean she does it the old-fashioned way." Lenore smiled and licked her lips in anticipation.

Daria laughed. "I haven't forgotten, and my mouth starts watering every time I think about it."

On her way home, Daria wondered again about Michael. Was Aunt Lenore right? Had the Lord brought him to her door for a significant reason? Could he be...

"Nah!" Daria laughed out loud. "That's wishful thinking, my girl. Wishful thinking."

Chapter Four

On Saturday afternoon, Michael stood on his mother's front porch and scanned his old College Park neighborhood. A lawn mower droned in the distance. Ranch style homes sat on neat lawns along both sides of the tree-lined avenue.

Amelia greeted Michael at the door wearing an apron over a comfortable earth-toned housedress. She gave him a big welcoming smile. "Hi, baby." Her black hair flowed back from her face and curtained her shoulders. Peek-a-boo strands of gray hair added class and character to her almond-toned face.

He hugged her and touched his cheek to her temple. "Baby? Moms, I'm a thirty-year-old man."

Amelia smiled. "I don't care if you're seventy years old. You'll always be my baby."

"It's good to be home again. I really missed your cooking while I was in Atlanta."

"Son, I'm glad you've moved back home. I don't know why you wanted to move so far away to begin with. Now I can keep an eye on you."

They moved into the kitchen, and Michael went straight to the stove and started lifting the lids off the pots cooking on the burners.

The savory smell of collard greens and chicken stock wafted up his nostrils.

As Michael knew she would, Amelia scolded him for his antics. "Get out of my pots!"

Michael laughed, replaced the lids, and kissed her on the cheek.

"Where is Sis today? I called her before coming over here, but I didn't get an answer."

"Brandon has a soccer game today, and Calyssa's probably still there."

"If I had known he had a game today, I would've gone. I wonder why Sis didn't tell me about it."

"You've been so busy. She probably didn't want to bother you." Amelia sat down at the table. "I've made some fresh-squeezed lemonade. Pour yourself a glass and come sit with me for a while." She pointed to the chair opposite of hers.

After Michael had poured his drink and settled at the table, she said, "I'm concerned about Calyssa. Ever since Alex's accident, she's been carrying a heavy load. She's trying to be both mother and father to Brandon, remain upbeat, *and* spend a lot of time at Alex's bedside." Amelia shook her head. "And Alex, that poor child, is just laying there."

Michael placed his hand on hers. "What are the doctors saying? Do they think Alex will come out of the coma anytime soon?"

Amelia shook her head again and exhaled deeply. "Honey, they don't know. They're doing the same thing we are—waiting."

They sat in silence for a few minutes, then Amelia patted his hand and asked, "When are you going to stop working on Sundays? You haven't been to church since you moved back. I understand that you have a responsibility to your job, but don't forget about the Lord. You wouldn't have that job if He hadn't blessed you with it."

Michael pulled on his earlobe, then took a long drink of lemonade. He wasn't about to tell his mother he didn't need to work on Sundays. Work had been a convenient excuse to stay away from church.

Michael may have chosen to walk away from God, but he wasn't an idiot. He knew that God had blessed him with his job. Guilt plagued him every time he used his job as a cover.

"I'll go to church with you tomorrow," Michael blurted before he could stop the words.

"Wonderful!" Amelia cried, and then searched his face. "I've been trying to find the right time to talk to you about something that's been worrying me. I think now is the time."

Michael knew what was coming. His heart picked up its pace.

His mom placed both of her hands over his, tilted her head to the side a little, and pinned him with serious eyes.

"When you were nine years old, you invited the Lord to be your personal Savior. God and the church meant everything to you." She squeezed his hands. "When you graduated and went off to college in Atlanta, you changed." A frown gathered between her eyes. "You became interested in everything but God and church. You let Satan sift all of that out of you."

Michael shifted in his seat and cleared his throat.

"You don't think I know it, but your lifestyle is totally contrary to the way you were raised." Amelia smiled. "I've told you and Calyssa time and time again—not much will get past a praying mother." Amelia shook her head. "Drinking, clubbing, and changing women like you're changing clothes."

Michael pulled back a corner of his lips and raised one eyebrow.

"Oh, yeah, I know all about your women. You can just wipe that smirk right off of your face. They're not even fit to bring home to your mama. I wasn't born yesterday. I know exactly why you're interested in *those* kinds of women."

Michael gave her a chagrined smile.

"You're not happy, son. Don't you think it's time to come back to the Lord? You know as well as I do that tomorrow is not promised to any of us." Amelia grimaced. "Just look at poor Alex. He was so full of life, had big plans for the future, but for the last three months, he's been lying in a coma in a hospital bed.

Michael's heart pounded. Tears filled his eyes. His mother's words confirmed everything that had been running through his mind.

David's question swirled to the forefront of his mind. *When are you going to stop running from God and surrender to Him?*

Amelia waved one of her hands. "I'm not talking about religion or just attending church. I'm talking about repenting, asking Christ to be the Lord of your life again, and seeking an intimate relationship with Him." Her hand came to rest on his arm. "Do you understand what I'm saying, son?"

"Yeah," Michael managed to answer around the knot lodged in his throat.

She went on. "I was a Christian a long time before I realized that I could get up close and personal with God. I loved your father, but nothing compares to having a close and honest, one-on-one relationship with the Lord," Amelia said with deep feeling. "Don't close your heart to the Lord. Let Him back in. If I could, I'd make this choice for you, but this is one choice you alone will have to make."

Amelia rose, walked around to Michael, and patted him on the shoulder. "I'll be back in a bit. I need to go into the den to find something for your Aunt Euvinia."

Michael sat at the table with his head bowed. His mother's words joined David's, and they spun like a whirlwind through his mind. His knee bounced as his heel jostled triple-time with nervous energy.

Why try to hang onto a way of life that had lost its appeal? He was tired of the struggle. He wanted peace, happiness, and contentment. He wanted the joy he knew only came from the Lord. He just wanted…to feel whole again.

Then he heard a voice he hadn't heard in a very long time. That still small voice he used to delight in hearing spoke into his spirit and said, *"I love you. I never stopped loving you. I'm married to the backslider. Come back to me."*

Michael began to weep brokenly.

He cried out, "Lord, I surrender! Forgive me! Come into my heart and fill me with Your Spirit once again!"

After this heart-felt plea, Michael felt the peace of God envelope him. The weights of discontentment, restlessness, and unhappiness dropped from his shoulders. Joy overwhelmed him.

When Amelia returned to the kitchen, Michael stood and turned his tear-streaked face to her.

Amelia shouted, "Hallelujah! My baby has really come home!" She ran over to him, wrapped him in her arms, rocked him, and cried tears of joy.

Later that afternoon, still basking in the joy of his spiritual renewal, Michael soaked up the peaceful familiarity of watching his mother shell peas on the back porch.

Birds chirped and flitted in and out of the birdhouse he'd built as a teenager. The smell of freshly cut grass drifted in the air. He could almost forget that he was in a large, bustling city.

Enticing smells drifted from the kitchen. *Home.*

"Has Aunt Euvinia settled in yet?" he asked his mother.

"Yeah, she didn't waste any time. Her house looks like she's been living there for years instead of just three weeks."

"That's great," he replied. "I thought moving to Orlando would be a challenge for her because she's so used to living in a small town. I'm glad she was able to buy a house right next to you. I'm sure she needed to be close to family after Uncle Calvin died." The old, weathered rocking chair Michael sat in squeaked as he set it into motion.

Amelia chuckled. "She sure surprised me. When Calvin died six months ago, she buried him; sold the home they'd lived in for thirty years in Hastings, and hightailed it to Orlando. I thought she loved the St. Augustine area too much to ever leave it." Peas shot rapidly into the bowl as Amelia's fingers flew over her task.

"She's what? Fifteen years older than you?" He continued at Amelia's nod. "She needs to be near us so that we can keep an eye on her."

Amelia sat the bowl aside, reached into her apron pocket, and pulled out an envelope. She smiled secretively as she handed it to him. "Go on over there and take this to her. She'll be glad to see you."

Michael gave his mom a puzzled look, took the envelope, and walked the few yards to his aunt's front door.

He rang the doorbell and waited.

When his seventy-year-old aunt answered the door, her hot-pink tracksuit shouted at him. His eyes widened at her elaborate, braided hairstyle. His aunt usually only wore dresses that fell below the knees, and she never *ever* wore plaits or braids.

"Hi, Michael. Why are you standing there staring at me like that?" she demanded. "Close your mouth and come on in." She snickered. "Thought you had me all figured out, didn't you? Well, there is a lot more to me than you've been seeing through the years."

"Uh…I see that you've been busy, Auntie," Michael said after he'd sat down on the bright red sofa in the living room. Knick-knacks littered every available tabletop.

She sat across from him in a bright blue armchair. "I've been busy finding myself. I put myself away for years for your Uncle Calvin. I lost myself and became the person he wanted me to be."

Michael wasn't quite sure how to react to her pronouncement. "So you're bustin' loose, huh?"

"You've got that right!" She nodded once and slapped her knee.

"Weren't you unhappy living that way? I know I would've been miserable."

"No, I wasn't unhappy. I thought that was what I was supposed to do, so I tried to be content. Don't get me wrong. Calvin wasn't a bad person, but he had some old-fashioned ways."

"I'm sorry, Auntie. I didn't know."

"You weren't supposed to know. My marriage was my business. I don't understand these young folk today who put all of their personal problems in the streets—all up on the television telling anybody who'll listen," she said, shaking her head in disgust.

"Girls these days don't have the patience to learn their man, so they can make them pay in ways that really matter. Take your uncle for instance. He could be mean sometimes. When he got on my nerves too bad, I'd cook pinto beans for dinner that night and take care of him real quick like." Euvinia giggled.

"See," she continued, lowering her voice as though telling a secret, "he couldn't eat pinto beans without getting indigestion in the worst way. I'd cook a *big* pot of them, enough for leftovers for the next day." Euvinia laughed and slapped her knee.

"Michael," she said, "that man did not believe in wasting food, so he'd sit there and eat those pinto beans. I'd sit there laughing under my breath the whole time, offering him more helpings." By the time Euvinia finished telling her story, tears were streaming down her cheeks.

Michael laughed. "Auntie, you're dangerous. Whenever I do get married, I'm going to make sure you stay away from my wife."

"Well, I did that kind of stuff before I became a Christian." She relaxed back in the chair and rested her hands on the arms. "After that I learned how to use a weapon more powerful than pinto beans—prayer."

Michael nodded, then smiled. "I have good news, Auntie. I came back to Christ this afternoon."

"Hallelujah!" she shouted, raising her hands toward heaven. "I'm glad for you. Listen, don't tell anybody," she leaned forward slightly as though she was about to impart a great secret, "but you're my favorite nephew."

"Auntie, I'm your only nephew," Michael retorted with a smile. He stood. "I guess I'd better get going. Moms sent this envelope to you." He handed her the envelope and walked toward the front door.

"All kidding aside," Euvinia said seriously as she followed him to the door. "Tomorrow's church service will be extra special because I'll be able to worship the Lord in one voice with my nephew." She hugged him and kissed him on the cheek.

Michael walked back to his mom's house chuckling over his encounter with Euvinia.

He'd thought she'd be elderly and needy. His aunt was bursting with energy and *life.*

The things she'd told him about her marriage were surprising to say the least. He really didn't believe he would've stayed in a not-so-happy marriage all of those years. He didn't have that kind of stick-to-it-ness when it came to relationships.

Oh , well, it's a good thing marriage is a vague event in my far distant future.

Chapter Five

The open casket sat in the middle of the room with a spotlight shining on it from somewhere above. The rest of the room was pitch black.

Peaches didn't want to go anywhere near the casket, but she was driven by an invisible force. She tried to resist, but she wasn't strong enough. In every fiber of her being, she knew that she'd be horrified by what she'd see.

She moved closer and closer. Her heart pounded. Sweat beaded on her brow. *Please, no! Not again.* She chanted in her mind.

Finally, the cold, metal casket pressed against her arms. She looked inside, saw herself lying still and silent on a white, silk pillow, and screamed, "Noooooooooo!"

Peaches Addison awoke from the nightmare with the scream still on her lips. She stumbled from her bed and into her master bathroom to splash cold water onto her face. Her heart pounded, and she gulped air between her sobs.

She looked in the mirror hanging over the bathroom sink, and hazel, bloodshot eyes stared back at her. The laughter that used to dance there was long gone. Her sandy-brown hair fell in tangles around her shoulders. The freckles sprinkled over her nose stood out more than usual because her light-brown skin was pale. Red blotches spotted her face.

Peaches sadly shook her head and turned away from the mirror. The usually welcoming burgundy, green, and toasted-almond décor of her bathroom barely registered as she walked back into her master bedroom.

She sat on the side of her rumpled bed with her head in her hands.

In four years, she'd gone from being a successful attorney, on her way to becoming a partner in one of Central Florida's most prestigious law firms to this—a drug addict.

Her life had started on a downward spiral when she'd met an attorney at a criminal-law convention in Philadelphia. She'd seen in him a kindred spirit—another adventurer who lived for laughs.

Her new *friend* had introduced her to crack cocaine. After binging on crack with him for three days at the convention, she was hooked.

Peaches lifted her head from her hands and peered at the picture that sat on her nightstand.

She smiled sadly and lifted the picture with a trembling hand. She and Daria—whom she affectionately called Ms. D—had taken the picture about five years ago, before she'd lost her mind and gotten hooked on drugs.

Ms. D wore a big, floppy, pink hat, and Peaches wore a big, floppy, white hat with tiny peaches dangling from it. Ms. D had laughed and called her Fruit Lady every time she'd glanced at the hat. They'd had fun that day combing the shops on the Daytona Beach boardwalk.

Peaches ran her fingers over the picture. "Ms. D, I've messed up big time." She hugged the picture to her chest and gently rocked back and forth.

Daria had immediately seen the changes in Peaches and had urged her to get help when Peaches had admitted she was experimenting with crack.

Experimenting? Peaches scoffed. *I was a bona fide crack head.*

She'd actually laughed at Daria's efforts. "Get help? For what? I don't need any help. There's nothing wrong with me. I've got it all under control." She'd laughed derisively. "You're way off base here."

Daria had continued to talk to her about getting help and about Christ, but her words had fallen on deaf ears.

Two years ago, Peaches' life skidded out of control. She started to miss a lot of work, and she dropped the ball on a lot of important cases. The firm had had no choice but to let her go.

Even without the job, she had no financial hardships. With nobody to support but herself, she'd saved and wisely invested money in the stock market. Her home and car had been paid off years ago from the legacy she'd received from her mother.

Instead of looking for work, she'd openly associated with known crack users and dealers. She'd hosted parties that lasted for days where sex, drugs, and alcohol had been abundant.

In spite of her brainlessness, Ms. D had kept right on loving her.

But will she continue to love me when she learns the truth?

Peaches let out a small sob.

Several months ago, she'd started having this recurring nightmare—at least twice a week. She hated to go to sleep because she was afraid she'd have the nightmare again.

A shiver snaked up her spine.

She glanced at the clock sitting on her nightstand. *11:00 P.M.*

She shuddered, picked up the phone, and dialed Otis Cartier, the only attorney at her old firm—Bolden, Bryant, Ford & Green, who'd still have anything to do with her. He'd given her his cell phone number. She hoped he'd meant it when he'd said she could call him at anytime. Maybe he wouldn't mind her calling so late on a Saturday night.

He answered on the second ring. "This is Otis." His voice sounded alert, so she didn't think she'd disturbed his sleep.

"Otis, this is Peaches. How are you?" She tried unsuccessfully to keep the tremors out of her voice.

"I'm doing great, but I'm concerned about you. How are you, Peaches?"

The genuine concern in his voice wrapped around her like a comforting blanket. "Oh, I'm hangin'."

"What can I do for you?"

His unconditional kindness brought tears to her eyes. "I want to meet with you to set up a will."

Otis had agreed to meet with Peaches on the following Wednesday, at an Italian restaurant located on Colonial Drive, to help her set up a will. He'd arrived first and had requested a table in a relatively private area.

"Thank you for meeting with me today, Otis," Peaches said as she sat in the chair he was holding out for her.

As usual, Otis was dressed in a simply cut, expensive suit. His short, black hair was neat and edged to perfection. A neatly trimmed goatee framed his mouth. His Rolex flashed as he gently pushed her chair closer to the table.

"It's my pleasure," he said. "It's been a while since I've seen you. What have you been up to?"

"I've been doing great," Peaches lied. "I'm still reviewing my options."

What was she supposed to say? That she'd made a mess of her life and was terrified she was going to die?

Peaches silently snorted. *Not hardly. I can front with the best of them.*

Actually, she felt like she'd been dragged up the highway by a semi. Because she wasn't sleeping well, fatigue was her constant companion. She had good days and bad days. Today was *definitely* not a good day.

She looked like a shadow of her former self. She'd lost twenty pounds. Her ponytail looked about as lifeless as she felt.

A little makeup would've toned down those red blotches on her face that were waving and screaming, *Hey, here I am. Look at me!* But putting on makeup was *not* an option. It had taken all of her energy just to get dressed, make her way to the restaurant, and plop herself down at the table.

Otis studied her face, but he didn't refute the obvious lie. "I wish you well," he said with a slight nod. "Would you like to order something to eat before we get started?"

Thank goodness, Otis is too much of a gentleman to tell me that I look like a hag.

"No, thank you. But I'd like to have some water." After the waitress filled her water glass, she said, "As I told you on the phone, I'd like to set up a will."

"May I suggest that in addition to a will that you set up a living trust? With a living trust your beneficiaries can avoid the expense and delay of probate court."

"You know, I never considered that option. Let's do that. Before we go any further, there's something I must tell you. I trust you, so I know that what I'm about to say will remain between us." Peaches took a deep breath. "Last year, I took an extended vacation in Georgia visiting my relatives, because…"

After she finished her story, Otis sat back in his seat with a stunned look on his face. For a few seconds, he just sat quietly and stared at her.

She never thought she'd see the day when the unflappable Attorney Cartier would be at a loss for words.

I'd laugh if it wouldn't take so much energy.

Finally, he cleared his throat. "To cover all of the necessary bases, we'll definitely need to complete a will *and* create a trust."

"Uh…um…Otis." She toyed with the napkin on the table, then sipped some of her water. "Would you consider being my trustee, as well as the executor of my will?" Peaches asked after they'd finished taking care of all of the tedious details.

He smiled. "I'd be honored to do that for you, Peaches."

Peaches exhaled the breath she'd been holding. "Thank you, Otis. I'd like to name Daria Simpson, my best friend, as your co-trustee and co-executor."

He nodded. "All right. Is she aware of your wishes?"

"Because of the sensitive issue involved, I don't want her to know yet. I'll tell her, but I need to take care of some things first."

"Okay. I can respect that. Is there anything else I can help you with today?"

Peaches reached into her purse, pulled out an envelope, and handed it to Otis. "This envelope contains a letter I want you to give to Daria if anything happens to me."

Chapter Six

As he pulled into a parking space in the church parking lot the next morning, Michael glanced at his watch and grimaced. *The first time I've been to church in years, and I'm ten minutes late!*

He threw the gear into park, grabbed his Bible from the passenger seat, and flung the door open. Hitting the lock button on his remote, he sprinted to the closest set of glass doors.

When Calyssa had called him last night to rejoice over his rededication, she'd told him where the family usually sat. He found them in the center aisle in the fourth row from the front and slipped into the open space at the end of the pew just as the congregation finished singing.

"You're late," Amelia chastened gently, and then kissed him on the cheek.

"I know. I was up late last night reacquainting myself with my Bible. I overslept this morning," he whispered into her ear.

"That's one excuse I'll gladly accept." Amelia smiled and patted his hand.

Michael focused on the platform as Calyssa walked out, followed closely by Daria.

Michael's heart lurched. *Daria's a member of this church?*

His eyes were drawn toward her. Her hair fell in loose, spiraling curls to her shoulders. Her red dress flowed over her curves just right.

Mmm-mmm, she's got it goin' on! Michael immediately castigated himself for the thought. *Man, you ought to be ashamed of yourself. You're in church. Take your eyes off of the sister and focus on the Lord!*

"That's Daria Simpson up there with Calyssa," his mother whispered. "She's a sweet girl. She and her Aunt Lenore are good friends of ours. You'll meet them today."

Still zoomed in on Daria, Michael couldn't form the words to tell his mom that he and Daria were neighbors and had already met.

Daria and Calyssa closed their eyes, raised their hands into the air, and belted out one worship song after another. They passionately sang songs all across the spectrum—contemporary, hymns, and traditional gospel.

Daria's lively movements across the platform invited the congregation to join her in praise.

The atmosphere became electrically charged. Michael had never experienced anything like this.

God's presence is in this place!

After getting over his initial awe, Michael joined the rest of the congregation in worshiping God.

At the conclusion of the worship service, Daria and Calyssa left the platform. Calyssa sat on a pew near the platform, but Daria left the sanctuary through a door to the left.

The pastor preached a soul-stirring message about the grace of God. Still basking in the grace that God had extended to him in allowing him back into His family, Michael soaked up the message like a sponge.

After the service ended, Michael turned to his mother and said, "Moms, my cup runneth over." He hugged her. "That was absolutely awesome! I can't find the words to express what I just experienced. I knew Sis could sing, but I had no idea she could do *that*."

"Your sister and Daria realize that being a worship leader is a ministry, and they take it very seriously." She nodded. "They told me once they feel like they're ushering the people into God's presence." She tapped his arm with her index finger. "Alex's accident has brought a deeper dimension into both Calyssa's and Daria's singing. They are so much more in tune with the Spirit in a heartfelt way. They—"

"Hey, y'all can talk later. I'm hungry. Let's get a move on," Euvinia interrupted.

Michael gave Euvinia an amused and indulgent smile. "Okay, Auntie. We'll feed you."

"Now, Euvinia," Amelia said, "you know that I can't leave here without introducing Michael to a few people. Just hold your horses. Make your way on out to the car, and we'll be there in about ten minutes," Amelia urged with a smile.

"All right. Ten minutes. Don't have me standing out there in the hot sun waiting for y'all," Euvinia grumbled as she moved to go around them into the aisle. "I tell you what, Amelia, give me your car keys so that I can start up the car and get the air conditioner going."

Amelia dug her keys out of her purse and handed them to Euvinia.

Euvinia smiled at her sweetly. "In ten minutes, I'm gone. If you don't see your car when you finally make it outside, catch a ride home with Michael." Euvinia walked off up the aisle, making a beeline for the sanctuary doors.

Amelia laughed and shook her head. "That woman is just too much."

Michael chuckled. "Yeah, but you've got to love her."

Amelia grabbed Michael's arm and started up the aisle. She introduced him to dozens of people, whose names he promptly forgot. It wasn't that he didn't think they were important. His mind was elsewhere.

Daria had never returned through the door she'd exited at the conclusion of the worship service. He'd enjoyed the rest of the service, but he'd also been aware of the fact that she'd never come back through that door.

Michael's eyes swept over the people still greeting each other. *Where is she?*

His mother stopped before an attractive, impeccably dressed, elderly lady. "This is Lenore Jackson, Daria's aunt. Lenore, this is my son, Michael. He recently moved back home from Atlanta."

Michael saw recognition flash in Lenore's eyes.

"I'm pleased to meet you, young man. Don't you live in the same complex as Daria?" Lenore asked.

"Yes, Daria and I met on Friday."

"You didn't tell me you'd already met Daria," Amelia remarked.

A grin spread across Lenore's face. "Would you care to tell us how that meeting came about?"

Lenore's question and expression told Michael that Daria had told her about Friday's incident. He wasn't about to discuss that in his mom's presence.

"Uh…maybe some other time." Michael glanced at his mom. Her quizzical look sent him scrambling for a diversion. "I think that we'd better get a move on before Aunt Euvinia sends out a search party."

Much to his relief, Amelia didn't ask any questions, but turned to move up the aisle.

Lenore fell into step behind him and said softly, "Maybe some other time my foot! I'm on to you, young man."

Michael pretended that he didn't hear her, but he couldn't pretend that he didn't feel her index finger poking him in the back, punctuating her sentences.

Calyssa was waiting at Amelia's car with Euvinia when they reached the parking lot.

Michael scanned the immediate area looking for Daria and was disappointed when he didn't even catch a glimpse of her.

Why are you so eager to see this girl? Michael asked himself.

Humph, considering how they'd met, a girl like her would probably run in the opposite direction if he came anywhere near her.

"Lenore, you and Daria come on over to the house," Amelia invited. "I prepared all of the food before church this morning, so we can start eating as soon as we get the food on the table."

Excitement zipped through Michael. *She's coming to dinner at Mom's!*

"Honey, as soon as Daria gets here, we'll be right behind you. We might even beat you there. I've been looking forward to this dinner all week. Wild horses couldn't keep me away from your table." Lenore grinned.

Michael was still standing close enough to Lenore to hear her say softly, "Oh, yeah, I've got a feeling that today's dinner is going to be very interesting indeed."

Michael snorted. *I wonder if Moms would box my ears if I barred this old lady at the door.*

On the drive to Amelia's house, Lenore asked Daria, "Amelia's son came to church this morning. Did you see him sitting with her?"

"No, I didn't." Daria removed her pumps and then settled back in the passenger seat. "After the worship service, I helped out in the nursery. They were short-handed today."

Lenore smiled. "Well, I met him after church this morning. I'm quite sure you'll meet him at dinner today."

When they arrived, Calyssa and appetizing aromas welcomed them into the house. "Come on in and get comfortable. The food is almost ready."

Lenore kissed Calyssa on the cheek. "Ooh, child, it smells good in here!"

Daria and Calyssa chuckled, then Daria asked Calyssa, "How is Alex? Has there been any change in his condition?"

A frown marred Calyssa's brown face, and sadness flashed in her dark-brown eyes. "No, there's been no change yet. We go to the hospital every day and talk to him." Calyssa exhaled. "We're trusting God to turn his condition around. Please continue to pray for him."

Daria gave Calyssa a quick hug. "That goes without saying. We know that God can do anything."

"We need a few more minutes to finish getting everything on the table. Go on into the living room and have a seat." Calyssa turned and went back into the kitchen.

As Daria and Lenore walked into the living room, Calyssa's son, seven-year-old Brandon, pounced on Michael, trying to take a hand-held electronic game away from him. "Uncle Michael, no fair! You're cheating!" Excitement radiated from his little nut-brown face, and his black eyes danced with enjoyment.

"Get him, Brandon!" Euvinia egged Brandon on from a recliner positioned near the window, well out of harm's way.

"Well, hello there," said Lenore as she sat down. "You two have way too much energy for me right now. Wait until after I eat dinner, and I'll give you a run for your money."

"Hi, Mrs. Jackson!" Brandon jumped up from the floor and ran over to Lenore. "This is my Uncle Michael from Atlanta," he said, pointing at Michael.

"Yes, I know. I met him after church today."

Daria froze. *It's him!*

A heated flush suffused her, and her breath hitched when she made eye contact with him. *Breathe, girl, before he has to give you mouth-to-mouth resuscitation. Wait. And that's a bad thing…how?*

"I think you two have already met," Lenore said.

Daria's eyes swung to Lenore. The word cheeky perfectly described the grin on her aunt's face.

"When was this?" Euvinia asked, looking back and forth between Daria and Michael. "Have I missed something?"

"Um…we live in the same complex, Auntie," Michael said before Lenore could say anything more.

"Okay…that's nice." Euvinia's tone said she knew there was more to the story.

"Michael, how are you?" Daria asked as she took a seat next to Lenore on the love seat.

"I'm doing great. How 'bout yourself?"

Daria smiled. "Oh, I'm doing very well. Thank you. I hear there was a female stalker around our complex on Friday. Have you heard anything about that?"

Brandon's brows snapped together in a confused frown. "I know what a female is, Uncle Michael, but what's a stalker?"

Michael shot Daria an exasperated look. "A person who follows somebody around without their permission."

"So, there was a lady following somebody around where you live without their permission? Why'd she do that, Uncle Michael?"

Daria's and Lenore's shoulders shook with silent laughter.

Euvinia intently watched them all from the recliner.

"Yeah, why'd she do that, Michael?" Daria asked, imitating Brandon.

At that moment, Amelia called them into the dining room, saving Michael from having to come up with an answer.

"Let's go wash our hands, champ." Michael grabbed Brandon, threw him over his right shoulder, and headed for the door. "Ladies, we'll go upstairs and leave the downstairs bathroom for you."

"Humph, tell me I haven't missed anything," Euvinia grumbled as she exited the living room. "I'd have to be a halfwit to believe that."

Daria and Lenore looked at each other and burst out laughing.

"This is going to be fun," Lenore said when she was finally able to speak.

After they'd finished saying grace, everybody served themselves collard greens, corn on the cob, black-eyed peas, seasoned rice, fried chicken, baked chicken, sliced honey-baked ham, candied yams, potato salad, and buttery corn bread.

"As always, you girls did a fantastic job today," Amelia complimented Daria and Calyssa.

"Made me want to dance," Euvinia added with a nod.

They all laughed.

"Auntie, that is something I'd want a ringside seat to watch." Michael chuckled, taking a big helping of collard greens.

"I believe I also speak for Calyssa when I say all of the glory belongs to the Lord. It's such an honor to be used by Him," Daria said. "Before we get up on that platform, we ask the Lord for his guidance and anointing."

Calyssa nodded. "We've offered the Lord our voices to bless His people." A sad, little smile formed on her lips. "Worship service has been a tremendous blessing to me, especially, since Alex's accident."

"Mommy, may I please have some peas?" Brandon was totally focused on filling his plate as quickly as possible. "Thank you," he said when Calyssa spooned some peas onto his plate. "Grandma, this sure looks good!" he added before shoveling a forkful of peas into his mouth.

"See, that boy knows what's important—takes after his uncle. Pass me that chicken, Sis." Michael reached for the platter.

Changing the subject, Calyssa said, "You know, Michael, you really need to slow down. You drive too fast. You passed my car on Colonial Drive last Friday evening, but you were going so fast you didn't even see me. Why were you in such a big hurry?"

"That had been a very difficult day, and I wanted to get home as quickly as possible," he answered.

"I can certainly understand that." After a pause, Calyssa continued. "There was a car on your tail when you passed me. It's a shame how aggressively people drive these days.

Michael glanced at Daria.

She gave him an angelic smile.

Michael quickly moved to another topic. "Mrs. Jackson and Daria, I want to share with you that I renewed my relationship with Christ on Saturday. I'd been in a backslidden state for years, but I've finally come back into the fold, as Moms would say," he said with a smile for his mother.

"That's great news!" Lenore exclaimed. "I'm happy for you."

Daria smiled. "That *is* good news." *Good-looking, employed, and saved. Oh my, what a combination!*

Brandon interrupted her thoughts. "Ms. Daria, I'm going to play with my friend Stefan this afternoon. We're going to have lots of fun."

"That's great, honey. May I come and play with you guys?" she teased.

"No, you're a girl," Brandon said with a wrinkled nose. His mouth was screwed up like he'd eaten something nasty. "It's no fun playing with girls."

"Let's see how long that sentiment lasts," remarked his mom wryly.

"Girls don't play fair. And they're stalkers," Brandon said seriously.

Michael had a coughing fit, and all of the other adults laughed.

"What do you know about stalkers, Brandon?" Calyssa asked with indulgent amusement. "Why do you think girls are stalkers?"

Brandon straightened in his chair and pushed his small chest out. "Uncle Michael said a stalker was a person who follows somebody around." He nodded. "There was a female stalker at his house on Friday," the boy finished innocently.

Michael groaned.

Daria tried desperately to hold in her laughter.

"Michael, what is this all about?" Amelia asked with concern.

"It's nothing, Moms. It was just a little, harmless incident last Friday," Michael hedged.

"Don't give me that. Tell me what happened!" Amelia demanded.

"Well…uh…see this lady came to my house looking for me." He paused and glanced at Brandon. Seeing that Brandon was focused on his food once again, he continued. "Um, she had a hard time accepting the fact that we didn't have a relationship anymore, so she wanted to talk to me about it."

Euvinia chortled, shaking her index finger. "I knew it! I knew y'all were trying to hide something."

"So what happened when you spoke to the lady?" Amelia asked.

Michael shot a glance at Daria. He squirmed in his seat and cleared his throat. "Uh…she left."

"Yeah, after she put on a big show," Daria mumbled with a chuckle.

Amelia's eyes swung to Daria. "What's that you said? What's this about a show?"

"Boy, spill it. If you don't, I will!" Lenore demanded, cackling.

"Okay," Michael said with resignation. "The lady tailgated me when I left my office…"

When Michael finally finished "spilling it"—always mindful of Brandon's little ears—he looked so uncomfortable that Daria felt sorry for him.

"I certainly hope you've learned a lesson. I've told you over and over again about messin' around with *those* kinds of women. Things could've turned out a lot worse."

Amelia turned to Daria. "Baby, I'm so sorry you had to go through that." Chuckling, she continued on a lighter note, "You should've hit him upside the head with something and ran him out of your house."

Michael smiled. "Oh, you don't have to worry about her. She's got some moves." His smile widened. "The thing is, I'm not sure whether they're karate moves or dance moves."

With a smile curving her cheeks, Daria picked up the steak knife that lay beside her plate. "Maybe I should've taken a leaf from Shaniqua's book." She playfully stroked the knife with her index finger.

Michael laughed appreciatively and gave her a mock salute.

The room seemed to shrink to include only the two of them as he stared into her eyes.

Daria's heart, already thumping at an alarming rate, kicked into overdrive when she saw heat ignite in his eyes.

She knew interest when she saw it, and this man was definitely interested. This handsome, fine, *saved* brother was interested *in her*.

Daria sent a quick prayer winging up to heaven. *Lord, in case You're wondering, I'm open to this.*

"Brother dear, I'll make sure you remember this one for years to come," Calyssa teased, unwittingly—Daria hoped—reminding them of the presence of the others.

Daria glanced around the table to see if anyone had witnessed what had just happened.

Lenore's gleeful expressions shouted, *Yes!*

Daria groaned. *I should've known. She doesn't miss a thing!*

"That girl sounds like a hoochie mama to me," Euvinia said.

Daria laughed. "Not you, too! Aunt Lenore said the same thing. I think the both of you need to have your television channels monitored."

"Mommy, what's a hoochie mama?" asked Brandon.

"We'll talk about that later. Finish your dinner." Calyssa glared playfully at Euvinia.

Euvinia rewarded her with a Mona Lisa smile.

Daria looked at Michael and found that he was staring at her. He smiled and winked. She interpreted the gesture to mean there were no hard feelings. She smiled back and slightly nodded her head to let him know she understood.

"Well, well," Lenore and Euvinia said in unison.

When Daria swung her eyes to them, she saw they were both looking back and forth between her and Michael with big grins on their faces.

Chapter Seven

The following Friday night, Michael decided to check in with David. It had been a week since they'd last spoken, so David didn't know that Michael had made a significant change in his life.

He dialed David's number and stretched out on his black, leather sofa.

"Monroe," David answered on the fourth ring.

"Whatup?" Michael asked.

"Hey, Michael. It's all good. I was just getting ready to go and shoot some hoops with the fellas."

"I'm glad I caught you. I've got some news for you," Michael said with a smile.

"Good. I hope."

"Yeah. It's good. I became a Christian last Saturday."

"You're joking, right?" David asked incredulously.

Michael laughed. "No, man. Seriously, I've become a Christian."

Michael held the phone away from his ear and could still hear David's delighted whoops.

"Man, that's tremendous!" David exclaimed. "What happened?"

"The things you said to me last Friday hit me like bricks. You said some things that had already been going around in my head. I was tired of my life being the way it was. As you said, I'd been runnin' from God for a long time. The day after we talked, I went over to Moms's house, and she hit me with some of the same *stuff.* I couldn't fight it anymore. Man, I didn't even want to. And you know what?"

"What?"

"It feels good!" Michael exclaimed joyously.

David laughed. "I feel ya', bro'. I'm happy for you. Now, you're asking yourself what took you so long to do this, aren't you?"

Michael chuckled. "You're right."

"So, now that you've made this change, what do you plan to do about your neighbor?" David fished.

"It turns out that she's a family friend, and she attends my family's church."

David chuckled. "This is getting interesting."

"You're telling me." Michael grunted. "Well, anyway, she and Sis led the worship service on Sunday, and they knocked my socks off." Michael smiled.

"They were that good, huh?" David asked.

"Man, I've never seen or heard anything like it. You're going to have to come and experience it for yourself."

"Is that an invitation to come and visit you?" David asked with a smile in his voice.

"No. Not yet. I'm just saying…" Michael answered half-jokingly.

David laughed.

"Anyway," Michael continued, "after church, Daria and her aunt had Sunday dinner with us."

"Uh-huh?" David asked slowly.

Michael laughed. "She and her aunt let the cat out of the bag about Shaniqua."

David chuckled. "Don't tell me. You got ribbed unmercifully, didn't you?"

Michael snorted and shook his head. "Yeah, Moms started talkin' about *those* kinds of women and my elderly aunt called Shaniqua a hoochie mama. Sis promised she wouldn't let me live the incident down for years to come."

David's laughter roared into Michael's ear.

Michael thought about the moment that had passed between him and Daria at the table. "But it wasn't all bad," he said softly.

"What gives?" David asked.

"I think Daria might be interested."

"In *you?*" David asked.

"Of course, in me. Who else would I be talking about?" Michael retorted.

"What makes you think she's interested?"

"She gave me the *look.*"

"*The* look?"

"Yeah, *the look.*" Michael chuckled.

"Wow! So, what are you going to do about it?"

"I don't know yet." Michael shifted his position on the sofa.

"What do you mean, you don't know yet? Have you lost your mind?" David yelled across the phone lines. "A beautiful, Christian woman is diggin' you, and you don't know what you're going to do about it?"

"Man, you know I don't mess with church girls," Michael answered out of habit.

"Michael, you idiot, listen to what you're saying." David's words shot into Michael's ear.

Michael paused, then said, "Oh."

David snorted. "Yeah. 'Oh' is right. What kind of girl *are* you going to be with now, if not a church girl?"

Michael chuckled. "Cut me some slack, man. I'm still trying to adjust to my new way of life."

"Yeah, well, I told you. I like the sound of this one. Don't mess this up," David said seriously.

"I've got to think about it. This is a whole new ball game. The rules are different," Michael said just as seriously. "If I do decide to make a move for Daria, I've got to be sure I'm doing the right thing."

"You've got me there," David said. "Well, I wish you the best, my brother."

"Thanks, man."

Later that night, Michael thought about their conversation. He was definitely interested in Daria. But should he pursue that interest?

Michael no longer wanted to date just for the sake of dating, and he had a feeling Daria didn't either. Was he ready for a commitment?

After so many relationships where there'd been no sexual restraints, would he be able to date and keep himself pure before God? Would he be a stumbling block for someone else?

Even though he and Daria had just met, he sensed that things between them could explode into something totally beyond his experience. When he thought about it honestly, that had him shakin' in his boots.

Friday night, two weeks later, Michael stood at his breakfast bar sorting through the mail that had accumulated while he'd been in Colorado overseeing the installation of new computer hardware at one of Kytech's branch offices.

At the last minute, he'd been asked to take on the task. He didn't mind because the timing had been perfect. He'd needed to put some distance between himself and Daria. She was too close—just a few steps away from his front door.

But still, he'd missed her. He'd missed seeing her scuttle to her car every morning dressed for success. He'd missed her delightful smiles, and that small wave she'd send him when their paths crossed.

Would he see her soon?

The ringing telephone interrupted his thoughts.

He checked the caller ID and groaned. *Sis.*

After Sunday dinner, he'd hightailed it out of his mother's house. He knew his sister well. At the first opportunity, Calyssa would hit him with a million questions about what had really happened.

"What do you want, Calyssa?" he asked in a no-nonsense tone of voice.

"Is that any way to talk to your big sister?" she asked playfully.

"It is when she's calling to get in my business," Michael answered.

"Since you know why I'm calling, don't make me work for my information," Calyssa said.

"It depends on what you want to know."

"Fair enough. Are you really through with that Shaniqua girl?" she asked.

"Yes."

"Good. Did she really threaten to cut you?" Calyssa asked with concern.

"Yeah, but don't worry. It was just an empty threat."

"I pray that you're right." She switched topics. "So, tell me, what do you think of Daria?" she asked.

"That's none of your business," Michael responded. "Next question."

"Mmm-hmm, I thought so," Calyssa said with satisfaction.

"You thought what?" Michael asked and instantly regretted that he had.

"You like her," Calyssa said with a smile in her voice.

"Mind your own business, Sis," Michael warned.

"Daria's my friend, so she is my business," Calyssa said with steel in her voice. "I know your track record with women, and I don't want to see her get hurt."

Doubting himself was one thing, but hearing his sister voice those same doubts irrationally sparked his anger.

"Have you forgotten that I've changed? Old things passing away, and all things becoming new, and all that," Michael retorted angrily.

"Just calm down. I'm not trying to hurt you, little brother," Calyssa said.

Michael felt another flash of irritation. She was only a year older than he, yet she never let him forget he was the baby of the family.

Calyssa continued. "I saw the look that passed between the two of you on Sunday. It was hot enough to burn toast." She chuckled. "I just want you to be careful with her."

Had they been that obvious? Had anyone else witnessed *the look?*

"Uh…has anyone else said anything?" Michael asked.

"No, but the aunties don't miss much. I wouldn't be surprised if they hadn't seen you guys trying to fry each other with your eyes. You know how Mom operates. Even if she'd seen you guys, she wouldn't say anything unless she thought it necessary, and then she'd come down on you like a ton of bricks," Calyssa said dryly.

"The wrath of Amelia." Michael chuckled. "I haven't experienced that in a long time."

"And you don't want to. The ol' girl can still set things off when she feels it's warranted." Calyssa chuckled fondly.

"Look, Sis, it's none of your business, but I'm not planning to hurt your friend. If I step to her, I promise you it'll be done right. Okay?" Michael said seriously.

"Okay, I'll have to accept that, buuut," Calyssa stretched the word out with a smile in her voice, "if you start making me nervous…" She paused for a heartbeat. "I'm telling Mom!" she ended with a laugh.

"Please don't do that. I don't want the wrath of Amelia to come down on me. I may never recover." Michael laughed.

"I'm glad you're home, Michael," Calyssa said warmly.

"I missed you too, Sis. And don't worry. I'm not going to hurt Daria," he said earnestly.

Chapter Eight

Saturday morning, Daria woke up with Michael at the forefront of her mind. Would she finally see him today?

It had been two whole weeks since he'd singed her with his eyes at his mother's dinner table, and she hadn't had a glimpse of him since.

When she'd left for work in the morning and returned in the evening, his SUV hadn't been in the parking lot.

Surprisingly, he hadn't been in church on Sunday, either. She hadn't had the nerve to ask his family where he was. There was no need to wave a red flag and shout, "I'm interested in Michael!"

Was he avoiding her?

She knew she hadn't imagined the interest in his eyes. He didn't strike her as being hesitant when it came to going after what he wanted, so why hadn't he tried to approach her?

I could adopt Shaniqua's technique and just show up at his door, demanding that he let me in. She smiled. *Nah, not my style.*

It had been a long time since a man had snagged her interest the way Michael had. *Could he be The One?* She didn't know, but she was no longer prepared to reject the idea outright.

Oh well, it was pointless to use up her brain cells trying to figure out something the Lord had already worked out. If Michael was The One, the Lord knew it and would bring them together in His own time.

But Lord, I just want to throw this out there: Today isn't too soon for me, and yesterday would've been excellent.

Daria laughed at her foolishness as she dressed in a pretty, soft-blue cotton blouse and a khaki skirt.

She decided to walk to the mail kiosk to pick up her mail and then go visit her aunt.

When she stepped outside, she glanced at Michael's door.

Get to steppin', Daria. Wishing is not going to make him appear.

When she reached the end of the walkway, her eyes swept over the parking lot looking for his SUV. They came to a screeching halt.

What in the world?

With her mouth hanging open wide enough to catch a family of flies, she walked over to Michael's vehicle.

It was coated from fender to bumper in what looked like flour. At least two-dozen shattered, raw eggs had dried in various places over the hood and windshield. One broken wiper lay at an awkward angle and the other held down a sheet of paper that rippled in the soft morning breeze.

Daria looked around to see if anyone was about, because there was no doubt about it, she was going to take a look at that sheet of paper.

When she didn't see anybody, she snatched the paper from under the wiper and promptly sneezed from the flour that flew up her nostrils.

From me to you, BOO!
With all my hate,
S

Daria's laughter rang out into the empty parking lot. *Shaniqua strikes again!*

Of course, Daria had to do the neighborly thing and inform Michael of the vandalism.

Thank you, Shaniqua, for giving me a reason to show up at his door, Daria thought with gleeful satisfaction as she headed toward the walkway that led to their entryway.

If she had the opportunity to speak with him again, maybe she'd be able to figure out what was going on in his head concerning her—them.

Her heart slammed in her chest, and she stopped in mid-stride. Would he think that she was chasing after him? Would he be friendly or unwelcoming?

She took a few deep breaths and started walking again.

She had a valid reason for showing up at his door. He could think whatever he wanted, as long as he didn't *say* the wrong thing. If he did, she'd make him wish he hadn't. She chuckled. She'd turn Aunt Lenore loose on him.

She stopped before his door and placed her hand over her pounding heart for a moment before knocking.

In what seemed like the longest minute of her life, Michael answered the door. And she promptly forgot how to breathe.

He was wearing a t-shirt that hugged the contours of his chest and denim shorts that left a lot of muscle showing beneath the hem.

Oh, have mercy! Ooh-ooh, look at those muscles. It should be against the law for anybody to look that good.

"Daria, is something wrong?" Concern wrinkled his brow.

Down, girl! Thou shalt not lust after thy neighbor.

Daria gave herself a mental shake. "Um…no…yes."

Michael questioned with a smile. "Which is it, yes or no?"

"Yes. Here." Daria handed him the paper that she'd snatched from his windshield.

"What's this?" he asked, reaching for the paper.

Daria smirked. "Shaniqua left you a present in the parking lot. That note was pinned onto your windshield, boo."

Michael read the note and groaned.

Daria chuckled.

"What did she do?" Michael asked with anger in his voice.

"Let's just say she gave your vehicle a makeover."

Michael's eyes widened, and then he sprinted off for the parking lot with Daria's laughter nipping at his heels.

Daria pulled the door shut and sauntered after him. When she reached the parking lot, Michael was standing—legs spread and hands fisted on his hips—and shaking his head in disbelief.

"I can't believe this!" Incredulous didn't begin to describe the expression on his face.

"Well, look on the bright side," Daria said, struggling to keep a straight face.

Michael scoffed. "What bright side?"

"Shaniqua could've slashed your tires," Daria said, attempting—she really was trying—not to laugh. She wasn't successful. Her laughter belted past her lips.

Michael grunted. "You're enjoying this, aren't you?"

"Just a little bit." Daria held up her hand, measuring out a small distance between her index finger and thumb. "About this much." She bent double as she howled her enjoyment.

Michael rolled his eyes in exasperation. "It's been two weeks since Shaniqua and I had that run in. Why now? I thought all of this drama was over."

"It probably would've happened sooner if she'd had the opportunity. You haven't exactly been around much lately," Daria said, and then mentally kicked herself.

Real smooth, Daria. Real smooth. You just told him that you've noticed his absence. She grimaced inwardly. *Maybe he'll have a man blip and miss my admission.*

Michael's eyes sharpened on her face. *So much for the man blip.*

"I'd been in Colorado for the past two weeks on business," he explained.

Ohhhh, so he wasn't avoiding me, she thought, suddenly happy.

"Oh, c'mon. Lighten up, Michael. It's not that bad. With a little soap, water, and some muscle, it'll be as good as new. That is, after you replace this poor, drunken wiper." She snickered, fingering the wiper.

She peeked at Michael, and the smile that kicked up the corners of his mouth reassured her.

"Are you going to do the Christian thing and help me wash my ride?" he asked with a gleam in his eye.

"Name the book, chapter, and verse that says I have to help you clean up this mess," Daria shot at him with mock fierceness.

"Michael 1:1," he shot back with a grin.

"That must be a lost book that didn't make it into the Bible because I've certainly never heard of it," Daria rejoined.

Michael chuckled. "C'mon, help a brother out," Michael begged with a playful twinkle in his eyes.

Did she really want to spend the next couple of hours watching him flex his muscles, or did she want to visit Aunt Lenore? Michael or Aunt Lenore? The pendulum immediately swung to Michael and stayed there.

I don't think I've ever looked forward to washing an automobile as much as I look forward to washing this one.

Daria bubbled with anticipation. "All right. I'll help you. I'll get changed while you get the supplies together."

With mixed feelings, Michael stood in the parking lot and watched Daria walk away. He'd missed her while he'd been gone and was pleasantly surprised to see her standing at his door this morning.

He wanted to spend time with her, but on the other hand, he felt he needed to keep his distance from her.

The escalation of his heartbeat when he'd opened his door this morning had told him that the past two weeks away had done nothing to reduce his attraction to her. She'd looked so fresh, so beautiful and desirable this morning.

Michael's nose twitched from the latest wave of air-borne flour.

He turned back to his SUV. Would he ever be rid of Shaniqua? Why wouldn't she just leave him alone?

He went indoors to collect the materials they'd need to wash away the mess.

When he returned, Daria was picking eggshells off his hood. He took one look at her and stumbled.

Michael squeezed his eyes shut. *This is a big, big mistake.*

Daria was wearing an old t-shirt and cutoff jeans. Nothing about her outfit was immodest, but, unfortunately for his peace of mind, it fit her perfectly in all of the right places. He was beginning to think she could wear a potato sack and pull it off with flair.

Michael moaned. *Lord, help me!*

Daria turned in his direction at that moment, so he made himself move.

"Hey." She sent him an engaging smile.

Michael forced a smile. "I've brought the stuff that we need." *Well, that's stating the obvious.*

He dropped the pails, soap, and sponges near the vehicle and went to connect the water hose.

After filling two pails with soap and water, they got to work.

Michael worked silently and tried to ignore the questioning looks Daria sent his way.

Just work, and you'll get through this unscathed, he instructed himself.

"Just like a man to mope because something has happened to his toy," Daria mumbled nearby.

"Just like a woman not to understand how important a man's ride is to him," Michael mumbled right back.

Daria stopped working and placed her hands on her hips. "What's wrong with you, man? I'm helping you wash *your* ride. Mine's sitting over there all nice and clean." Daria gestured over her shoulder at her red, mid-sized Toyota. "You act like I'm the one who started making a cake on your SUV," she continued indignantly.

Michael felt a quick jab of guilt. In his efforts to keep a distance between himself and Daria, he'd unintentionally hurt her.

There was no way he was going to admit the real reason for his behavior, so he grabbed at an obvious explanation.

He moved closer to her, his eyes pleading with her to accept his explanation. "I'm being a jerk, and I'm sorry. It's just that I thought this thing with Shaniqua was over."

Daria exhaled sharply. "You've got to be kiddin' me. Haven't you heard the saying about a woman scorned and all of that? This woman in particular promised you retribution."

"I thought she was just making idle threats," Michael responded.

Daria rolled her eyes. "Well, you were wrong."

"Hopefully, this is the end of it."

Thinking that all was forgiven, Michael got back to work. He was soon disabused of that idea, by a cool blast of water hitting him in the face.

"Argh!" Michael shouted, wiping at his face. "What's wrong with you, woman? Why'd you do that?" he yelled.

Looking as cool as a cucumber, Daria said, "I thought you looked hot and needed to cool off a bit. Did I do something wrong?" She gave him a sweet smile.

"You thought…" Michael didn't even finish his sentence. He dipped his sponge in his pail and lunged for her.

Daria shrieked and lit out across the parking lot with Michael in close pursuit.

He threw the sponge and hit the bullseye. It smashed into the center of her back and left a wet trail down her legs as it fell to the ground.

She stopped, breathing hard from her exertions. "You…sir…are not…a gentleman," she puffed.

Michael smirked. "I am when I want to be."

"Yeah?" Daria kicked up a brow. Her chest rose and fell with her efforts to draw in enough air.

"Yeah," Michael answered, unconcerned.

Daria walked back toward the SUV with Michael trailing behind her. When she reached it, she shot him a mischievous look over her shoulder and dove for the water hose.

"Oh, no you—" Michael's words were cutoff by the blast of water that hit him from the nozzle of the hose.

Daria's shouts of laughter mixed with his yells of outrage—that is, until he lunged for her again.

He grabbed her from behind and tried to wrestle the hose out of her hand. The exact moment their play turned serious, he didn't know.

It seemed like the air around them stood still.

Their laughter and shouts quieted.

Slowly, Daria dropped the hose and turned to face him.

The firm hold Michael had had on her upper arms shifted into a soft caress, as he stared intently into her eyes.

With fire dancing in her eyes, Daria stared back at him just as intently.

He moved closer, zeroing in on her lips.

She lifted her lips slightly, giving him full, unimpeded access.

Lord, help me. I'm going down. I know it, and I can't stop myself.

He lowered his head toward hers and—

Beep! Beep! Beep!

Jerking back from Daria, Michael swung his head in the direction of the intruding noise and cringed. *Aunt Euvinia!*

Michael heard Daria groan softly.

Euvinia rolled her car window down and grinned at them. "Whatcha doing, Nephew?"

"Uh…hi, Aunt Euvinia." Michael paused to clear his throat. "How are you?"

"Fine. Just fine," she responded, still grinning from ear to ear. She zoomed in on Daria. "How are you today, Daria?"

"Fine, Mrs. Pearson," Daria croaked.

"Honey, call me Aunt Euvinia. We're all family, after all—or will be before long if I don't miss my guess." Her eyes pinged back and forth between Michael and Daria.

Michael's heart nosedived.

"What can I do for you, Aunt Euvinia?" Michael asked, trying to distract her.

"Not a thing. I was just out driving around and thought I'd swing by this way." If it was at all possible, her grin turned up a watt. "I didn't know my drive would be so interesting when I set out."

Michael rubbed his ear and ran his hand over his wet head. "We were just washing my truck. It was vandalized last night," he said, hoping to change the subject.

"Is that what you young folk are calling it these days? And here I thought you were about to kiss Daria," Euvinia said sarcastically.

Michael groaned.

Daria giggled.

"Sorry about your truck. Was there any major damage?" Euvinia asked with concern.

"No, nothing major. I have to replace a wiper and give it a good washing," Michael answered.

"Good," Euvinia responded with a nod. "Any idea who did this?"

He grunted. "Yeah. Shaniqua."

"That hoochie! I should've known," Euvinia said.

Daria chuckled, drawing Euvinia's attention back to her. "Does your aunt know that you're helping my nephew *wash* his truck?"

"Um…no, I haven't spoken to her this morning," Daria responded.

Euvinia cackled. "Don't worry about it. I'll call and tell her all about it just as soon as I get home."

Daria moaned as if she were in pain.

"Do you have to call her, Auntie?" Michael asked, hoping that she'd relent.

Euvinia chuckled. "Of course I do. It would be right selfish of me if I didn't tell Lenore about all of the sights that I've seen on my drive today." She paused and beckoned Michael and Daria closer with her hand. "Y'all be careful, you hear. Flesh is a mess when you don't keep it in check."

Michael lifted his eyes toward heaven, praying for divine intervention.

Shaking with laughter, Euvinia rolled up her car window and slowly pulled away, leaving them standing in the parking lot.

Michael turned to Daria, not really knowing what to say. "Daria, I…I'm…"

With her eyes fastened on his face, she slowly backed away from him. "Yeah, me, too." She smiled and walked away.

Chapter Nine

The following Monday, the telephone rang as Daria walked through her front door after a long day at work.

She answered the phone to hear, "Hey, Ms. D!"

"Peaches!" Daria cried. "How are you? When did you return from Haven?" With a pleased smile, Daria flopped into the nearest chair and kicked off her heels.

"I'm fine. I returned earlier this week. I've been busy running around trying to wrap up some legal matters. I've decided to get my affairs in order. I've set up a living trust and written a will."

"You finally got around to taking care of that. Good for you. You've put that off for years. It wasn't as painful as you thought it would be, was it?"

"Actually, I hated it. So many details. Ugh!"

Daria could imagine the look of disgust on Peaches' face.

"Well, if you were like me and didn't have anything to leave anybody but a bunch of bills, it would've been a piece of cake," Daria joked. "Girlfriend, you are going to leave me all of your worldly goods, aren't you?" she asked playfully.

"Ms. D," Peaches said with a note of seriousness, "I'll be leaving you everything that I have. You can count on that." She paused, then asked, "Do you remember Otis Cartier?"

"Yes, of course I do. The three of us had lunch together a few times when you worked at Bolden. What red-blooded woman *could* forget that debonair brother?"

Peaches chuckled. "Girl, he's still got it goin' on. He's just as suave as ever."

"I never could figure out why you two didn't hook up. It was obvious he was interested in you." Daria removed her jacket and draped it over the arm of the chair.

"Otis was too serious for me. He's the kind of man you want to settle down with. Settling down is the furthest thing from my mind."

"Why'd you bring him up anyway?" Daria asked, massaging her aching instep.

"He's agreed to be my attorney. He's really been cool about…everything. The rest of those suits at the firm act like they'll catch the plague if they come within ten feet of me." Peaches' words oozed contempt.

"I'm not surprised Otis is willing to stand by you. He's definitely his own man." Daria ran a hand through her hair.

"That he is. And a fine one at that, too." Peaches laughed softly, then her tone turned serious once more.

"Well, anyway, Otis is one of my trustees as well as one of the executors of my will. I mailed you his business card this morning. If anything should happen to me, please call him immediately. Immediately, Ms. D. Okay?"

"Okay, okay, but this is way too morbid. Let's talk about something else, like when are you going to go to church with me again?"

"You know, it has been a while since I've seen Sister Mavis catch the Spirit." Peaches sniggered. "That alone is worth a visit to Prayer Tabernacle. Ms. D, does she still wind up her arm like she's about to pitch a fast ball when she feels the Spirit?"

"Peaches, stop. You're too much," Daria said, trying to stifle her laughter. "I do want you to come to church with me, but not to laugh at Sister Mavis."

"Yeah, I know. You want me to come because you want me to give my life to Christ," Peaches said soberly. "It may surprise you, Ms. D, but I do think about that sometimes."

"That's great! Let me know if I can answer any questions for you. You know that I'm praying for you, right?"

"Yes, I know. I've never told you this, but I really appreciate all of the love and concern you and Aunt Lenore have shown me. I know I don't act like it sometimes—like when I tell you to step off and mind your own business." Peaches chuckled. "But I really do appreciate it."

"We know you do, Peaches, but we're very concerned about you. Uh…" Daria hesitated. "Have you thought anymore about going into rehab?"

"I've thought about it." Peaches paused. "But I think I'm doing all right on my own. I'm not going to lie to you and tell you that I've stopped smoking crack completely, but I have cut back some. Six months ago, I went without it for about four months. I did smoke some after that, but I haven't had any in about a month now."

"Peaches, that's fantastic! You know Aunt Lenore and I will help you in any way that we can."

"I appreciate that. But you know me. I want to try to do it on my own."

"It seems like you're in Georgia more than you're here in Florida these days. I miss our girlfriend chats."

"Actually," Peaches said, "I'm going back to Georgia in a few days to visit my relatives for a while."

"I think it's great that you and your relatives are getting to know each other, but I'm starting to feel jealous," Daria joked with a chuckle. "I don't see enough of you. How long will you stay this time?"

Peaches laughed softly. "Oh, you know you're still my girl. I'm not sure how long I'll be gone this time—maybe a month."

"Not being able to even talk on the cell phone has been lousy. Is the cell phone reception any better in Haven yet?"

"Unfortunately, no."

"Okay, just call me whenever you can to let me know how you're doing."

"Will do. Before I go, tell me the truth. Is your new neighbor *really* as good-looking as you say he is?" Peaches asked with a smile in her voice.

Daria laughed. "He's definitely eye candy. Looks good enough to eat."

"Have you talked to him yet?"

"Mmm-hmm. We talked for the first time three weeks ago," Daria said with a smile.

"Don't hold out on me. What's he like?"

"Well, he wears a suit to work every day and carries a briefcase. Translation: The brother's got a good-paying job. Now, girl, you know that's important." Daria laughed.

"Mmm, I know you're right!" Peaches agreed with a soft chuckle.

"He has this smoky, baritone voice that sends shivers down my spine."

"Ooh, talk to me now!"

"Aaaaand." Daria paused and smiled because she knew that Peaches was chomping at the bit for more information.

"What? What? Don't play with me, girl. Tell me!" Peaches demanded.

"This is very important, so listen closely." Daria crossed her legs and jiggled her dangling foot.

"Ms. D, don't make me jump through this phone and pull the words out of your mouth," Peaches threatened good-humoredly.

Daria laughed. "He's a Christian!"

Daria held the phone away from her ear until Peaches' shrieks subsided. "You better nab him, Ms. D. You know he's not going to be on the market long once those single sisters at Prayer Tabernacle find out about him.

"You're joking, but it's true. Some women hang out at churches just to find a 'good' man. When they spot one coming through the church doors, hunting season is open.

"But you know, Peaches, if the Lord doesn't send him, I don't want him. It's either my sisters don't know, or they've forgotten that Proverbs 18:22 says, '*He who finds a wife finds a good thing...*'"

"Preach, Ms. D!"

Daria laughed. "Okay, I'll stop. It's your fault. You got me going. Listen, I haven't told you everything. You're going to love this." Daria waved a hand in the air.

"Yeah? What?!" Peaches demanded with anticipation ringing in her voice.

"Girrrrl, let me tell you..." Daria told her about the Shaniqua incident, and the subsequent ribbing Michael had gotten when they'd had Sunday dinner with his family.

Peaches howled. It took her a while to stop laughing. When she could finally speak, she said, "Ooh, I wish I could've witnessed that. I bet Aunt Lenore enjoyed herself. His Aunt Euvinia sounds like she's just as eccentric as Aunt Lenore. He didn't stand a chance, poor guy. Have you seen him since the dinner?"

"Yep." A wide grin stretched across Daria's face.

"I'm sensing that something big has happened. What have you left out?"

Daria tried to sound nonchalant, but failed terribly. "I helped him wash his SUV on Saturday."

"Daaaria," Peaches said with a warning note.

"Okay, okay, Shaniqua vandalized his truck..."

Peaches didn't interrupt during Daria's entire rendition of the episode.

"That's it?!" Peaches' voice exploded in Daria's ear. "Don't tell me you guys didn't pick up where you'd left off before his aunt interrupted you."

Daria giggled. "No, we didn't."

"And why not?!" Peaches asked with disbelief.

"The moment was lost." Disappointment laced Daria's statement.

"Have you seen or spoken to him since then?"

"Seen him? Yes, I saw him in church on Sunday. Spoken to him? No." A smile pulled up the corners of her lips. "But I sure do have a hankerin' to hear his voice. With that voice of his, he could read to me out of the dictionary, and I'd eat up every word."

Peaches laughed. "Girl, you've got it bad."

"I'm just kidding. He's a nice guy."

Daria didn't mention that she grew more and more attracted to him after each of their encounters. He seemed to be genuine in his renewed relationship with Christ. Their conversations were easy, and he had a great sense of humor.

"It's been a long time since you've been this interested in a man. I have got to meet this brother," Peaches said.

"When you meet him, you'll see why I just can't help myself." Daria laughed softly.

Peaches' laughter rang across the phone lines.

After their laughter had subsided, Peaches said, "Well, I guess I'd better be going. I love you, Ms. D, and don't you forget that. When you see Aunt Lenore, tell her I said that I love her and to behave herself."

"I will. Peaches, this has been fun. Just like old times. I love you, too, Fruit Lady. Don't forget to call me to let me know how you're doing."

Peaches chuckled. "You haven't called me that in a long time."

"Yeah, I know. Michael asked me about that picture we took in Daytona Beach, and it brought back memories of the fun we had that day. That reminds me. He said that he may have met you before."

"I don't think so. If I'd met the man you've been goin' on and on about, I'd remember him." Peaches paused a moment. "Well…I'd remember him if I wasn't in the c-zone when we'd met."

In the c-zone—meaning stoned, Daria thought sadly. "Don't worry about it. It's highly improbable that you guys have ever met."

"Okay. Bye, Ms. D, and I hope you get your man."

Daria chuckled as she replaced the receiver. "She sounded like the old Peaches."

Later that night, as Daria prepared herself some dinner, she thought about how her feelings for Michael had changed. She'd gone from being totally convinced he wasn't for her to fervently hoping that he was.

Saturday had been totally unreal. *They'd almost kissed!*

She was very, very, *very* disappointed that the kiss hadn't happened.

She could tell from Michael's reaction that he'd been just as flabbergasted as she'd been.

This delicious thing that had sprouted between them was far from over. Before all was said and done, she might still get that kiss.

A grin slowly creased her faced. *Lord, You know what I want, but I pray that Your will be done in this situation. Uh…I'd like to add, if I may, that it would sure be nice if Your will and mine were the same concerning Michael.*

Chapter Ten

On Thursday night, the doorbell rang just as Daria started to remove a pan of baked pork chops from the oven. She finished removing the pan and carefully set it on the counter on top of a potholder. The doorbell rang again as she turned to head for the door.

"I'm coming. I'm coming. Hold your horses," she muttered.

She peeked through the security hole, and her heart skipped a beat. *Michael!*

Although they had waved to each other across the churchyard on Sunday, she hadn't spoken to him since last Saturday when they'd almost kissed. If ever her short supply of patience had been tried, it had been since that day. She'd wanted to talk with him about it—dissect it move by move, but she had enough sense to know she wouldn't get that from Michael.

Instead of confronting him about the incident, she'd prayed for patience and waited. Of course, it had helped a whole lot that she'd been out of town on business since Tuesday morning.

She'd hoped that Saturday would be the beginning of something special between them. Since then, she'd had a strong feeling of inevitability. She felt like this *thing* with Michael was serious business, and she was open to the Lord's will.

She patted her hair, made a lightening inspection of her blouse and chinos, took a deep breath, and plastered on a big smile.

"Hi!" she said when she opened the door. "Come on in. What can I do for you?"

Yummy!

Michael was wearing jeans and a short-sleeved denim shirt.

Down, girl!

"I don't need anything. Can't I stop by just to say hello?" Michael asked with a smile. "I haven't seen you since last Sunday, so I thought I'd stop in to say hello."

She hadn't left for her workshop until Tuesday morning. He could've seen her plenty of times since Saturday if he'd tried. *Though I guess I have to give him points for indirectly admitting that he's missed me. He is such a man!*

Would he discuss the almost-kiss, so they could clear the air? Would he pretend that the incident never happened? If so, why was he here? She decided to wait and see where he'd end up on this path he'd chosen.

"Sure, you're welcome to stop by at any time. I'm cooking dinner. Come on through to the kitchen." Daria turned and headed toward the kitchen. "I just got back from a Data Workshop in Jacksonville. Hotel food is all right, but I'm ready for a home-cooked meal." They moved past her gleaming dining room table. The candle pyramid sitting in its center reflected on the dark wood.

I missed you while I was away, she thought, but didn't dare say.

Michael stopped at the breakfast bar. "What are you cooking? It sure smells good, and I'm starved." He closed his eyes, inhaled deeply, and rubbed his stomach.

Daria laughed, then checked on the cooking pots. "Are you fishin' for an invitation to dinner?"

"Well, it is your Christian duty to feed the hungry," Michael teased.

She smiled. "I'm cooking yellow rice, baked pork chops, and string beans. I always cook too much, so there's plenty. Would you like to join me?"

"Yes." Michael accepted with a quickness that caused her to blink. "Thanks, you're truly a saint. What can I do to help?"

Hmm, interesting. Maybe he's as eager to be here as I am to have him here. This is promising.

"You can set the table. The napkins are on the counter, and the silverware is in the top drawer." She pointed to a set of drawers next to the stove.

"So, what was the workshop about?" Michael asked as he carried out his assigned task.

"First, let me tell you what I do for a living." Daria set the serving dishes on the table. "I work for the Information Technology Department at the state university. All of the state universities and community colleges have to periodically submit data to the Department of Information Resource Management in Tallahassee. The data is then collated, analyzed, and presented to the Florida legislators to help them make decisions concerning our education system. I'm responsible for maintaining the computer applications system that collects my university's submission data."

"Impressive." Michael's praise, coupled with the admiration shining in his eyes, sent delicious warmth spreading through her heart.

They sat down at the table. "I'll continue after we say grace. I don't want you to die of hunger," Daria teased with a smirk. "Would you bless the food?"

Michael reached across the table for her hand. She placed her hand in his, and they said grace. Daria was pleased with his heartfelt prayer.

Daria passed him the platter of pork chops.

"I'd like to hear more about your job." Interest shown in Michael's eyes. "Please continue."

Daria smiled, warmed by his genuine interest. "Annually, representatives from all of the state universities meet somewhere in the state to discuss data reporting requirements, and any data issues that have occurred during the year. This year the workshop was hosted by the state university in Jacksonville."

"Your work impacts our educational system. You have a remarkable job."

"Thanks. I love my work."

"I also work with computers. I'm a Systems Programmer and Hardware Specialist for KyTech International. I work at the main headquarters in Maitland, and my job is to make sure that the computer network purrs. It can be stressful sometimes, but I love what I do."

Michael took a bite of pork chop. "You're a good cook. This is delicious," he said with appreciation.

"Thanks, I'm glad you're enjoying it."

Okay, he gets more points for complimenting the cook. But would he ever get to the reason for this visit?!

After a few minutes of companionable—in Daria's case, impatient—silence, she asked, "How's your family?"

"They're doing fine. There's still no change in Alex's condition. We're praying for a miracle." A grin spread across his face. "Aunt Euvinia is…well, Aunt Euvinia. Yesterday, she told me that she's thinking about going on a trip. She doesn't know where yet, but she wants to go somewhere exciting."

"You know, Aunt Lenore wants to go on a European vacation, but she doesn't want to go alone. Do you think Mrs. Pearson…*Aunt* Euvinia…would be interested in going?"

Daria deliberately changed her reference to Euvinia, trying to jar Michael into addressing the *incident.*

He hesitated briefly, but didn't address her change in reference. "She'd probably jump at the chance."

Oh, so he hasn't forgotten that she told me to call her Aunt Euvinia on Saturday. I guess he wants to pretend that he's having a man blip. Okay, we'll keep playing this his way—for now.

"I'd love to go to Europe, but that's not possible right now. Maybe someday," Daria stated with a genuine note of wistfulness.

"What else would you like to do that you've been putting off until later?"

Talk about that almost kiss! Daria yelled silently.

"Well, I want what most girls want—a husband and children," she answered sweetly. "I'm not exactly putting that off. The opportunity has just never presented itself."

Michael gazed into her eyes and said, "You're a kind, beautiful woman, and I'm quite sure that you will marry and have children one day."

Daria squirmed in her chair trying to stifle the shivers that ran up her spine. *Ooh, that voice is lethal! Okay, he gets a whole lot of points for that one.*

Daria had to clear her throat before she could say, "Thank you."

"Do you have any other relatives living in the area besides Mrs. Jackson?" Michael asked after a pregnant pause.

Oh, c'mon, do we have to talk about this now? Daria griped to herself.

"No. Uncle Charles, Aunt Lenore's husband, died three years ago. They don't have any children. My parents were killed in a gun-shooting incident when I was eight, and I'm an only child." Daria was amazed that she could carry on this conversation and not show her frustration at the fact that they hadn't addressed the parking lot incident yet.

"That's tragic. I'm so sorry. That must've been a really difficult thing for you to deal with at such a young age." His expression echoed the kindness in his voice.

"It was hard, but I had Uncle Charles and Aunt Lenore. They loved me and raised me like I was their own child."

"That's great—very commendable."

She smiled. "I also have Peaches, my best friend. She's also an only child. We struck up a sistership when we were kids and have held each other close ever since."

"Does she attend Prayer Tabernacle?"

"Occasionally, but she hasn't attended in a while. Peaches is not a Christian. She's addicted to crack cocaine. She was a brilliant attorney until she got hooked on drugs." Daria shook her head sadly.

"That's such a waste."

"It is, but I'm hopeful. She's acknowledged that she has a problem, and she's trying to do something about it."

If he'd been planning to divert her, he'd been successful. Peaches and her plight was a worry spot for Daria, so it had been very easy for her to lose herself in the conversation. There was no way he could've known that, but then again, what woman didn't want to talk about her girlfriend?

They ate in silence until Daria decided to take matters into her own hands. *That's it! I can't take it anymore!* She screamed to herself when her minute of patience ran out.

She laid her fork down. "Are you ready to talk about what happened on Saturday?" she challenged. "That *is* why you're here, right?"

Michael exhaled and placed his fork beside his plate. "I still don't quite know what to say about what happened in the parking lot." He paused as if thinking carefully about what he was going to say. "I'm obviously *very* attracted to you. I've fought it, but I can't seem to banish it," he admitted.

Daria frowned and bristled. "So, you *don't want* to be attracted to me?"

"Yes, but *only* because of my past relationships—the lack of restraint and boundaries. Do you understand what I'm saying?"

Daria smiled, appeased by his explanation. "You mean scratchin' itches as Shaniqua so eloquently put it?"

Michael laughed sheepishly. "You heard that, huh?"

"Uh-huh." She smirked, then continued in a no-nonsense tone of voice. "And you know there won't be any of that with me, right?" Daria asked.

"Oh, absolutely. I wouldn't step to you if that were what I was looking for. I don't want to be a stumbling block for you, nor do I want to sully my relationship with Christ," he responded earnestly.

Step to me?! He's stepping to me?! Daria—her heart soaring—accepted this with a regal nod of her head. *Play it cool, girl!*

"I no longer want to date just to be dating. I don't believe you want that either. Am I right?"

"Yes." Daria gave a nod for emphasis.

"I'm tired of fighting a losing battle. I want to spend time with you and get to know you better. I want to see where this thing between us will go. Are you open to that?" Michael eyes never left hers.

Daria snorted silently. *Like, yeah!*

"Yes, *very*," Daria answered with what she hoped was poise because inside she was doing cartwheels. *Breath in. Breath out. In. Out. Keep cool!*

Michael smiled and nodded. "Are you going to the singles' Bible study tomorrow night?"

"Yes."

His warm gaze caressed her face. "Would you go with me?"

"I'd like nothing better," Daria accepted from her lofty position on cloud nine.

He gave her a slow wink." Okay, it's a date."

Oh, be still my heart. It's a date! If I'm dreamin', don't wake me up!

Chapter Eleven

Michael was as contented as a tick on a dog. He was with his lady, and all was right with the world. A weight had lifted from his shoulders when he'd finally stopped fighting his attraction to Daria. His step was lighter, and his mind was at ease. They hadn't talked much since they'd left their complex, but it was a comfortable silence.

"Stanley and Briana Candle are excellent Bible study leaders. I wish more singles would attend," Daria said as Michael's SUV pulled into the church parking lot. "The Candles met at Prayer Tabernacle while attending singles' events, so they're well-known by the other singles at the church. I'm not sure what they have lined up for tonight, but I'm sure it will be interesting."

"I've only been able to attend once, and I really enjoyed the session," Michael said.

They slid into their seats just as Stanley began to say the opening prayer.

After he'd finished praying, Stanley said, "A few months ago, Briana and I were counseling a Christian teenage couple. They told us that they hear all the time that Christians are not supposed to have sex outside of marriage. But they said nobody had ever told them how to date as

Christians and avoid that pitfall. They put the question to us and we were stymied. We knew spouting Christian platitudes at them wasn't good enough.

"We couldn't pass on advice that had been given to us, when we were dating because we hadn't received any. We set up another meeting with the couple to give ourselves time to seek God about answers for them. The information we're going to share with you tonight is what we shared with them."

Michael's heart kicked into a faster gear. There was no way this was a coincidence. This was a God thing. It had to be. The Lord knew of his struggles and fears in this area. This session was an answer to his prayer.

"Tonight is going to be a departure from how our Bible studies usually go, but we really feel like the Lord is leading us in this direction tonight," Briana added.

"We have quite a bit that we want to cover, so we're going to go ahead and get started. Briana and I think it's more appropriate for her to speak to the ladies and for me to talk to the men. So, gentlemen, please follow me into the adjoining room." Stanley gestured toward a door to the right.

The guys trooped out of the room behind him. Michael hoped that he didn't appear to be as eager as he felt to hear what Stanley had to say.

Daria thought about her conversation with Michael last night about scratchin' itches and sent up a silent prayer of thanks for this Bible study topic. She chuckled inwardly. *Yep, this is all You, Lord. You don't miss a beat.*

At the front of the room were some balloons and a helium tank. Briana walked over to the tank and attached a balloon. When she'd finished, she'd faced the group.

"Ladies, I don't want to preach at you tonight. I want to share with you. Only two short years ago, I was walking in your shoes. Believe me..." she grinned and rolled her eyes, "...I know what you're going through."

The group laughed.

"This is not a lecture, so please feel free to interject your thoughts at any time," Briana invited. "Okay, I need you to use your imagination. This balloon is a monster." She fingered the deflated balloon.

The group chuckled.

"I know. I know. Just work with me." She grinned. "The monster's name is Lust and Sexual Impropriety. Every time you allow yourself to get caught up in inappropriate situations, you feed the monster."

To illustrate, she let a little air flow into the balloon from the helium tank.

"The more you feed the monster, the bigger it gets, and pretty soon, it'll take complete control. In the case of our balloon here, it'll explode." She smiled.

"Here is a scenario: An unmarried couple goes out on a date to a romantic restaurant and has a wonderful time. He gives her a single red rose, stares into her eyes, and tells her that she's special, and he loves her."

Daria visualized this scene with Michael and her as the couple. The picture was so vivid a thrill shimmied up her spine.

"All right now! Who is this man, and where can I find him?" Sonja Grey asked, causing the room to erupt into laughter. Sonja was known for her outrageousness.

Briana laughed with them, and then continued. "They leave the restaurant, and he holds her hand as he drives her home."

Oh, yeah, I'm seeing this. Daria smiled to herself.

"They know it's late, but they don't want the night to end. She invites him in, and they cuddle on the sofa with the lights turned down low."

Daria shifted in her seat. *This too.*

"Soon, this isn't enough for them, and they want to get closer, so they start kissing and touching."

The scene flashed before Daria's mental eyes. *Bad eyes!*

"Before the night is over, they end up in bed," Briana finished laying out the scenario.

Hold it right there, sister! That I ain't seein'.

"Where do you think this couple went wrong?" Briana asked.

"Well, they shouldn't have done the deed since they're not married," Sonja piped up.

After the group's laughter died down, Briana said, "You're correct, but they started to feed the monster long before that. It was late when he drove her home. The night should've ended at her door. When he entered her home at that late hour, they fed the monster." Briana let some air into the balloon. "Can you point out anything else they should've done differently?"

No one said a word.

"Ladies, don't clam up on me now," Briana said.

"Okay," she continued when no one from the group said anything. "They moved into even more dangerous territory when they started cuddling on the sofa with the lights turned down low. They fed the monster some more." Briana let more air into the balloon.

"All right, by this time, they were both a bit hot and bothered, but they didn't stop. They escalated things by kissing and touching. They fed the monster some more."

"Ladies, if your date is not your husband, as a rule of thumb, you shouldn't touch him anywhere that you wouldn't touch your father or brother." Briana inflated the balloon some more. "That's deep, ain't it?" she asked with a chuckle.

Several of the ladies in the group—including Daria—responded, "Mmm-hmm."

"Well, if they were already hot and bothered before they started kissing and touching, it's no surprise they ended up in bed." Briana inflated the balloon to the point that it exploded with a loud bang. Everybody, even Briana, jumped at the sound, and then they all laughed.

"There is nothing wrong with giving your man a kiss," Briana said.

"Thank the Lord for that," Sonja said, giving the group another laugh.

Amen! Daria seconded to herself.

"But you need to use wisdom. If kissing your man deeply—and y'all know what I'm talking about—gets you all hot and bothered, limit your kissing to the cheek."

Briana paused because the group was laughing loudly.

"If that is a problem for you, don't kiss him at all.

"If you still have a problem, put your name in the prayer box because you need some serious prayer."

The group howled with laughter.

"Please, please do not sit with your man and talk about sex and how much you desire each other. That will escalate to conversations that include statements like 'If I weren't saved, I would…' You don't want to go there.

"Ladies, we love romance, don't we? A romantic, candlelit supper with soft music makes us all mushy and warm inside, right?"

"Oh, yeah," the group agreed.

"There is nothing wrong with that. But, sisters, if he is not your husband, please have that romantic candlelit supper in a restaurant where there will be many chaperones instead of in your home alone."

"I hear you, sister," responded Sonja, sparking more laughter.

Daria thought about the heat she'd glimpsed in Michael's eyes on occasion and about how attracted she was to him. She nodded her agreement. *It's a good thing we're both of the same mind to stay pure before God, or I'd be in serious trouble.*

"I've talked enough," Briana said after the laughter died down. "I want to hear from you. Do you have any questions or comments?"

"I don't have any questions, but I just want to say that I really enjoyed your talk. You've given us a lot of food for thought," Daria said earnestly.

"Daria, if that hunky specimen you came to Bible study with was my man, I'd be in serious need of prayer tonight," Sonja jested.

"Girl, you need to repent," Daria said, laughing and shaking her head.

Aunt Euvinia's words of wisdom popped into her mind and quieted her laughter a bit. *Flesh is a mess when you don't keep it in check.*

Oh, God, help me—us—to stay pure before You!

In the adjoining room, Stanley had given the men the same scenario. He'd also used a balloon and helium tank.

"Brothers, you know yourselves and your bodies better than anybody. You know your limitations. Don't get in trouble by being stupid," he said with a chuckle.

"If you know kissing your lady passionately is going to get your engine revving, limit your kisses to her cheek. If that still gets you going, man, don't kiss her at all. If your engine starts going at full throttle by just being anywhere near her, you're pathetic."

The group erupted with shouts of laughter. Michael joined them, but his laughter was more restrained.

"A word of advice concerning touching: Don't touch her anywhere you can't touch your mother or sister."

He paused at hearing groans emanate from some members of the group.

"Man, are you serious?" one of the guys asked.

"Dead serious. Think about it. Touching your lady anywhere else is only a prelude to other things. Don't go there," Stanley advised seriously.

Michael thought about his past relationships and nodded his agreement.

"Fellas, if your lady is not your wife, she doesn't need to hear about how much you desire her," Stanley continued. "Bottom line, no sex talk whatsoever."

Stanley smiled. "One last word of advice: If you're with your lady and you start to get monster alerts, run! Exit stage left."

The room erupted in laughter.

Michael silently prayed, *Lord, help me to keep my flesh in check.*

Chapter Twelve

"That was interesting," Daria remarked as they pulled out of the church parking lot.

"Very. I don't think I'll ever think about monsters in quite the same way again." Michael chuckled.

Daria shot him an amused glance. "Yeah, me neither."

"I need to pick up a few things from the grocery store on the way home. Do you mind?"

"No, not at all."

They rode in easy silence until Michael pulled into the parking lot of The Pantry.

"I'll go in with you," Daria offered.

"Great! It won't take me long."

Inside, Michael walked toward the produce section.

Daria fell into step beside him. "Take your time. I'm in no hurry." *No hurry at all.*

After Michael selected some grapes and bananas, they headed for the meat section.

He had just selected a package of ground beef when they heard the rapid clatter of footsteps approaching from behind. They looked back over their shoulders and turned as one to see Shaniqua tripping toward them in high-heeled boots, with daggers shooting from her eyes.

Michael groaned audibly.

Oh-oh, drama on stilettos! Daria chuckled to herself.

Shaniqua wore a sheath that fell only five—six at the most—inches down her thighs.

Shaniqua stopped in front of them with anger burning in her eyes. "Oh, so now I see what the real deal was. You just wanted to get with her! Talkin' about you wanted somethin' more. She can't give you nothin' that I can't." A flash of her long fingernails in Michael's face accompanied each sentence.

"Shaniqua, please don't make a scene," Michael pleaded.

"Don't make a scene! Just who do you think you are?! I'll turn this sto' out!"

She turned to Daria. "And you…"

Daria stiffened and shot Shaniqua her "don't go there" look. Shaniqua stopped in her tracks. *Smart girl. 'Cause if you do go there, I'll go there, too, and I promise you that you won't like what'll happen when I get there.*

Daria guessed that Michael must have interpreted the look because he inched closer to her and lightly placed his hand on her arm. *Hmm, I'm going to have to watch him. He doesn't miss a whole lot.*

"Well…uh." Shaniqua turned away from Daria back to Michael. "Now that you're with *her*, you're trying to act like you're all that, when you ain't 'bout nothin'."

"This is not about her. This is between you and me," Michael responded.

"Excuse me, Michael. Would you please give me your keys?" Daria interrupted. "You handle your business. I'll be waiting outside."

"Sure." Michael reached into his pocket for his keys and handed them to Daria. "I'm sorry," he apologized softly.

Daria took the keys, turned, and walked away without a backward glance.

"Touching," Shaniqua sneered.

Michael focused on her, and he could feel anger and disgust radiating from him in waves. Daria was a lady, and the fact that she was a victim of Shaniqua's antics made him livid.

"Look, Shaniqua, I don't know what your problem is, but you're way out of line. First, you stalked me like somebody crazy, then you vandalized my ride, and now you're harassing me in public."

"You—"

"No! Just listen. This is it. If you ever come near me again, I'll get a restraining order against you." He backed a step away from her. "I hope that I've made myself perfectly clear, Shaniqua." He turned and walked away.

He heard Shaniqua suck her teeth in his wake.

On the way to his SUV, Michael said a quick prayer. *Lord, I don't know where things are going with Daria, but I've come to care for her. I know, in the past I've avoided commitment, but Daria is special, and I don't want to mess things up with her. Lord, if this thing growing between us is Your will, I ask that You give me the wisdom I need to make things right.*

When Michael reached the vehicle, Daria unlocked the door so that he could get in.

"Daria, I can't begin to tell you how sorry I am," Michael began as soon as he'd closed the door. "Tonight is the first time I've seen Shaniqua since the Friday she showed up at our complex. When I told you things were over between us, that was the truth." He reached across and took her hand. "I have the utmost respect and admiration for you. I'd never do anything to hurt you. Do you think we can move past this?" He brought her hand to his lips and kissed it softly.

When his lips touched Daria's hand, a grin blossomed on her face. "That depends on whether I'm going to have to deal with any more Shaniquas."

Michael chuckled. "You won't. I promise."

Thank You, Lord! Michael sent up silent praise as he drove toward their complex.

When they stopped in front of Daria's door, Michael asked, "How about catching a movie on Saturday night?"

"Sounds like fun. I'd love to go."

"Great! I'll stop by at seven o'clock. Well, I guess this is good night." Michael searched her face intently.

The banked flames in her eyes ignited under his gaze.

Michael groaned, leaned in close—careful to keep a respectable distance between them—and brushed his lips across hers.

"Goodnight, sweet lady," he whispered as he backed away.

On Saturday, Daria and Lenore had another crab boil. This time, they met at Daria's condominium.

Much to Daria's relief, Lenore hadn't mentioned the incident that had happened in the parking lot last Saturday. Daria was beginning to think Aunt Euvinia had mercifully changed her mind about calling Aunt Lenore with the news.

"Peaches called me the other day." Daria cracked open a crab claw. "I hadn't spoken to her in a while, and it was really good to hear her voice."

"How is she?" Concern blanketed Lenore's face.

"She sounds good. Actually, she sounded more like the old Peaches. She told me that she's had some successes fighting her addiction."

"Oh, well, praise the Lord! That's great news." Lenore's eyes sparkled with delight.

Daria smiled. "She asked me to tell you that she loves you. She also asked me to tell you to behave yourself."

"Behave? Where's the fun in that?" Lenore teased.

"Aunt Lenore," Daria laughed, shaking her head. "you're too much."

"That was delicious. The crabs were really full today." Lenore drank the last of her soft drink, and then wiped her hands.

"Yes, they were. I'm stuffed." Daria got up from the table and began to clean up the shells.

"I'm going home to take a long nap. What do you have planned for the rest of the day?"

"I'm going to the movies with Michael tonight." Daria tried to sound as casual as possible. "By the way, I have some good news for you. Michael told me that his Aunt Euvinia wants to go on a trip. He said that she hasn't locked in on a destination yet, so you may be able to get her to go to Europe with you."

"Is that right?" Lenore asked with interest. "I'll mention it to her and see what she says. That would be great. I think we'd have a lot of fun together."

"Knowing the two of you, I'd say *too* much fun," Daria teased. "I can't imagine turning the two of you loose on Europe."

Mischief danced in Lenore's eyes. "What are you talking about? We're just two sweet, little old ladies. What harm can we possibly do?"

"Yeah, right."

Lenore dropped her crumpled napkin on the table and pinned Daria with a stare. "Do you see much of Michael?"

So much for Aunt Lenore forgetting about her remarks regarding Michael.

"We went to the singles' Bible study together last night."

Daria prudently omitted all of the other instances that she and Michael had interacted. Especially, about the kiss last night. *Mmm, that is one smooth brother!*

She forced herself to refocus on Aunt Lenore. Every time she'd thought about that kiss, she'd jettisoned up into the clouds.

"That's nice," Lenore responded in an innocuous tone. "Does Michael get many visitors? I mean does his family stop by to see him?"

Daria instantly went on the alert. *Aunt Euvinia! That ol' tattle-tell.*

She refused to give those two busybodies ammunition. Aunt Lenore could fish all she wanted to. She'd get nothing out of her!

"His Aunt Euvinia stopped by last Saturday. Why do you ask?" Daria strove to match Lenore's tone. *C'mon out with it, Auntie!*

"Considering the way things are going between the two of you, I think you need a chaperone." Lenore chuckled.

Daria groaned and winced.

"Burning each other up with your eyes and getting into clinches in the parking lot." Lenore's chuckles dissolved into laughter.

"Aunt Lenore!" Daria covered her face with her hands. "We were not in a clinch in the parking lot!"

Lenore grinned. "That's not what I heard."

"Well, you heard wrong." Daria tried to look forbidding. It didn't work.

"All right. *You* tell me what happened."

The corner of Daria's mouth kicked up in a half smile. "Not a chance."

Lenore nodded once as though she'd come to some kind of decision. "Why don't you bring Michael over to the house for our next crab boil?"

"I don't know if he eats crabs, but I'll ask him." *Now, what is she up to?* Not for a minute did Daria believe Lenore's invitation was innocent.

"Good. I'll look forward to him joining us."

The smile on Lenore's face made Daria a tad uneasy.

Michael had never enjoyed a movie quite so much. He was in-touch with himself enough to admit that the true source of his enjoyment was his lovely date.

Michael pulled into his parking space at their complex. "That was a good movie." The movie had been about a creature from Hades who joined humans in the battle against evil on the earth.

Daria shot him a look of disbelief. "Well…if you say so."

Michael laughed softly. "It was good. You just missed a lot of it because you had your hands over your eyes."

Daria smiled. "The next time, I'll pick the movie."

"The next time. Hmm, sounds promising. That'll give me a chance to redeem myself. I'm sorry you didn't enjoy the movie."

Daria's smile stretched wider. "The evening wasn't all bad."

The fact that he was spending time with her made the evening exceptional to him. Michael reached for her hand as they walked toward her door. She placed her hand in his and squeezed it lightly.

"Would you like to come in for a cup of coffee?"

Michael was not ready for the night to end. "I'd love to."

Daria busied herself preparing the coffee while Michael lounged on the couch in the living room.

"I told Aunt Lenore that Aunt Euvinia might be interested in going on vacation with her. She was delighted."

"That's great. I can see those two now—taking Europe by storm."

Daria served the coffee and sat down near Michael on the couch.

"Uh…by the way…um…Aunt Lenore asked me to invite you over to her house for our next crab boil."

"Did she?"

Mrs. Jackson wasn't extending a casual invitation. She was far too wily for that. If he accepted the invitation, he'd be making a statement of intent.

He thought about how much he enjoyed Daria's company. When he was with her, he felt a level of contentment he'd never experienced in any of his past relationships. He knew he was falling fast and hard for her, and it scared him spitless.

What were his intentions? Did he want the *M word* or an indefinite dating relationship? He glanced at Daria and snorted. *Get real, man, you'd never survive an indefinite dating relationship with her and keep your relationship with Christ intact.*

Deep down, he knew he wanted more than that with Daria. Would the possibility of the *M word* with her be so horrible?

One thing was certain—he didn't want to lose her.

He thought she enjoyed his company, but he wasn't sure about her feelings for him. Were her emotions engaged to the same degree as his?

Daria was a smart lady. She had to know what Lenore was up to. "How do you feel about that?" he asked cautiously.

She gave him a direct look. "I'd love for you to come."

Michael grunted his satisfaction with her reply. He set his cup down on the nearest table and took her hands in his.

"I've come to care a lot for you." Michael watched her face intently. "I don't know where this relationship is going, but I feel the Lord has brought us together for a purpose. Do you feel the same way, or am I alone in this?" His intensity demanded a sincere and honest answer in return.

"I feel the same way. I also believe God has brought us together. I care a lot for you, too, but I believe we should continue to seek God's will concerning our relationship."

"I agree whole-heartedly." He rose to his feet, bringing her with him. "I'd better get going." He walked toward the door holding her hand.

When they reached the door, he turned and pulled her into his arms. "You're one special lady." He kissed her softly on the lips.

She feels so right! Michael's chaste kiss quickly became passionate.

Daria's embrace tightened, and she pressed closer.

The words *Monster Alert!* popped into his head. He ended the kiss, but still held her close.

"Daria, Daria, Daria…"

"Hmm?" She clung to him.

"*Monster Alert!* It's time for me to go."

Daria shook with laughter in his arms.

Chapter Thirteen

The following Saturday, Michael found himself sitting with Lenore in her living room while Daria prepared the crabs for their crab boil.

"Has there been any change in Alex's condition yet?" Lenore asked him.

"No, he's the same. The doctors told us he still has a 50-50 chance of coming out of the coma. There's no telling what shape he'll be in when he does emerge from it. Calyssa's trying to remain positive, especially around Brandon. We continue to go to the hospital and talk to him." Michael pulled on his earlobe. "We'll just have to keep believing God for his healing."

"That's all we can do." Lenore moved on to another subject. "I talked to Euvinia about going to Europe with me. She told me she'd love to go." Satisfaction rang in her voice and sparkled in her eyes. "You wouldn't believe the trouble I've been having trying to find someone to go with me on this trip. We still need to iron out the details, but I'm looking forward to it."

"I'm quite sure the both of you will enjoy yourselves," Michael said with a smile. *Okay, this isn't as stressful as I thought it would be.*

"Michael," Lenore pointed toward the closet in the entry foyer, "look in that closet there and give me my baseball bat."

Baseball bat? Michael quickly did a mental replay of all of his encounters with Daria as well as his current conversation with Lenore. Nothing jumped out at him that would prompt Lenore to use a baseball bat on *him*, so he retrieved the bat from the closet as instructed.

Someone had used a marker to draw hair, a face, and clothing onto one side of the bat.

"Thank you," Lenore said upon receiving the bat. "Daria tells me you've been seeing quite a bit of each other," she commented after he'd returned to his seat. She absently twirled the bat in her hand, drawing Michael's eyes to it.

"Has Daria told you what happened to her parents?" Lenore inquired after a brief pause.

"She told me they died in a tragic gun-shooting incident."

"No one should ever have to endure such heartbreak." Lenore frowned and shook her head. "Daria was just a baby!" Lenore's hand sliced through the air.

"I didn't witness everything that happened that night, but I've been able to piece it all together from conversations I've had with Daria, my husband, and a family friend. It's all so vivid in my mind it seems as though I *did* witness it all first hand.

"I was so sick that night," she went on. She shook her head again and absently rubbed her chest. "Charles had rushed me to the emergency room because we thought I was having a heart attack.

"He had telephoned Daria's mother, Evelyn, and asked that she and Ralph meet us there. Evelyn told Charles that Ralph wasn't at home, but she knew where she could find him. She told him not to worry; they'd be at the hospital as soon as possible.

"Ralph had told Evelyn he would be working late, so she called his office thinking she'd find him there. When she didn't get an answer, she called Bernard Clemmons, a family friend and Ralph's co-worker, to find out if he knew where she could find Ralph. Bernard's wife told her that earlier that evening after work, Bernard and Ralph had gone to the Do Drop In bar, located on Ivey Lane.

"Evelyn tried to call the bar to let Ralph know that I was sick, but there was no answer."

Lenore's eyes had a far-away look in them. She seemed to be lost in the past—reliving the night all over again. "Well, after Evelyn hung up the phone…"

"He's lied to me, again!" Evelyn fumed as she hung up the phone. "He told me he'd be working late. I don't know why that man can't stay at home sometimes. Look what's happened. His sister is sick and needs him, and he's not even here," she muttered angrily as she rushed around looking for her purse and keys.

"Mommy, what's the matter?" eight-year-old Daria asked.

"Your Auntie Lenore's sick, and I have to find your daddy so that we can go to the hospital to be with her."

"Can I go, too?"

"No, baby. I have to go by the bar to get your daddy before we can go to the hospital, and I don't want to take you to that place. I wish I didn't have to go there either. I'll ask Mrs. Addison if you can stay with Peaches until we get back home."

Evelyn went off to find her husband after giving Daria a big kiss and leaving her next door with Mrs. Addison.

The parking lot was packed when Evelyn arrived at the bar. She parked illegally on the curb. About twenty-five people were standing outside around the entrance. She spotted her husband's hefty friend, Bernard, standing among them. But Ralph wasn't with him.

She sprinted toward Bernard. "Bernard, where's Ralph?" she gasped, breathing heavily.

He avoided her eyes. "Uh…He's still inside."

"Lenore's sick," she said. "Charles is taking her to the emergency room and has asked us to meet him there. We really need to leave right away."

She started toward the entrance, but Bernard grabbed her arm. "Evelyn, please don't go in there. Ralph riled up this bad dude who carries a gun. I tried to shut Ralph up, but you know how he gets when he's had a few too many. Everybody started moving outside when they realized what was going down."

She snatched her arm away. "Has anyone called the police? I have to get him out of there!" Before Bernard could stop her again, she dashed toward the entrance.

He took off after her.

Inside, Ralph and another man were facing each other just a few feet away. Ralph's back was turned toward them. His stance was very rigid, like he was poised to pounce.

The other man looked to be about six feet tall and weighed about two-hundred-fifty pounds. He had massive shoulders. His face was like stone.

Just as Evelyn opened her mouth to call out to Ralph, the man reached behind his back, pulled a gun from his belt, and started firing.

Ralph was shot in the head and died instantly. Evelyn was life-flighted to Orange County Medical Center with a gunshot wound to her abdomen.

Before Evelyn was flown away from the scene, she was conscious long enough to beg Bernard to go to the Addison's home, get Daria, and bring her to the hospital. She gripped his arm until he promised, then slipped into unconsciousness.

Lenore let out a long breath and shook her head as though trying to shake off the cobwebs of the past.

"I was diagnosed as having gastric reflux and treated with a cock-tail—a mixture of several types of antacids—and released, so I was able to sit with Evelyn in the critical care unit.

"Evelyn regained consciousness twice. The first time, she asked for Daria. When Daria approached the bed, Evelyn told her that she loved her.

"I think one of the hardest things I've ever had to do was to tell Evelyn—a dying woman—that her husband had just died. To know that she was about to leave her child parentless had to be a horrendous, heart-wrenching feeling.

"The last time she regained consciousness, she called for Daria and me. She could only speak above a whisper, but she managed to ask me to take care of Daria for her. Again, she told Daria that she loved her and admonished her to be a good girl for me. Shortly after that, Evelyn died.

"So, you see, Daria is my daughter in every way that matters. She's had enough pain to last a lifetime. I don't want to see her hurt or trifled with. If you're not ready to commit to her, leave her alone—now. Do you understand what I'm saying to you?"

"Yes, ma'am," Michael answered meekly.

"Good." Lenore nodded once. "And another thing: Don't ever lie to Daria—deliberately or by omission. My brother was guilty of doing that to both Daria and her mother. Daria won't tolerate that—not even a little bit."

"All right," Michael responded.

Lenore turned the bat around so that the drawn face was facing toward him.

"Let me introduce you to Clifford." She pointed to the bat. "If you hurt my baby in any way, I'll make sure you become *very* acquainted with Clifford." Lenore raised an eyebrow. "Understand?" Her smile sent chills through Michael.

"Perfectly." Michael cleared his throat. "I understand you perfectly, Mrs. Jackson." He rubbed his palms together. "You don't have to worry, because I'd never hurt Daria. I admire, respect, and..." His words trailed off as he tried to find the right expression to convey how special Daria was to him.

His heart thumped hard and took off at a sprint. *I'm in love with her!*

He was as certain of that, as he was that Mrs. Jackson would be all over him with that bat if he said the wrong thing.

He swallowed past the lump lodged in his throat. "I'm in love with her, and I'd like nothing more than to spend the rest of my life showing her how much she means to me."

I'm in love with Daria! He wanted to yell it from the rooftops, and at the same time, he wanted to run for the hills.

Lenore took her time answering. Her eyes were glued to his face as though she could see the level of his sincerity written there. "You have my blessing. You can call me Aunt Lenore. We are going to be family after all." She paused a beat and smiled. "But, son, make sure you save some of that *showing* for after the I Do's."

Michael laughed shakily. "Yes, ma'am."

"Does Daria know how you feel about her?"

"She knows that I care for her, but she doesn't know that I'm in love with her." *I just figured it out myself.*

"When do you plan to tell her?" Lenore asked.

After I get used to the idea myself! Michael thought, but said, "When I feel the time is right."

Panic clawed at Michael as he felt lock-down looming ominously in his not-so-distant future.

Chapter Fourteen

Two weeks later on Thursday evening, the phone rang as Michael sat in his den reading his Bible. He absently picked up the receiver. "Greer."

"Hey, man, how's it goin'?"

A smile creased Michael's face. "Great. David, man, it's good to hear from you. It's been a while."

"That it has. What's been goin' on with you? Are you staying out of trouble?" David's voice held a hint of concern.

Michael knew David was really asking how his walk with Christ was going.

"Yeah, it's all good, man, it's all good." Michael's answer was quick and sincere.

"I'm glad to hear that," David responded with a gust of relief. "You hadn't called in a while. I'll be honest with you. I was beginning to worry."

"You can rest easy. I'm not going back out there. At times, I wonder why I backslid in the first place. I have more peace, joy, and contentment now than I've had in years. I still have difficulties and disappointments, but I feel like the Lord has my back, and that makes a big difference." Earnest wonder filled Michael's voice.

"I hear you, man."

"There have been some developments since we last spoke."

"Yeah? Good I hope."

Michael smiled. "Shaniqua vandalized my ride."

David's disgust zinged across the phone lines. "How come I am not surprised? She vandalized your ride? Man, that's low. You don't mess with a man's ride."

Michael chuckled.

"How can you possibly find humor in that?" David asked incredulously.

"You know that verse in Romans that says all things work together for our good?"

"Yeah. What about it?"

"Shaniqua may have meant to cause me harm, but in the end a good thing came out of the whole mess."

"Man, you're talking in riddles. How could anything good possibly come out of her vandalizing your SUV?" David's annoyance was evident in his voice.

"Shaniqua baptized my SUV in flour and eggs. Except for a broken windshield wiper, she really didn't do much real damage."

"Damage is damage. Are you going to get to the point?" David's caustic question zipped through the phone lines.

"Daria helped me wash my truck." Michael smiled in satisfaction.

"Ah, now I'm beginning to get the picture. What happened?"

"Let's just say things got intense."

"*Good* intense or *bad* intense?" Anticipation permeated David's voice.

"Good and bad. Good in that I almost kissed her senseless in the parking lot in front of God and anybody that cared to look on. Bad in that it catapulted me down the path toward lock-down."

"Man, are you serious?!" David yelled.

Michael laughed. "I gave up. I couldn't fight my attraction to her any longer."

David chortled. "I told you that you wanted that sister. Was I right or what?"

"You were right. But you know what?"

"What?"

"I never knew surrender could be so sweet."

David laughed. "Michael Greer, ladies' man extraordinaire, is considering the M word."

"Yeah, it boggles the mind doesn't it?"

"You know it. How far along are things? I mean, should I start airing out my tux?" David asked with a chuckle.

"No, we're just getting to know each other and enjoying each other's company. Though I have had The Interview."

David laughed heartily. "How'd it go?"

"Her aunt introduced me to Clifford," Michael responded deadpan.

"Who is Clifford? A cousin, uncle, brother, or somebody else you need to be afraid of?"

Michael chuckled. "Some*thing* else. Clifford is her baseball bat. Man, she's drawn a face and clothes on the thing."

David guffawed.

"You laugh, but I was choosing my words very carefully. Her aunt told me if I hurt Daria, Clifford and I would become *very* acquainted. Man, I believe her, too. She had this blood-thirsty look in her eyes."

David's howls rang unchecked into Michael's ear. "Man, there's never a dull moment with you."

Michael sobered. "Daria and I went to the singles' Bible study together shortly after that scene in the parking lot. The topic was Christian dating and avoiding the pitfall of pre-marital sex."

David whistled. "Heavy stuff."

"Yeah, but timely. David, man, I just see God's handprints all over this thing with Daria and me. The things the instructors said have been a sustaining force." Michael chuckled. "My old auntie hit the nail on the head when she said, 'Flesh is a mess when you don't keep it in check.'"

David laughed. "She's right."

"Man, you've been saved a long time now. Help a brother out. How do you manage to date and keep yourself spiritually clean?"

David made a sound that sounded like the combination of a laugh and a snort. "I don't date."

"What do you mean, you don't date?"

"I don't. I tried, but it never felt *tight*." David paused a few seconds. "I've decided that when it's time for me to make that move, God will send *the* lady into my life. In the meantime, I'm not shopping around."

Michael grunted his approval.

Later that night, he thought about what David had said about God's timing. He knew God's hand was guiding his life. He also knew God's grace had placed Daria in his life at this time. "Lord, please help me to walk worthy of Your great gift."

On the following Saturday evening, Daria's cell phone rang as she and Michael sat on his couch watching a chick-flick and munching popcorn.

Daria checked the display, and her lips turned up in a wide smile. "Peaches! What's up, girl?"

"Where are you, Ms. D?" Peaches asked. "I've been trying to reach you at home all afternoon. I finally gave up and called you on your c-phone."

"I've been over at Michael's place all afternoon. Where are you? Are you still in Haven?"

"I'm back in Florida. I got back late this morning."

"Great! Will you be here for a while, or will you be going back soon?"

"I'm planning to go back in a couple of weeks. Since I'll only be up there for a day or two, I was thinking about asking you to ride up there with me."

"Sounds like fun. I'd love to go with you. Just give me the dates, and I'll put in for some vacation days at work."

"Thank you, girlfriend."

Daria leaned forward and propped her elbow on her thigh. "How've you been?" Daria hoped that none of the apprehension she felt came through in her voice. She knew she'd get an honest answer from Peaches, but she wasn't sure she really wanted to hear the answer. She wanted so badly for Peaches' addiction to be a thing of the past.

"I've been doing fine. I'm still clean. It's not easy, but I'm taking it one day at a time."

Daria slowly released the breath she'd been holding. "Fantastic! You know I'm pulling for you." Daria settled back in her seat.

"Girl, I know you've got my back and will help a sista' out any way you can," Peaches acknowledged. "Other than that, I've got a bad case of indigestion that will *not* go away. I've taken several different kinds of antacids, but none of them have given me any relief."

Daria frowned. "You should talk to Aunt Lenore about that indigestion. Maybe she can suggest something that'll take care of it."

"I'll do that. I haven't spoken with Aunt Lenore in a while. It's past time I called her anyway." Peaches changed the subject. "It's been several weeks since we've talked. You said you've been at Michael's place all afternoon. I know you didn't think I'd let you throw out that little nugget of information without giving me any details. What's going on over there?" Peaches asked with a smile in her voice.

"Well..." Daria started, then looked over at Michael. "Please hold on a minute, Peaches."

Daria addressed Michael. "I'll be right back. I need to go over to my place for a few minutes."

Michael smirked. "I know why you're leaving. Just don't say anything too bad about me to Peaches." Michael reached for the remote control and changed the television channel to a sports channel.

Peaches had heard Michael's comment. Daria could hear her laughing over the phone. "I won't," Daria said with a grin. "And we *will* finish looking at that movie when I return."

Michael winked and sent her an air kiss.

Pleasure snaked up Daria's spine. She caught the kiss in her hands and placed her hand over her lips. She blew him a return kiss before leaving.

Daria entered her condo and sat down in the nearest chair. "Girrrl, let me bring you up to date. Shortly after you left for Georgia, I attended a Data Workshop in Jacksonville. When I returned, Michael showed up at my door—"

"Don't tell me he was running from another woman," Peaches interrupted.

"No, not this time." Daria laughed. "He just wanted to say hello."

"Interesting. Tell me more."

Daria kicked off her backless shoes. "I invited him to dinner, and he asked me to ride to the singles' Bible study with him that Friday night."

"You had a date? You go, girl!"

Daria folded a leg beneath her. "Bible study was a bit different this time." She smiled. "We talked about monsters." She waited for Peaches' reaction.

"Monsters? What do monsters have to do with the Bible?"

When Daria stopped laughing, she answered, "More than you know. The session was actually about Christian dating and avoiding the pitfall of pre-marital sex. Our Bible study leaders used a balloon and a helium tank to…"

After Daria finished, Peaches chuckled. "That was so clever. I'll never think about balloons in quite the same way."

Daria unfolded her leg and sat forward. "That's not all," she continued. "After the Bible study, we stopped by The Pantry, and you won't believe whom we ran into." She had to pause, because she was laughing so hard.

"Who?! Who?! Tell me!"

"Shaniqua!" Daria sputtered and smacked her thigh.

"No!"

"Yes, and she went on the attack. She said…"

"You've got to be kiddin' me. What did Michael have to say about all of this?" Peaches asked after Daria had finished telling her about the latest Shaniqua incident.

"When he got in the truck he apologized, and…are you ready for this?" Daria teased with a satisfied grin.

"What?"

"He told me that he respected and admired me. And then he ever so gently kissed my hand."

"Ooh, I'm seeing green. That is just too sweet!"

"Yeah, I thought so, too." Daria smiled and continued. "When we got back here, he walked me to the door and kissed me good night. Girl, you know it took me a while to come down out of the clouds after that."

Peaches giggled. "Hmm, I believe it."

Daria moved to the sofa. "It gets even better." She folded both legs onto the chair and propped her elbow on the arm. "Aunt Lenore invited him over for crabs." She chortled.

Peaches laughed. "Uh-oh."

Daria swiveled, placing her back against the arm of the chair, then drew her feet up close. "Peaches, she introduced him to Clifford." She howled.

When Peaches could finally control her laughter, she said, "No…she didn't. Aunt Lenore is too much."

"Since then, we've been spending as much time together as possible."

"I'm so happy for you, Ms. D. You deserve all of the pleasure that comes your way."

"Thank you, Peaches."

"So tell me, have there been any monster alerts?" Peaches asked with a teasing note.

"Mmm-hmm." Daria laughed.

After Peaches finally stopped laughing, she said, "I'm going to go to church with you tomorrow, Ms. D. Why don't you and Michael come over here for dinner after church? I think it's time for me to check this brother out."

"I'd love too, but I'll have to check with Michael to see if he already has plans. I'll head back over that way." Daria stuck her feet back into her shoes. "Hang on while I lock up." She exited and closed the door behind her.

She knocked on Michael's door.

"Michael," she said when he opened the door. "Peaches would like for us to come over to her place for dinner after church tomorrow. Would you like to go?"

Michael asked playfully, "Can she cook?"

"Peaches, Michael wants to know if you can cook," Daria said into the cell phone.

Peaches chuckled. "Tell him to come over and find out."

Daria laughed. "She said to come over and find out," she passed on, then added, "Peaches is a very good cook."

Michael smiled. "I'd love to come."

"Michael would love to come. I'll see you at church on Sunday. Take care." Daria ended the call.

Michael captured Daria's hand and walked over to the couch. She sat down beside him, leaving her hand in his.

"That was a long call. We missed the rest of the movie."

Daria huffed. "As if you really wanted to see it anyway."

Michael laughed and squeezed her hand. "What did you ladies talk about?"

Daria gave him a saucy wink. "This and that. Believe me, you don't want to know."

Michael put his arm around her and pulled her closer to his side. "I missed you."

Daria gazed into his eyes and smiled.

Michael started to slowly trail soft kisses all over her face. When he pulled back and looked into her eyes, the flames he saw there scorched him.

"Michael," Daria said with deep feeling and lightly placed her hand on his cheek.

Michael kissed her on the lips, and the kiss rapidly deepened in intensity and seared them.

Daria broke away first. "Uh...Michael?"

"Yeah?" Michael's mind was totally focused on his task—nuzzling Daria's neck.

"*Monster Alert!*" she uttered softly with a hint of desperation.

He rested his forehead against hers and groaned. "You're right. It's time to call it a night." *Oh, man, these monster alerts are happening too often.*

They walked to her door in silence.

After Daria opened the door and stepped inside, Michael gently turned her around so that she faced him.

"I think we need to set some boundaries. Those monster alerts are happening too often." Michael searched her face for a reaction.

Daria exhaled and then smiled. "I agree. As we walked over here, I was trying to think of a way to tell you the same thing."

"Good!" he said with relief. "Let's mull it over and then put our heads together. Between the two of us, I believe we can come up with something that'll help us."

She nodded her agreement.

"Okay, I'll say good night." He kissed her on the cheek and walked away.

Peaches got up at six o'clock Sunday morning to finish cooking her dinner. The service started at ten o'clock, so she had plenty of time to finish cooking before she needed to leave for the church.

She had prepared the pork roast, turnips, fruit salad, and chocolate cake the night before. She only needed to make the potato salad and the macaroni and cheese.

She grimaced as she walked into the kitchen. She loved to cook and spent a lot of time in her kitchen. The welcome familiarity of the burgundy-apple decorating theme usually soothed her. Today, she didn't even notice it.

"Why won't this indigestion go away?" she asked out loud as she reached for the bottle of antacid she'd left on the counter the night before.

She was still taking different kinds of antacids; hoping one of them would give her some relief. She had even asked Lenore for some suggestions about what to take. Lenore had suggested a few medicines, but when Peaches had told her that she'd tried them already, Lenore had told her she needed to see a doctor.

Peaches hated to go to the doctor and avoided it like the plague. She was fed up with doctors because she'd suffered through too many doctor's appointments where the doctor handled her with impatience instead of really listening to her complaints.

As she stood at the counter opening the medicine bottle, the pain intensified. It felt like a tight band wrapped around her chest. She felt lightheaded and started to sweat profusely. She decided to sit for a few minutes, hoping the pain would subside.

"What's wrong with me?" Peaches voiced her worry as she sat down in a chair at the kitchen table.

Instead of subsiding, the pain got even worse. It radiated from her chest down into her left arm and to the fourth and fifth fingers of her left hand.

At that point, Peaches realized what was happening to her. She was having a heart attack! *I've got to get help!*

Clutching her chest and panting, she stood and headed toward the telephone hanging on the wall on the opposite side of the kitchen.

Lord, help me! She pleaded over and over again in her mind as she slowly moved toward the phone.

When she reached it, she leaned against the wall and tried to catch her breath. She lifted the receiver, and pain, like none she'd ever experienced before, ripped through her chest and down into her left arm.

Peaches dropped to her knees with a grimace. The phone fell from her hand onto the floor.

Before that pain could ease, another seized her. She fell over onto her side and drew herself up into the fetal position.

"Oh, God!" she mouthed silently as blackness closed around her.

Chapter Fifteen

After church Daria, Michael, Lenore, and Michael's family were standing in the church parking lot talking.

"Peaches told me she was going to come to church today. Have you seen her?" Daria asked Lenore. She scanned the parking lot.

"No, I haven't. Are you sure she came? She called me last night complaining of indigestion. She wanted to know if I could recommend a medicine that would give her some relief. She'd already tried everything I suggested. I told her she needed to see a doctor and get herself checked out."

Well aware of Peaches' aversion to doctors, Daria said, "You know how much she hates doctors, so I can imagine how she reacted to that suggestion."

"She may not have indigestion," Lenore grumbled, shaking her head. "It could be something a lot more serious. Humph, you young folk today think you know everything. Can't tell you nothin'."

"I hope it's nothing more serious than that," Daria said with concern. "She invited Michael and me over to her place today for Sunday dinner. I guess we'll head over there in a few minutes."

"Just let me know when you're ready to leave," Michael said.

Euvinia winked at Michael, and then said to Daria, "Since you and my nephew are an item, why don't you stop by the house sometime and visit me? Don't bring my nephew with you. I want to talk with you about some things—give you a few tips."

Daria smiled, warmed by the invitation. "Sure, I'd—"

"Oh, no," Michael interrupted. "You don't need to give her any tips, Auntie. She's doing just fine. She doesn't need you to corrupt her." Michael shook his head, stressing his objection to the idea.

Euvinia laughed and slapped her thigh.

Daria frowned and looked at Michael. "Michael, what are you talking about?"

"Don't worry about it. It's just a little something between Aunt Euvinia and me," he answered with a chuckle.

Euvinia grinned. "I'm just having a little fun at Michael's expense. But I do want you to feel free to stop by and see me anytime you want to. You don't have to wait for Michael to bring you over. I'm quite sure Amelia feels the same way."

Amelia had been watching the by-play between Euvinia and Michael with an indulgent eye. "Absolutely. Anytime. Seeing the two of you together makes me very happy." Amelia gave Daria a warm smile. "I couldn't have chosen better for Michael myself."

Daria intercepted a look between Calyssa and Michael that she didn't understand. "Yes, little brother, you finally got something right." Calyssa turned mischievous eyes on Daria. She thought she must've imagined the note of seriousness she'd heard in Calyssa's voice when she'd addressed Michael. "Daria, we do need to talk, though, so I can fill you in on a couple of things."

The group laughed.

Michael touched Daria's arm. "I think it's time for us to go before they turn you against me."

"Let me call Peaches to tell her we're on our way." Daria took her cell phone out of her purse.

She moved a few steps away from the group and dialed Peaches' home phone number. She got a busy signal. That was strange because Peaches had call waiting. She dialed again, just to make sure she hadn't misdialed the number. Again, she got a busy signal.

Daria tried to reach Peaches on her cell phone, but she didn't answer that either. When voice mail picked up, Daria left a message telling Peaches that they were on their way and would be arriving shortly.

Daria returned to the group perplexed and troubled.

"Is there a problem?" Michael asked, lightly placing his hand on her arm.

"I can't get her on either of her phones," Daria answered.

Michael frowned. "Let's head on over there and make sure everything is all right."

Forty minutes later, Michael whistled softly as he pulled his SUV into the driveway of Peaches' Lake Mary home, beside her Lexus. "Nice place. Nice ride."

Her house was a huge, single-level home, built in the latest colonial style. Red brick covered the exterior, and the woodwork was trimmed in a cream color.

There were two large windows in the front of the house bracketing beautifully crafted, double doors at the entrance. The blinds were open in both windows.

"Peaches has done very well for herself." Daria's voice held a mixture of pride and sadness. "If only she hadn't allowed her adventurous spirit to lead her down the wrong path, there's no telling what she would've achieved by now."

"I'm looking forward to meeting her. I'm also hungry, so can we go in now?" Michael asked on a lighter note.

The corners of Daria's mouth lifted in a ghost of a smile. "Let's go."

Daria rang the doorbell and waited. When Peaches didn't answer, she rang it again. Two minutes later, Daria was near tears.

She walked to the window on the right side of the front doors. "The lights are on in the kitchen, but I don't see Peaches." Daria sniffed. "You can see the living room through that window." She pointed to the window on the other side of the doors. "Please take a look and tell me if you can see anything."

Michael looked into the window. "Nothing. The lights aren't even turned on."

Lines of worry formed on Daria's brow. "This doesn't feel right."

"Try calling her again," Michael suggested.

Daria tried to call Peaches again, but still got a busy signal.

"It just doesn't feel right. I know where Peaches hides a key. I'm going in." The urgency Daria felt rang in her voice.

She walked along a stone walkway around to the side of the house. When she reached the fourth stone, she lifted it up and retrieved a key case, which was enclosed in a tiny plastic bag.

She unlocked the front door, and they entered the house.

"Peaches?" Daria called out.

There was no answer. They walked into the living room. It was empty.

"Peaches, are you here?" Daria called out again.

Still, no answer.

"Let's check the kitchen. There's a light on in there," Michael said.

They walked across the hall into the dining room, then straight through into the kitchen.

Peaches was lying on the tiled floor beside the telephone receiver.

"Peaches!" Daria cried as she ran to her.

Peaches was in the fetal position with her hands fisted near her chest.

Daria shook her frantically trying to rouse her, but Peaches didn't respond.

"Is she breathing?" Michael asked.

Daria checked Peaches' nose and chest for signs that she was breathing.

"No," Daria answered on a sob.

Michael pulled out his cell phone and dialed 911. He told the dispatch operator what they'd found when they'd walked into Peaches' kitchen.

"What's the address?" the operator asked.

When Michael gave her the address, the operator asked whether Peaches had a pulse.

Daria was leaning over Peaches crying, so Michael gently laid his hand on her shoulder and said, "Daria, please let me check her pulse. The dispatch operator needs to know if Peaches has a pulse."

Michael knelt down beside Peaches' inert body and hesitated. He scanned her face, taking in her pale, light-brown skin and experienced a vague feeling of recognition. *Could this be Fruit Lady?*

The lady he hazily remembered had been about twenty pounds heavier, but still…

The only features he remembered clearly were Fruit Lady's light skin and hazel eyes. Peaches' eyes were closed, so he couldn't check the color.

Nah. That's impossible. Michael gave himself a mental shake, dismissed the possibility, and proceeded to check for a pulse.

When he touched Peaches, her skin was warm, and she was a little stiff. He felt her neck for a pulse, but couldn't find one. He reported his findings to the operator.

"Was Ms. Addison ill, or had she been complaining of any kind of pain?"

Michael remembered Daria's and Lenore's conversation after church about Peaches' indigestion and relayed the information to the operator.

"I've dispatched an emergency unit. They should be there in a few minutes."

"Thank you." Michael ended the call.

"Michael, she's gone, isn't she?" Daria asked through her tears.

"I'm afraid so. Come here." He helped her to her feet. He wrapped her in his arms and tried to soothe her by rocking her.

"How could this happen? She was just getting her life back on track."

"I don't know." He shook his head. "I don't know."

The room was silent except for Daria's sobs. After what seemed like an eternity, they heard sirens wailing in the distance.

"They're almost here. I'll go and let them in." Michael kissed her softly on the cheek and then gently released her.

When the paramedics arrived, they asked Michael and Daria to move out of the kitchen, so they could have the space to evaluate the patient.

They stood in the doorway of the dining room and watched the medics work. One came over to them with a clipboard and asked questions about Peaches' health. Daria answered as many questions as she could.

"Ma'am, Ms. Addison is deceased," the paramedic said. "She appears to have been dead anywhere from four to six hours. We've contacted the Medical Examiner's Office for transport."

When the field investigator from the Medical Examiner's Office arrived, he and the paramedics discussed the information they had gathered during their evaluation. The investigator did his own preliminary assessments, then asked Daria more questions about Peaches.

"From the symptoms she was having—the acute indigestion—and my preliminary observations, I believe she had a heart attack," the investigator said. "We'll be able to make a more definitive diagnosis after the autopsy."

Ten minutes later, the investigator and paramedics departed with Peaches' body.

"Are you okay?" Michael asked Daria.

"No, I'm not okay." A broken sob escaped her.

"I know, but we'll get through this," Michael promised.

"I know we will, but it hurts so much." Daria cried uncontrollably.

"Come here, Daria," Michael commanded softly and opened his arms.

When she walked into his arms, he wrapped them around her in a comforting embrace. Daria's deep wrenching sobs ripped through him, tearing at his heart. A prayer rose from deep within and tumbled from his lips. "Dear Lord, I come to You on behalf of Daria. Because of Peaches' death, she's sad and hurting. As much as I want to help her, I can't give her what she needs. Father, she needs You. I'm asking that You comfort her and bring peace to her heart. Lord, I know You love her and will minister to her needs, so I'm going to praise You in advance. Hallelujah! Hallelujah! Hallelujah!"

After Michael finished praying, he blinked away the unshed tears that swam in his eyes.

He held Daria until she gained a small measure of control. Then he locked up the house and led her outside to his SUV.

After he settled into the driver's seat, Michael placed his hand on Daria's arm. "Do you want to go to Lenore's house, or do you want me to take you home?"

She sniffed. "I need to tell Aunt Lenore what's happened, but I want—no, *need*—to be home right now. *Please* take me home. I'll call Aunt Lenore and ask her to come over when I get there."

"Okay. Home it is." Michael held her hand as he drove them home.

By the time they reached their complex, Daria was weeping brokenly again. Michael took her key and opened her door. "I'm going to call Lenore for you."

Daria kept a directory of phone numbers beside the telephone that sat on her desk in the den, so he went in there and turned on the light. He looked through the directory until he found Lenore's number.

Michael prayed Lenore was up to receiving the shocking news of Peaches' death over the phone. Somehow he thought she would be. Yes, she was elderly, but he sensed she had an iron constitution.

Lenore answered on the third ring. "I'm afraid I have some bad news, Lenore," Michael said.

"Is Daria all right?" Worry and fear filled Lenore's inquiry.

"Yes, Daria's fine." Michael paused. "Peaches is dead."

"Dead?! What happened?" Disbelief and horror warred in Lenore's voice.

"When we arrived at her house earlier this afternoon, she didn't answer the door, so we entered the house with a key that Daria had access to. We found Peaches dead on the kitchen floor." Michael rubbed his forehead with his thumb and index finger. "The investigator from the Medical Examiner's Office believes she had a heart attack. One of the paramedics told us she'd already been dead several hours when we found her. Apparently, what she was calling indigestion was actually heart trouble."

"Oh, no!" Lenore exclaimed. "When that child had started foolin' around with those drugs, I'd feared something like this was going to happen to her. But I'd hoped…" Lenore's exhale gusted through the receiver.

Michael could imagine her shaking her head in disappointment.

"Peaches and Daria were as close as sisters. How's Daria handling this?" she asked anxiously.

"Not well at all. I don't think she should be alone tonight. It's not proper for me to stay here with her all night. Would you please come and be with her?"

"Of course. I'll be there in thirty minutes."

"Great, I'll see you then."

When he hung up the phone, he noticed an envelope laying on the desk with the words *Peaches' Attorney* written across it in red ink. He picked up the envelope and returned to the living room.

Daria was still sitting where he'd left her, but her sobs had subsided.

"Daria, I know you don't feel like dealing with this right now, but I found this envelope lying on your desk. Whenever you're feeling up to it, you'll need to notify Peaches' attorney of her death."

Daria reached for the envelope. "Peaches sent this to me last month." She inhaled a shuddering breath. "She'd just finished setting up her will and wanted me to have her attorney's phone number in case something happened to her. She made me promise to call him immediately if anything happened to her."

"If that's what Peaches wanted, I think you should call him today."

Daria let out a shaky breath. "You're right. I'll call him now." She punched the speaker button on the phone on the table near her chair.

She opened the envelope and pulled out the business card. Peaches had highlighted and starred Otis's cell phone number. Daria dialed that number.

He answered on the second ring. "Otis Cartier."

"Otis, this is Daria Simpson."

"Hello, Daria. What can I do for you?"

"I called to let you know that Peaches...died of a heart attack this afternoon," Daria told him.

"I'm so sorry to hear that." Sympathy filled Otis's voice. "Was she ill?"

"Saturday, she said that she had indigestion really bad. But it wasn't indigestion. She was having heart problems." Daria crumpled the envelope.

"Was she in Florida, or was she visiting her relatives in Haven?"

"She returned from Haven on Saturday morning. I went over to her house after church today and found her...on the kitchen floor. She'd already been gone a while before I found her." Daria paused and cleared her throat. "Last month, she told me to call you immediately if anything ever happened to her," Daria ended on a sob.

Michael stepped behind her chair and gently laid his hands on her shoulders.

"I'm glad you didn't wait to call me. Peaches named you and me co-trustees of her trust and co-executors of her will," Otis said in a business-like voice, softened with sadness.

"Peaches has already made arrangements for her memorial service. She's chosen a mortuary, paid for a memorial service," he went on, "and she purchased a burial plot. I'll call the mortuary right now and make arrangements with them to pick up her body. I also need to meet with you as soon as possible to discuss the terms of Peaches' trust and will."

Michael felt Daria flinch when Otis said the words *trust* and *will*.

Otis's voice softened even more. "Can you meet with me at my office on Wednesday at two o'clock?"

She placed a hand on top of Michael's. "Do we have to meet about that so soon?"

"I know it's difficult, but it's imperative that we meet right away."

Daria exhaled. "Okay, I'll be there."

"I'll see you then. Take care."

Chapter Sixteen

After ending the call with Daria, Otis closed his cell phone and sat unmoving for several minutes. He sighed out a deep breath, then rubbed the heels of his hands into his eyes.

He'd gone into the office to review and sign some paperwork that his Personal Assistant, Beatrice Howard, had left on his desk on Friday evening. He'd been tied up in probate court all day Friday and hadn't had time to take care of the documents.

They lay forgotten on his desk as he thought about Peaches.

When Peaches had worked at his firm, he'd admired her greatly as a colleague and as a woman. He'd known that she had what it took to be successful and was going to make her mark as an up-and-coming attorney.

As a woman, he'd thought she was gorgeous, and he'd been very attracted to her. Before she'd started using drugs, he'd entertained the idea of the two of them becoming romantically involved.

"Ah, Peaches," Otis sighed with deep feeling. He rubbed his hand over his face, then reached for the telephone receiver.

"Beatrice, Otis here."

"Hi, Otis. Don't tell me you're working today. Whatever you're doing could've waited until tomorrow," Beatrice reprimanded him gently.

Beatrice had been Otis's Personal Assistant for six years. Otis considered her top notch and indispensable. She was in her fifties, and treated Otis—with his tacit permission—like he was one of her sons.

"Beatrice, Peaches died today," he said sadly.

"Oh, what a shame! I always liked Peaches. I know you were fond of her. Are you okay, Otis?" Beatrice's motherly concern touched him in a special way.

Otis pinched the bridge of his nose and cleared his throat. "Yes, I'm okay. Thank you." He cleared his throat a second time and continued, adopting a business-like tone. "You typed up all of the papers pertaining to her will, so you know that we need to move quickly."

"Yes, what do you want me to do?" Beatrice asked without hesitation.

"I'm going to need you to travel with me to Haven, Georgia. Can you do that on such short notice?"

"Absolutely. When do you want to leave?"

"Tomorrow morning. Get us the earliest flight you can arrange. We'll need to fly into Savannah and drive to Haven from there, so you'll need to reserve a vehicle for us at the airport. I don't know what we'll find when we get there, so you'll need to rent something with plenty of cargo room—a van or SUV. We'll drive back to Orlando in the rental."

"How long will we be gone?"

"I've asked Ms. Simpson to meet with me on Wednesday afternoon. I'd like to be back here by Tuesday night."

"I'll make the reservations right now and call you on your cell phone as soon as I've finalized everything. Your first appointment tomorrow is at eleven o'clock. I'll reschedule it and clear your calendar through Thursday morning."

"Beatrice, you're priceless." His voice conveyed his fondness and genuine gratitude.

"Oh, I know it. Now, go home!" Otis could hear the smile in her voice.

"Now, who's that knocking on the door at this time of morning?" Lenore grumbled as she headed for Daria's front door. She peeped through the security hole. "I should've known."

She opened the door. "Didn't you just leave here a little while ago?" she asked with mock fierceness.

"Good morning to you, too, Lenore." Michael entered the door, closed it, and kissed her on the cheek.

"Is Daria awake yet? Did she get much sleep last night?" Michael asked anxiously.

"She's still sleeping. No, I don't believe she got much sleep last night. I'm going to wake her up in a little while so that she can call her job." Lenore looked at Michael quizzically. "Shouldn't you be at work?"

"I'm taking the day off to be with Daria."

Lenore nodded her approval. "Since you're here, you might as well make yourself useful. You can cook us breakfast this morning."

Michael smiled. "You don't think I can cook, do you?"

"I'm quite sure you can cook something. The question is, will it be edible?" Lenore teased, then added soberly, "If you cook breakfast, I might have a better chance of getting Daria to eat something this morning. She'll eat because she doesn't want to hurt your feelings."

Michael smiled and shook his head. "I've got to make certain you don't ever become my enemy because you're too cunning."

"Just make sure that you treat my baby right, and you'll be safe from me...and Clifford." Lenore chuckled.

Michael went into the kitchen, washed his hands, and located a skillet.

Assured that he could at least get started on his assigned task without her looking over his shoulder, Lenore headed for Daria's bedroom.

She sat on the side of Daria's bed and worriedly studied the younger woman's face. Daria had dried tear tracks down her cheeks, dark circles under her eyes, and a puffy face.

She'd cried so much last night that Lenore feared she'd make herself sick. After much coaxing, Michael had given her some aspirin and convinced her to go to bed.

"Daria, you need to wake up." Lenore shook her gently.

Daria groaned. "What time is it?"

"It's eight o'clock."

"Oh, no! I've overslept! I'm late for work." Daria threw the covers back and moved to scramble out of bed.

Lenore placed her hand on Daria's shoulder, hindering her efforts. "Daria, you're not going to work today. Call your job and let them know that you need to take some time off to make funeral arrangements for a close friend."

"Peaches has already made the arrangements."

"Yes, I know. But you may still need to take care of some things that she didn't think about," Lenore explained patiently.

"But—"

"No buts! Girl, you're not going out there on that job and cry all over those people. Humph, you're not going out there and embarrass me. Now, are you going to call them, or am I?"

Daria gave her a watery smile. "All right, all right, Auntie. I'll call them."

Thank You, Lord. She's going to be all right! Lenore sent up a silent, earnest prayer of thanksgiving.

Lenore kissed Daria lightly on the cheek. "That's my girl." She patted Daria's shoulder. "After you make your call, come into the kitchen and get yourself some breakfast."

"You've cooked breakfast?"

"No. Michael showed up at your door thirty minutes ago to check on you, so I put him to work in the kitchen."

Daria blinked at her. "Auntie, you didn't!"

Lenore smiled. "Well, I want to see what he can do. So far, he's doing okay. He knows the difference between a frying pan and a saucepan."

Daria called her immediate supervisor and got approved leave for the entire week. She showered and dressed in jeans and a knit top. When she looked at her face in the mirror and saw the dark circles and puffiness, she shrugged her shoulders at her image and pulled her hair back into a ponytail.

She pulled a face. *I look as washed out as I feel. Michael's going to have to take me as I am today.*

Lenore was sitting in the den when she came out of her room. Walking into the kitchen, she saw Michael standing over the stove.

He smiled when she entered the kitchen. "Good morning, gorgeous."

Pleased by his gallantry, Daria returned his smile. "Gorgeous? I saw myself in the mirror, and that is not a word I'd use to describe myself right now."

"You always look gorgeous to me." Michael shot a quick look in the direction of the den, enclosed her in a loose embrace, and kissed her on the cheek. He sobered and searched her face. "But seriously, how are you this morning?"

"Okay, I guess. But I know that it's going to take a while for the pain of Peaches' death to lessen. I'm really going to miss her." Daria laid her head against his chest, taking comfort from his steady, strong heartbeat.

"Of course you will, but you don't have to go through this alone. I'm here for you. Lean on me."

"Thank you, Michael." Daria squeezed his waist a little, emphasizing her appreciation.

"I called my family last night after I arrived home to tell them what happened. They told me they'd be calling you later today. They want you to know they're here for you and are just a phone call away, if you need their assistance with anything."

"That's sweet of them." Still in his arms, she looked into his face with concern wrinkling her brow. "Hey, shouldn't you be at work?"

"I wanted to be here for you." Michael shrugged. "I took the day off."

She smiled her gratitude. "You're a sweetie."

Michael cocked a brow. "Sweetie?"

Lenore cleared her throat loudly as she walked into the kitchen. "Isn't that food ready yet? What's taking so long?" She stopped and ran her eyes over them. "Humph, I see what's taking you so long. Turn my niece loose and finish doing what you're supposed to be doing. That food isn't going to cook itself," Lenore scolded, and then softened the rebuke with a wink.

Daria and Michael chuckled.

Not taking any unnecessary chances, Michael obediently ended the embrace.

"It's ready. I just finished making the last of the French toast. Both of you get out of my kitchen and have a seat at the table. I'll have everything on the table in a minute."

Michael had cooked French toast, scrambled eggs, and bacon. When he'd placed the food on the table, and they'd said grace, he asked Daria, "Do you know how to get in contact with Peaches' relatives in Georgia?"

"No, I don't. As a matter of fact, I don't even know their names. Peaches never told me much about them. I was surprised when she asked me to go up there with her on her next visit."

Reaching for a slice of bacon, Lenore remarked, "Peaches could be very closed-mouthed when she wanted to be."

Daria scooped a child-size serving of eggs onto her plate, then sipped some orange juice.

"Maybe her attorney will know how to get in touch with them," Michael offered.

"I guess I won't know much of anything until I meet with Otis on Wednesday," Daria said.

"At least she had the foresight to make a will. You'll know what her wishes are and won't have to guess about them," Michael said, using his fork to cut a bite of French toast.

Daria pushed the eggs around on her plate. "Peaches just completed her will last month." She told them. "When I think back on how she spoke about it, and how insistent she was that I call Otis immediately if anything happened to her, I wonder whether she had a feeling she would die soon."

She gave her head a quick shake. "No, forget I said that. My mind is racing in all kinds of directions trying to make sense of it all."

"Eat, Daria," Lenore coaxed gently, then continued when Daria ate a forkful of eggs, "There may very well be some truth in that. We'll never know."

"Recently, Peaches told me she'd thought about accepting Christ as her personal Savior. I didn't push her to talk about her thoughts, but maybe I should have." Daria's voice was thick with regret.

"Baby, don't torture yourself this way." Lenore reached over and patted Daria's hand. "You knew Peaches better than I did. If you'd pushed her in any way, she would've thrown up a wall."

"You're right, but I just wonder whether she accepted Christ before she died." This unanswered question had woven itself through Daria's grief and magnified it. It was tragic that her best friend had died so suddenly and unexpectedly. It would be beyond horrific if she hadn't made her peace with God before she'd died. Daria shuddered at the thought.

Michael reached across the table and lightly laid his hand on her arm. "Peaches was around you, Lenore, and Prayer Tabernacle long enough to know the way to Christ. You shared Christ with her and prayed for her. There wasn't anything else you could've done. Maybe she did have time to accept Christ before she died, and then again, maybe she didn't. We don't know, but what's more important is that, God does."

Daria inhaled a deep fortifying breath to push the gloominess away. "You're right, Michael."

"Well, young man, that was a tasty breakfast." Lenore got up from the table and looked at Michael with mischief sparkling in her eyes. "Now, let's see how well you can clean up a kitchen."

Michael and Daria chuckled as Lenore walked away.

Later that afternoon, Lenore opened Daria's door, and Michael walked in laden down with bags. Lenore had sent him out to a local restaurant to pick up food for a late lunch.

"Is Daria still napping?" Michael asked as he walked into the kitchen and set the bags on the counter.

Lenore followed him. "Yes, the poor thing is worn out. Hopefully, she'll feel better when she wakes up."

"I hope so. She seemed to be in better spirits this morning, but I'm still worried about her."

Lenore nodded.

"Is that you, Nephew?" Euvinia's voice called from the den.

He glanced at Lenore's grin and headed for the den. "What are you doing over here?" he asked with delight as he and Lenore walked into the den. "I didn't know you were coming over today." He hugged Euvinia, kissed her cheek, and then sat at Daria's desk.

Euvinia teased, her eyes bright with laughter. "Well, I don't tell you everything. I've got to have some secrets. I needed to come over here and check up on you anyway, to make sure that you're behaving yourself."

Her lips trembled with suppressed laughter. "Have you washed your truck lately?"

Michael coughed to cover his embarrassment. "Nah." His eyes fell on the travel brochures that were scattered about Daria's desk, and he leaped at the chance to change the subject. "I see you two are planning your European vacation. Are you making any progress?"

Euvinia stated, "We're trying to decide which countries we want to visit. Lenore wants to go to Great Britain, but I want to go to Scotland."

Michael smiled. "Auntie, Scotland is a part of Great Britain," he explained.

"You don't say," Lenore said, sharing a surprised and pleased look with his aunt. "Well, that solves that problem. Great Britain it is then."

"I'd also like to go to France," Euvinia said.

"Do you want to go to Paris, or do you have someplace else in mind?" Michael asked.

The ladies shared a glance. Both shrugged their shoulders.

"Paris sounds good to me," Lenore answered.

Euvinia asked, "Can we drive to France from Great Britain?"

"I don't think you should drive while you're over there," Michael said. "Driving over there is a bit different than it is here."

"I don't see why not," Lenore objected with indignation shimmering through her voice. "We both have licenses. We can rent a car and drive anywhere we want to go."

Michael tried again. "In England, they drive on the opposite side of the road. You're not used to driving that way."

"You've got a point there, Nephew," Euvinia said.

"I suggest you ladies let a travel agent help you plan your trip. It may be easier for you if you purchase a tour package. An agent can put together a package for you that'll include every country and city you want to visit." Michael hoped they'd accept his suggestion. The thought of those two running loose all over Europe was *very* scary.

"That's a good idea, Michael," Lenore conceded.

"Yeah, that sounds good to me." Euvinia punctuated her agreement with a nod. "We can let a travel agent do all of the work. All we'll have to do is show up and enjoy. Now, that's my kind of vacation."

"Now, back to the subject of that truck-washin' business." Lenore redirected the conversation in a stern voice.

Michael's eyes swung to Lenore. The laughter he saw glinting in her eyes didn't match her tone of voice. He groaned to himself because this did *not* bode well for him.

"In my day, Nephew," Euvinia said, drawing his attention to her, "when a fella was standing as close to his girl as you were that day in the parking lot, he had marriage on his mind." Euvinia's eyes gleamed with amusement. "Wouldn't you agree, Lenore?"

Daria, please wake up! These old ladies are about to make minced meat out of me!

Lenore smirked. "If he didn't, he would have by the time her daddy got through showing him the business-end of his shotgun."

She said that with entirely too much enthusiasm.

"Nephew, you're the only male Greer left. It's up to you to carry on the name." Euvinia threw Lenore a sly grin, then leaned forward. "So, Nephew, when are you and—"

That's it. I'm outta here!

Michael stood abruptly and headed for the door. "Uh…excuse me, ladies. I need to…I'll be back."

Their laughter pelted him in the back as he hightailed it out of there.

Chapter Seventeen

M s. Simpson, it's good to see you again." Beatrice clasped Daria's hand as she greeted her on Wednesday afternoon.

Daria had met Otis's pleasant assistant on several occasions when she'd visited Peaches at this firm. As always, Beatrice was impeccably dressed, her salt-and-pepper hair coiffed, and exuding comfortable motherly warmth. A welcoming smile shone from her caramel-toned face and dark eyes—eyes that were even now moving over Daria's face with concern.

Every time Daria had seen her, Beatrice's outfit complemented the dark-blue, brown, and burgundy color scheme of Otis's plush office. Today, Beatrice was wearing a brown suit with a silk scarf that had brown, blue, and burgundy swirls.

Daria smiled. "It's always a pleasure to see you, too, Mrs. Howard. How are those grandbabies?"

Beatrice loved to talk about her grandchildren, ages five to seven. Her office desk was covered with pictures of them.

"They're doing just fine. Growing like weeds. They have so much energy; they wear me out in just a couple of hours. One of the joys of being a grandparent is that you can spoil the kids rotten, and then send them home with their parents," Beatrice said with a chuckle.

Their conversation was interrupted when Otis, looking like he'd just stepped off the pages of *GQ*, opened his door and walked out. His black suit fit so perfectly, it had to have been tailor made. The splashes of red in his black tie added dash to his conservative ensemble.

"Daria, sorry to keep you waiting." Otis extended his hand to her.

Daria smiled and shook his hand. "That's quite all right. Mrs. Howard was telling me about her grandbabies."

Daria thought about Peaches' comments about Otis a few weeks ago. It was hard for Daria to grasp the fact that she was actually standing in his office today to discuss Peaches' death. This whole situation just seemed surreal.

"Come into my office, and we'll get started," Otis invited, motioning for Daria to precede him.

A diaper bag, baby bottle, and rattler sat on Otis's high-gloss, mahogany desk.

She gave Otis a puzzled look. "Are you babysitting today, Otis?" Daria asked as she sat in one of the ultra-comfortable chairs facing his desk.

"Only for the last ten minutes or so." Otis pointed toward the sitting area in his office, where a small infant slept in a carrier seat. Daria couldn't see very much of the baby, because it was wrapped in a blanket.

"Otis, are congratulations in order?" Daria gave him a quizzical half-smile.

"Yes, but not for me." His eyes and tone were serious.

Daria picked up on his seriousness, then was distracted because the baby began to stretch.

"I guess nap time is over." Otis walked over to the baby and gently lifted it out of the seat with confident ease.

"I'm impressed. You lifted that baby like a pro."

Otis smiled. "Beatrice gave me a crash course in baby handling a few days ago." He walked toward Daria with the infant.

"Daria, I'd like for you to meet Nicole Alexis Addison—Peaches' daughter. Peaches called her Nicki."

Shock resonated through Daria. "Did I just hear you say Peaches' daughter?"

"Yes. She's three months old. She's been living in Haven, Georgia, with Peaches' relatives."

A frown wrinkled Daria's brow. "I don't understand. I didn't even know Peaches was pregnant. When did she have the baby?"

"Peaches was three months pregnant the first time she went on an extended visit to Georgia."

"But…I'm her best friend. Why didn't she tell me?" Daria couldn't hide the hurt that ripped through her heart. *Why had Peaches hidden this from me?*

"I don't have all of the answers for you, Daria. But I'm sure Peaches felt like she had valid reasons for handling things the way she did."

"May I hold her?" Daria walked over to Otis and Nicki.

"Certainly." Otis carefully transferred the infant into Daria's arms.

Daria returned to her seat with the baby. When she pulled the blanket back from the baby's face, she gasped. "She looks just like Peaches!"

Like Peaches, Nicki had sandy brown hair, light brown skin, and hazel-colored eyes. Her nose…no, that wasn't Peaches' nose. Nicki's tiny nose had a rounded tip and flared nostrils. Except for that nose, she was the image of Peaches.

Otis nodded. "The resemblance is quite remarkable."

Daria stared down into the baby's beautiful little face and fell instantly in love.

"She's adorable," Daria said with a teary, admiring smile.

Nicki scrunched up her little face and emitted a few tiny squeaks.

"Nicki's diaper will probably need to be changed. I'll ask Beatrice to change her so that we can continue."

At Otis's request, Beatrice came in to get Nicki. Daria reluctantly released the baby to her.

"If Nicki has been in Haven since her birth, how and when did she get here?"

"Beatrice and I went to Haven on Monday and brought her to Florida last night. Beatrice kept her overnight and brought her into the office thirty minutes before you arrived." Otis sat down behind his desk.

"What's to become of Nicki now?" Worry pulled the muscles around Daria's eyes tight. She rubbed her temple.

"In her will, Peaches appointed you Nicki's legal guardian. If anything happened to her, she wanted you to raise her child."

Daria's head spun. She was supposed to raise a child that she didn't even know existed a half-hour ago?

Why didn't Peaches tell me about Nicki?!" Daria cried.

"She would've eventually. She wanted to get her life together before she brought Nicki home to Florida. She wanted to offer Nicki more than a mother who was addicted to drugs."

"I wouldn't have judged her. I would've supported her in any way that I possibly could. She didn't have to go through that by herself." Daria fought overwhelming sorrow as she struggled to maintain some semblance of control.

"Daria, we're talking about Peaches here. She had to do things her way, and her way was to try to do everything alone."

Daria exhaled and shook her head. "You're right."

"Are you willing to take on the huge responsibility of raising Nicki?"

"Peaches was family. Nicki's family. Family takes care of each other. I wouldn't have it any other way," Daria said earnestly. "Didn't Nicki's caregivers object to her being removed from their custody?"

"Yes, they did," Otis answered dryly. "But Peaches had put measures in place to override any of their possible objections." He looked at Daria with questioning eyes. "How much do you know about Peaches' relatives in Haven?"

"Actually, very little. Peaches never talked about them. One thing I learned about Peaches over the years is that she'd tell you what she wanted you to know when she wanted you to know it. I didn't pry. I figured she'd tell me about them when she was ready."

"The only family that Peaches had left in Georgia was a cousin and her husband. I gather from what Peaches told me, they were not the kind of people she would usually seek to have in her orbit. They were very mercenary—always looking for a fast dollar. If she had not been in a position to send a little cash their way every now and then, they wouldn't have welcomed her or Nicki for very long. Don't get me wrong. They didn't have criminal tendencies or anything like that, but they *loved* money."

"Peaches went to Georgia so often that I thought she was really enjoying getting to know her family. I was wrong. She went there to be with Nicki."

"Peaches left you a letter. The letter was sealed when she gave it to me, so I'm not aware of the contents." Otis opened a file, removed the letter, and handed it to Daria.

"Would you like something to drink?" he asked.

"I'd like to have some water, if I may," Daria responded absently, fingering the envelope.

"I'll get the water while you read the letter." Otis exited the office, closing the door behind him.

Daria opened the sealed envelope. Her eyes immediately went to the date on the letter. The date was a few days before Peaches had called to tell her about the will.

Daria read the letter, savoring every word. This would be the last time she'd ever "hear" Peaches' voice again.

June 15, 2004
Dear Ms. D,

If you're reading this letter, I've gone on to the great beyond. Was that solemn enough? ;-D

Seriously, Ms. D, I have a lot to tell you. Since I don't know when you'll be reading this letter, I'll start at what I feel is the pertinent beginning.

Ten months ago, I found out that I was three months pregnant. During that time, I was throwing wild parties and dating indiscriminately. I had no idea who the father was. I still don't.

Because of the type of men I was associating with at that time, I thought it best not to even try to find out who the father was. I figured my baby didn't need to have two messed up parents. One was bad enough.

Although, there was this guy that I met one night in Atlanta. I'm sad to say I was in the c-zone when I met him, so I don't remember a whole lot about him—you know, important stuff like his name, what he looked like, or where he lived—but I do remember sensing that he was safe and nice. I wouldn't mind at all if he was the father of my precious daughter. Do you know what's really pathetic? I don't know if I'd recognize him if I ever saw him again.

When I learned I was pregnant, I felt like I'd let you down, and I couldn't face you. I planned to get my act together, and then tell you about the baby.

I found my cousin Thelma's phone number and called her. I thought that if I went to Georgia for a while, it would give me the time I needed to pull myself together before the baby was born.

I'd heard horror stories about crack babies, and I didn't want to subject my child to the pain and agony of being born addicted to drugs. I thought that if I got away from my drug buddies, I'd be able to break the addiction.

Ms. D, I have never in my life met anybody as money-hungry as Thelma and her husband, Paul. They will do anything for a dollar. :-D

When they realized I had a little money, they welcomed me like I was a long-lost child. :-D

They thought they were using me, but in the end, we used each other. I'll get to that later.

Well, as you already know, I stayed in Georgia for five months before returning to Florida. It was very hard, but I didn't smoke any crack for the last four months of my pregnancy. I also made sure I got good prenatal care.

I only carried Nicole—I call her Nicki—for eight months, but she was a healthy baby.

A few weeks after Nicki was born, I left her with my cousin and returned to Florida to start getting everything ready for her so that I could bring her home.

I knew my cousin would take good care of Nicki, because she wanted to keep me happy.

As long as I was happy, the money flowed. By then, I'd learned how to use their greed to my advantage.

When I traveled to Florida, I never told them how long I'd be away, because I wanted them to care for Nicki with the expectation that I could walk in the door at any time.

Last year, I started having occasional nightmares seeing myself lying dead in a casket. Lately, they've started occurring more frequently, so I decided to get my affairs in order—just in case.

I've chosen you to be Nicki's legal guardian, because I know that you will love her and teach her good values.

You don't have to worry about my relatives giving you any problems over Nicki. I've authorized Otis to give them five thousand dollars in cash in exchange for their signature on a document stating that they'd make no future claims against my estate, or interfere with your guardianship of Nicki in any way.

When Nicki is old enough to understand, please tell her about me. Tell her that I loved her very much.

I love you and Lenore dearly.

> *Love,*
> *Peaches*

Daria held the letter in a fierce grip as Peaches' words vibrated through her mind. Bitter tears ran unrestrained down her cheeks as sobs racked her body.

"Oh, God, help me!"

Chapter Eighteen

A half-hour later, Otis returned to his office with a bottle of water in his left hand and Nicki held securely in the cradle of his right arm.

Daria guessed he'd taken longer than necessary to return to his office in order to give her some privacy to read Peaches' letter.

She was thankful for his delay in returning, because it had given her a chance to compose herself and repair her makeup. The corner of her mouth kicked up in a half-smile. She could imagine Peaches saying, "Girlfriend, you need to do something about your face, because that red, swollen, raccoon-eyed look is *not* workin' for you."

Oh, Peaches, I'm going to miss you!

Otis placed the water bottle on his desk and passed Nicki to Daria.

Nicki beamed a wet, gummy grin at her. The smile was a salve to the raw ache that had settled around her heart.

"You are so adorable." Daria buried her face in Nicki's tummy.

Nicki gurgled and worked her limbs.

"Ouch!" Daria exclaimed because Nicki's tiny fingers had gotten tangled in her hair.

Nicki's smile seemed to grow wider.

"You little stinker. If I didn't know any better, I'd think you did that on purpose." Daria smiled down into the baby's hazel eyes.

Otis chuckled. "Beatrice told me that it's time for Nicki to be fed." He rummaged around in the diaper bag for a bottle.

"I don't know anything about Nicki—when she eats, sleeps, or anything else that I'll need to know to take care of her." Dismay filled Daria's voice.

Otis nodded. "Mrs. Jones gave Beatrice all of that information before we left Haven. She'll go over all of that with you." He passed Daria the bottle.

"Good," Daria said with relief as she popped the nipple into Nicki's mouth.

"You're handling her very well. Have you had much experience with babies?"

"I often volunteer in the church nursery, and, occasionally, I've baby-sat infants for friends." Daria pulled a wry face. "That limited experience in *no* way prepared me for this. I pray I'm up to the task."

Otis gave her a reassuring smile. "I'm sure you'll do fine."

"I'll have some help. I'm quite sure my aunt will lend a hand."

"Great! I'm glad you'll have some support. You know I'll assist you in any way that I can."

Daria smiled. "I hope you mean that, because Nicki may need to spend some time with her Uncle Otis."

Otis chuckled. "If you ever need a sitter, just give me a call." He paused a beat. "And I'll arrange things with Beatrice for you."

Daria's smile broadened into a grin. "Beatrice might have a thing or two to say about you arranging her free time."

Otis gave a crack of laughter. "More like four or five." He sobered and said seriously, "I feel confident in saying that you can call on her if you need her assistance. Beatrice is a gem."

"Okay," Daria said with a nod.

Reverting back to the business at hand, Otis said, "The mortuary picked Peaches' body up from the Medical Examiner's office on Tuesday afternoon. The memorial service is scheduled for next Wednesday at eleven o'clock. Will that work for you?"

"Yes, that's fine."

"I'll arrange for a car to pick you up and take you to the service. The car will transport four people comfortably, so feel free to invite someone else to ride with you."

"Thank you, Otis. Did the autopsy confirm that Peaches died from a heart attack?"

He nodded. "Yes, she did die from a heart attack." He rubbed the back of his neck and cleared his throat.

Daria realized that Otis was hurting as well. She'd been so blinded by her own grief that she hadn't seen his. Of course he was hurting! He'd been very fond of Peaches.

"Otis, please forgive me for being so self-involved. I know you were fond of Peaches. Are you okay?"

Otis waved away her concern. "Yes, I'm fine."

Not! Daria wanted to retort. Men and their need to appear stoic!

Before she could address his feelings again, Otis said, "I'll officially read the will after the memorial service. But I want to go over some key points with you today. I'll give you a copy of the will and trust documents to take with you, and you can call me if you have any questions. Is that acceptable?"

She'd never get him to open up to her. She didn't know him well enough to pry, so she said a quick prayer. *Lord, give him peace and solace.*

"Yes," Daria replied, lifting Nicki to her shoulder to burp her. She made sure the blanket covered her shoulder.

Otis smiled. "I learned to do that the hard way. They're messy little creatures, aren't they?"

Daria returned his smile. "Yes, they are. But they're also precious."

"In a nutshell," Otis went on, "Peaches has set up a trust fund for Nicki. Nicki will take control of the trust when she turns eighteen years old.

"You already know that Peaches appointed you Nicki's legal guardian. Since Nicki doesn't have any known parents living, she'll become a ward of the State until the courts appoint a legal guardian for her. The Florida courts won't allow Peaches to give Nicki away, but the courts will consider Peaches' appointment when they legally appoint a guardian for Nicki.

"By signing a document stating that they wouldn't interfere with your guardianship of Nicki, the Joneses have removed themselves as possible appointees. Any questions so far?"

"I'll ask them later. Please continue."

"Over the years, Peaches invested wisely in the stock market, and her stocks are doing very well. The stocks will be transferred to you. You can continue to receive the dividends, or you can sell the shares. She wanted you to have the stocks as a means of support for Nicki.

"Peaches also left you the remainder of her assets—her home, jewelry, and car."

Ms. D, I'll be leaving you everything that I have. Peaches' statement flashed through Daria's mind, and she closed her eyes as a wave of pain crashed through her.

Oh, Peaches! She wailed inwardly.

She realized Otis was plowing doggedly on through the details and struggled to focus on what he was saying.

"Peaches had started to set up a nursery for Nicki in her home, so it may be more convenient for you to relocate there as soon as possible.

"Now, I'll answer any questions you may have," he finished.

"How long do you think it'll take the courts to legally appoint me as Nicki's guardian?"

"I think the issue of guardianship, along with anything else involved in carrying out the terms of the will and disbursing the property and assets of the trust, can be resolved in a few months. I'll do everything

I can to expedite things so that you and Nicki can get settled as soon as possible."

"Thank you, Otis. I don't have any more questions for you at this time, but I'm sure I'll have some later. Right now, I just can't absorb it all."

"That's okay. You've been hit with a lot today. Review the will, and if you have any questions or concerns, please feel free to contact me."

Daria's shoulders rose and fell with the deep breath she inhaled, then slowly released. "I guess we'd better get going."

"All of Nicki's things are in the vehicle we drove back from Haven. If you don't mind, I'll follow you to your home and unload her things there."

"No, I don't mind at all. I've got a feeling I'm going to need all the help I can get until I can find my feet." Daria stood and carefully strapped Nicki into her carrier.

They collected all of Nicki's things and placed them in her diaper bag. Otis put Daria's untouched bottle of water in the bag as well.

He pressed the intercom button and asked Beatrice to bring in the list of instructions for Nicki's care.

"Here you are, Ms. Simpson." Beatrice handed the list to Daria. "I wrote down the information Mrs. Jones gave me about feeding and sleeping schedules. I've also included a few notes of my own. I've written my home phone number and the name of a good pediatrician at the top of the list. Please feel free to contact me if you need any assistance," Beatrice finished with a smile.

"I will, and thank you for everything," Daria said sincerely.

"Beatrice, I'm going to leave for the day. It's five o'clock, so why don't you call it a day as well. I'm going to follow Daria home in the rental and unload Nicki's things. I'll turn in the rental tomorrow morning on my way to the office."

Nicki cooed and played with her hands all the way to Daria's complex.

When Daria pulled into the parking lot, she scanned the lot for Michael's SUV. *I guess he's working late,* Daria thought with mixed feelings when she realized it wasn't there.

She wished he were there so that she could lean on him—draw from his strength—but on the other hand, she wasn't ready to announce to him that she now had a child. What was she supposed to say? *Michael, I've got good news! While you were at work today, I became a mom?*

She parked her car, and Otis pulled alongside her into the adjacent parking space. She climbed out of the car. "I'll unlock the door, so we can start unloading Nicki's things." Before walking away, she peeked at Nicki to make sure she was still content.

Daria unlocked the door and walked back to the car.

Otis removed his suit coat. "You get Nicki," he instructed, rolling up his shirtsleeves. "I'll unload her things."

By the time Daria had gotten Nicki out of her carrier and the car, Otis was ready to carry in the first load. She grabbed her purse and the diaper bag and headed for her door.

"You can just put everything in the den." Daria pointed to the room to their left.

Otis returned to the living room after depositing his load. "Nice place you have here."

"Thanks," Daria said over her shoulder as she and Nicki started back outside.

"Where are you going?"

"We're going to get some stuff and bring it in."

"You don't have to do that. I'll take care of it."

Daria smiled and responded by addressing the baby. "We want to help, too, don't we, Nicki? We want to flex our muscles, too, don't we, pumpkin?"

Nicki responded with a gurgle and a smile.

"Did you see that?" Delight rang in Daria's voice. "She smiled because she agrees with me."

Otis threw up his hands. "I'm outnumbered." He motioned for them to precede him outside.

With Nicki's and Daria's questionable help, Otis finished unloading the SUV twenty minutes later.

"Thank you, Otis. You've been great!"

"It's been my pleasure. Please call me if you need my assistance with anything."

"All right. I'll see you next Wednesday."

"Okay. Don't forget to review your copy of the will and the trust documents, so we can go over them after the memorial service."

After Otis left, Daria changed Nicki's diaper and laid the baby in the middle of her bed. She changed into sweat pants and a t-shirt while Nicki entertained herself by playing with her hands.

After Daria finished changing, she sat on the side of the bed and called Lenore.

"Hi, Aunt Lenore."

"Hi, baby. How did things go with that attorney?"

"Are you sitting down?"

"Yes, why do you ask?"

"Because what I'm about to tell you may knock you off your feet." Daria grinned.

"Okay, let me have it."

"Peaches has a three-month-old daughter."

"What?! You mean to tell me that Peaches had a baby and hid it from us?"

"Yes, she left me a letter explaining her actions. I'll let you read it later. The baby's name is Nicole Alexis Addison."

"Cute. Her first name is Peaches' middle name. Her middle name is the same as yours."

"Auntie, she looks just like Peaches."

"How do you know who she looks like? Have you seen a picture of her?"

"Have I seen a picture of her? She's lying right here in the middle of my bed."

"Daria, what's going on? Where did she come from, and why is she in the middle of your bed?"

"Nicki was living in Georgia with Peaches' relatives. Otis, Peaches' attorney, and his assistant went to Georgia on Monday, picked Nicki up, and brought her back to Florida."

"You still haven't explained why the baby is with you," Lenore prompted with impatience.

"Peaches named me as Nicki's legal guardian."

"She did what?!"

"She wants me to raise Nicki."

"Oh, have mercy. This is a lot to take in at one time. Child, that's a big responsibility. Are you okay with that?"

"Of course I was shocked when I first found out, but when I held Nicki for the first time, I fell in love with her." Daria caressed the infant's cheek. "She's adorable, Aunt Lenore."

Lenore snickered. "Yeah, they usually are...when they're not crying."

Daria chuckled. "I've yet to hear her cry, but I'm quite sure I will eventually." She went on seriously, "I'm all she has, Auntie, and I'm going to do the best I can to give her a good life."

"I know you will, child, and I'll help you in any way that I can. Just please try not to need any help during the time I plan to be in Europe on vacation," Lenore teased.

"I know you've got a lot of questions, but I'm going to have to go now. I need to get Nicki settled for the night. We'll talk more tomorrow. I love you, Auntie."

"I love you, too, baby. I'll be praying for you. Call me if you need me. I'll be over there tomorrow morning." Lenore ended the call.

"All right, Ms. Nicki, let's check out your goods." Daria picked Nicki up and headed for the den.

Today's drama was far from over. If anything, it was about to intensify. Michael would be showing up at her door at any minute, and she had absolutely no idea what she was going to say to him.

Butterflies took flight in her stomach. "Lord, please…" Her voice trailed off into an inarticulate moan because she didn't even know what to ask for.

Chapter Nineteen

Daria found a portable crib, a case of diapers, baby formula, a bathtub, a box of clothes, and a box of other assorted baby items.

"Look at this, Nicki." Daria held up a little pink, lace-trimmed dress.

Lying on a blanket on the floor, Nicki responded by making noises and bicycling her legs.

"This is just too cute."

After Daria finished going through the boxes, she finally allowed herself to think about Michael and his possible reaction to Nicki.

They'd never spoken of love, commitment, or the future. Yes, Michael had told her that he cared for her, but how deep did that sentiment go? Maybe he was content with their current relationship. He'd certainly never given her any indication that he wanted to make it permanent.

She snorted. If he had, she'd be Mrs. Greer by now because she would've had him down the aisle so fast, his head would've spun.

Now that Nicki was a part of the equation, would he walk away?

Her guardianship of Nicki was not negotiable. Michael would have to accept that.

Who was she kidding? The man hadn't committed to her before Nicki came on the scene, and now? Pshhh. Michael was as good as gone. There was no way he'd want to continue their relationship.

After she told him about Nicki, his swift departure would generate gale force winds.

Despair weighed her shoulders down like a heavy cloak. When he finally walked away, it would be unbearable. Maybe she should just end things now—tonight. It would be pure agony to wait for him to walk away and, at the same time, pray he never would.

It would be even worse if he made promises, then didn't follow through. A pain knifed through her abdomen. She moaned. Yes, it was best to terminate their relationship tonight.

The doorbell rang, setting off a volley of unease and fearful anticipation in her stomach.

"Come on, Nicki." Daria scooped the baby up from the floor. "Let's answer the door. We've got a visitor."

There could only be one person at the door—Michael.

"Hi, Michael. Come in," Daria said after opening the door. "Did you have to work late tonight?"

Michael kissed Daria's cheek and glanced at Nicki. "Hi. No, I stopped by Moms's house and picked up some grub." He held up a container of food. "She made us some chili. How was your day today?" he asked with concern as he entered and closed the door.

Daria gave him a wry look. "Full of surprises."

Questions crowded Michael's eyes.

Nicki chose that moment to start whimpering. Daria jiggled the infant in her arms and walked toward the kitchen. "Nicki's about to demand her meal. Come on through to the kitchen."

"Who's your little friend?"

"This is Nicole Alexis."

"So, you're babysitting tonight. Who are her parents?"

"Well…" Daria popped the rubber nipple into the baby's mouth and sat down at the dining room table. "Nicki is Peaches' daughter." She searched Michael's face for every nuance of his reaction.

Michael frowned. "I didn't know Peaches had a kid."

"I didn't either—until a few hours ago." She took a deep breath before continuing. "Not only did I find out that Peaches had a daughter, I also found out that she named me as Nicki's legal guardian."

Michael's eyes grew wide, and his mouth fell open. "You…uh… You're her guardian?" He cleared his throat. "What does that mean exactly?"

Okay, here we go!

Daria stiffened. "It means exactly what I said. I'm her guardian. Peaches wanted me to raise Nicki if anything ever happened to her."

"Wow." Michael exhaled, clearly still reeling from her announcement. "How did all of this come about?"

"Peaches had Nicki three months ago in Georgia, and Nicki's been living there ever since."

"That would explain why Peaches went to Georgia so often."

Daria nodded. "She left me a letter explaining everything. She didn't tell me about Nicki because she felt that she'd let me down. She wanted to get her life back on track before she told me about the baby."

"Amazing." Wrinkles grooved his forehead. "That's a big responsibility. What about Nicki's father? Where is he?"

Daria blinked and narrowed her eyes. "Peaches wasn't sure who Nicki's father was. She didn't want to know, because there was a possibility that he was a druggie. She wanted better than that for Nicki. That's why she was trying to get her life back on track."

"What about Peaches' relatives in Georgia? Evidently, they were already a part of Nicki's life." Michael leaned forward. "Wouldn't it be more appropriate for them to raise Nicki?"

Daria's anger boiled, rising quickly to the words-pop-in-your-head-and-straight-out-your-mouth temperature.

Was he asking these questions because he wanted her to make Nicki someone else's responsibility? If so, he could forget it. Nicki wasn't going anywhere. She was staying right here with her!

"You know, Michael. It doesn't matter who Nicki's father is," Daria bit out. Her neck moved, accenting her words. "And Peaches' relatives don't play into this at all. Peaches wanted *me* to take care of her daughter, and I'm going to do it." Steel clang in Daria's voice. "I'm not asking *you*—"

Michael held up his hands in a placating manner. "Whoa. Don't get upset. Bring it down a notch." A frown clustered between his eyes. "I'm just trying to understand. This is going to change your life in a big way."

She gave him a long, hard look, then blew out a breath, trying to release her irritation. "You're telling me. But I believe I can handle it."

She told him everything Otis had discussed with her that day about the memorial service and Peaches' trust and will. "You know, it's really eerie. She was having nightmares about dying. That's what prompted her to get her affairs in order."

Daria lifted Nicki to her shoulder and gently patted her back.

Nicki let rip a big burp.

Michael laughed. "That was impressive. You need to enter her in one of those belching contests. I think she has a chance at coming in first place."

Daria laughed half-heartedly. "I need about thirty minutes to get her ready for bed. Can you wait that long for your chili, or are you starved?"

"I can wait. Is there anything I can do to help?"

"Sure. Nicki's things are in the den. Would you get the portable crib and set it up in my bedroom?" Daria gestured toward the master bedroom.

"Consider it done."

Nicki patiently endured Daria's fumbling as she sponged her off.

After Michael finished setting up the crib, he said, "I'll go and start warming up the chili."

"Okay. I'm almost finished here. We'll be out there shortly."

Lord, I don't want to lose him. I don't want to hurt him. I don't want to be hurt. I'm a total mess! Please give me the strength I need to end this relationship.

Positioning Nicki on her stomach so that she could sponge her back, Daria saw a small, diamond-shaped birthmark between her shoulder blades.

"Cute birthmark, Nicki. Does this mean you're going to have expensive tastes? If you're going to be anything like your mother, you definitely will."

Daria dried Nicki with a fluffy towel, and dressed her in a yellow sleeper. Nicki started to yawn and whine as Daria finished up. *Just in time!*

"Nicki, I promise you I'll get better at this." Daria shook her head at her ineptness. "I sure can't get any worse."

They joined Michael at the table.

"This is delicious," Daria said after eating a spoonful of the chili. The chili turned into lead in her already churning stomach. She really wasn't hungry, but she knew she needed to eat in order to keep her strength up. She had to stay healthy for Nicki.

Michael smiled. "Yes, it is. I'm glad you like it."

Lying in Daria's arms sucking a pacifier, Nicki was almost asleep.

When they finished eating, Daria said, "Michael, we need to talk. Can you stay a little while longer?" Tears pooled in her eyes, and she tried desperately to blink them away.

Michael frowned slightly. "Sure. Why don't you go and put her to bed while I clear all of this away?"

He had just finished up in the kitchen when Daria returned.

"Michael, I've enjoyed the time we've spent together. Now that I have the responsibility of raising Nicki, my priorities have changed. Nicki's my first priority." Daria paused and took a deep breath.

"I can appreciate that."

"Well," Daria continued, "now that Nicki's a part of my life, the dynamics of this relationship have changed. I'm a single mother now."

"Daria, I am not sure I understand what you're trying to say."

Tears rolled down her cheeks. "I'm saying that I don't think we should continue to see each other."

"What?! How could you possibly think such a thing?"

"Michael, it's going to happen sooner or later. Most men don't want to get involved with women who have kids. They think there are too many issues to deal with in that kind of relationship."

"Daria, since when have I become 'most men'? Have I said or done anything here tonight to make you think I'm going to walk away from you because of Nicki?"

"No, but—"

"You've tried and convicted me without giving me a chance to defend myself." Michael rubbed a hand over the back of his neck.

"Michael, you may stay for a while, but eventually you'll leave. The longer we continue this relationship, the harder it'll be for me to let you go when that time comes."

"Daria, I'm not going anywhere. I—"

"Michael, don't." She waved her hands to stop him. "Don't make any promises." A sob broke through. "Don't make this any harder for me than it already is. It's over. Please, just go," she pleaded though her tears.

Pain, swiftly followed by determination, flashed in Michael's eyes before he slowly turned away and walked out.

I don't think we should continue to see each other.

The words haunted Michael. He sat in the recliner in his dark living room, feeling like he'd been run over by a semi.

How many times had he said those exact words to girlfriends in the past? Did those ladies feel the same level of devastation as he was feeling right now?

A mocking laugh burst from Michael's lips. *Well, once again, I can see that God's word is true. In my past relationships, I sowed devastation, and now, I'm definitely reaping it.*

The pain in his heart reflected an image of himself that sickened him. He was ashamed of the way he'd handled his past relationships. He'd been selfish and unkind. He'd used women for his own gratification, never considering their feelings.

How many women had he hurt with his arrogance and callousness? How many hearts had he scarred?

He knew Daria would never deliberately hurt him. He also knew she believed the things she'd said to him. She honestly thought he'd walk away from her because of Nicki.

Didn't she know that she'd stolen his heart? Didn't she know that she was as dear to him as the air he breathed? Didn't she know that he loved her? Didn't she know…

He scoffed. *How could she possibly know these things, you idiot, when you've never told her?*

He was no fool. Apart from his renewed relationship with Christ, falling in love with Daria was the best thing that had ever happened to him. He was not about to give her up without a fight.

Michael pushed a button and the footrest rose. He shifted until he found a comfortable spot.

Okay, now Daria was a single mom. Did that make him love her any less? No! She's the same person she was yesterday. Her ability to readily love and embrace Nicki made him love and admire her even more.

He scrubbed a hand across his face.

The ten-million-dollar question was this: Could he handle a ready-made family? Was he ready to have kids? Until just a few short months ago, he was doing everything in his power to dodge commitment. He'd just accepted the fact that he was in love with Daria and wanted to marry her. If he still wanted Daria—which he did—he'd have to also accept the responsibilities that went along with Nicki.

He lowered the footrest.

Nicki was a part of Daria. He loved Daria, and, given time, he knew he'd grow to love Nicki as well. He loved children. Nicki was just a small munchkin, and a beautiful one at that. How could he not grow to love her?

Michael bowed his head and steepled his fingers. "Lord, before I ask for anything else, I ask that You forgive me for my arrogance and the pain I've caused others. I know those relationships were in the past, but I didn't recognize the extent of the damage I've caused until tonight. I ask that You heal any hearts I've scarred.

"Lord, I feel with everything within me, that You brought Daria and me together. I love her, and I don't want to lose her. I don't know how to fix this situation, so I am surrendering it to You. You've never failed me before, and I know You won't fail me now. Lord, Your will be done—not mine."

After Michael finished praying, peace filled him. He sat quietly and meditated in the peace after the storm.

Be patient.

Those two words resonated through Michael's spirit. Joy exploded in him like a rocket, because he knew everything was going to be all right. He jumped to his feet and raised his palms toward heaven. "Hallelujah! Thank You, Lord!"

Chapter Twenty

L ater that night, jarred awake by Nicki's shrill cries, Daria jackknifed up in bed and glanced at the clock sitting on the nightstand. She groaned. "Three o'clock in the morning! I just went to sleep."

In the darkened room, Nicki's cries increased in strength and volume.

"Okay, Ms. Nicki. I'm coming." Daria turned on the lamp on the nightstand and dragged her tired body out of bed.

When she peered into the portable crib, she saw that Nicki had turned red from her exertions—crying, waving her arms, and pumping her legs.

Daria lifted her out of the crib and held her close. "You poor pumpkin. Let's get you dried and fed."

Hearing Daria's voice seemed to calm Nicki. Her cries turned into whimpers and snuffles.

Daria changed the baby's diaper and, with Nicki in her arms, went into the kitchen to get a bottle. When the bottle was ready, they returned to the bedroom.

Daria piled her pillows up against the headboard, rested her back against them, and popped the rubber nipple into Nicki's mouth.

Inevitably, her mind gravitated to Michael. Tears pooled in her eyes and spilled down her cheeks unchecked as she thought about their break-up.

Her heart belonged to Michael, and she knew she wouldn't get over him any time soon—if ever.

She knew she'd hurt him and deeply regretted that. What else could she have done? Pain was inevitable in this situation.

Oh, Michael! I'm going to miss you so much.

After Nicki finished her bottle, Daria maneuvered the crib closer to her bed. Satisfied with the placement, she put Nicki in the crib, dimmed the lights, and climbed back into bed.

By the moonlight streaming through the window, Daria watched Nicki play with her hands and make noises until she fell asleep.

Daria awoke four hours later and looked into the crib. Nicki was sleeping peacefully. The cobwebs in her foggy mind told Daria she could use just a tad more sleep. But knowing she needed to shower while Nicki slept, she got up and headed for the bathroom.

She grimaced when she saw her reflection in the bathroom mirror. Blood-shot, swollen, dark-rimmed eyes stared back at her. She cast her reflection a half-smile. "Girl, you're scarin' me." She chuckled, shook her head, and turned from the mirror.

When she reentered the room ten minutes later, Nicki stretched out her limbs, signaling that night-night time was over.

Daria grabbed the nearest article of clothing she could find and quickly pulled it on. Not bothering to look in the mirror, she ran a comb through her hair and pulled it back into a ponytail. She finished right on time. Nicki squawked her displeasure, summoning Daria to the crib.

She lifted Nicki out of her crib and bussed her tiny cheek. "Good morning, Princess Nicki. Your breakfast will be served momentarily."

She made quick work of changing Nicki's diaper and headed for the kitchen.

By nine o'clock, Daria had managed to dress Nicki in a cute little jumper. She had just finished grooming Nicki's hair when the doorbell rang.

She scooped Nicki up and went to answer the door. When she peeked through the security hole, she saw Lenore standing at the door.

"Good morning, Aunt Lenore."

Lenore's eyes slowly traveled over Daria.

When her gaze finally traveled back up to Daria's shirt, one of her brows lifted.

Daria looked down at her outfit, and saw that she was wearing a neon-pink t-shirt and a pair of red sweats. A closer look at the sleeves of her shirt revealed that, in her haste, she'd put the thing on inside out.

Oh, good grief! Daria rolled her eyes and then shrugged. *It doesn't matter. I ain't got no man, so I don't have to dress to impress.*

Lenore flashed a smile. "From the looks of you, I'd say you finally got around to hearing Nicki cry."

A yawn interrupted Daria's tired smile. She waved Lenore in with her hand.

"Have you eaten breakfast yet?" Lenore asked.

"No, I haven't had a chance to fix anything. I'm not really hungry."

"Here, give me that baby. You're going to have to eat something. How do you expect to keep your strength up if you don't eat? Go and fix yourself something." Lenore removed Nicki from Daria's arms, walked into the living room, and sat down.

"Now, young lady," Lenore said to Nicki, "it's time for us to get acquainted. I'm your Auntie Lenore."

Nicki smiled and cooed.

"My, except for that nose, you do look a lot like your mother. You're going to be a beauty."

Nicki made some more baby noises.

"Daria, have you thought about what you're going to do about child care?"

"No, I really haven't given it any thought." Daria removed two slices of toast from the toaster.

"You really need to give yourself some time to find your feet. Why don't you take some time off from work?"

Daria opened the refrigerator and took out the butter. "I think I qualify for parental leave. I'll call my supervisor and discuss it with her."

"How much time will they give you?"

Daria buttered a slice of toast. "Six weeks. I believe." She bit into the bread.

"That would be great. Do you have everything you need for Nicki?"

"Mmm." Daria swallowed. "I have enough for about a week or so. After that, I'll need to restock my diaper and formula supply. Otis told me Peaches had started to set up a nursery for Nicki. I have a key to Peaches' house, and I want to check out the nursery to see whether I can use anything there."

Lenore kissed one of Nicki's tiny hands. "Why don't we check it out today?"

"Okay. We can head on over there after I finish my breakfast."

Lenore swept Daria with her eyes once again. "Nicki and I don't want you embarrassing us, so we're going to ask you to do something about your 'look' before we leave."

Daria laughed. "Far be it from me to embarrass you ladies. I'll make myself more presentable."

Peaches had used four basic colors throughout her house—deep burgundy, dark green, soft white, and toasted-almond.

The nursery had white walls with a colorful border going all the way around the room two feet above the floor. Frolicking, deep burgundy, dark green, and toasted almond colored teddy bears played along the white border. Matching deep-burgundy wall-to-wall carpet covered the floor. Dark-green and toasted-almond oversized throw pillows were scattered on the burgundy window seat cushion.

Daria turned in a tight circle in the middle of the room. "This is beautiful."

"That child always did have good taste, didn't she?" Lenore asked.

"Yes, she did. Expensive taste. It's a good thing she was wealthy." Daria smiled in fond memory.

The room contained a small, white, four-drawer dresser, a changing table, an adult-sized white rocking chair, and a seat the baby could sit in and play.

Daria walked over to the seat. "The angle of this seat can be adjusted, so Nicki can recline in the chair and see the things going on around her."

"Mmm." Lenore was busy checking out a large box leaning against a wall. "Come and take a look at this. What kind of new fangled thing is this?"

Daria moved closer to give the box a thorough examination. "That's an unassembled baby crib."

"I know that," Lenore snapped. "But what *kind* of crib is it."

"The crib will grow with Nicki. When she becomes a toddler, it can easily be converted into a toddler bed."

"Is that right? I've never seen anything like it. It'll definitely come in handy. Peaches certainly put a lot of work into this room. I agree with Otis, it makes sense for you to move in here as soon as possible. She'd almost completed this nursery. How long will it be before you can get Nicki settled in here?"

Daria sat in the rocker and set it into motion. "Otis said we should be able to get everything settled in a couple of months." She frowned. "Peaches asked me to go to Georgia with her on her next visit. She must've decided to tell me about Nicki. I wonder if she was going to bring Nicki home on that visit."

Lenore peered into a few drawers. "I believe she was ready to bring her baby home. Do you see anything you want to take with you?"

"Yes. I'll take the little seat. That will free up my hands some."

"Okay. You grab the seat. I'll take Nicki out to the car."

As Daria drove them back to her house, Lenore asked, "Has Michael met Nicki yet?"

"Yes…he stopped by last night."

"What was his reaction?"

"Well…uh…he was definitely surprised. I was busy with Nicki much of the time that he was there. He didn't stay long."

"Daria, you don't sound right." Lenore shifted in her seat. "What are you not telling me? And don't try to fob me off with nonsense either. Now out with it."

"Michael and I are no longer seeing each other."

"When did this happen?"

"Last night."

"Does this break-up have anything to do with Nicki?"

"Yes."

"Girl, you're about to get on my last nerve." Exasperation filled Lenore's voice. "I'm not going to play twenty-questions with you. Tell me what happened last night!"

"Well…now that I have a ready-made family, I knew Michael would eventually walk away. I didn't want to suffer through the agony of wondering when he'd finally make that move, so I decided to end the relationship last night."

"Did Michael agree with your decision to end the relationship?"

"Not exactly…He argued against it."

Lenore leaned forward. Daria glanced at Lenore's narrowed eyes, then looked back at the road. "Uh-huh. Did he say or do anything last night to support your belief that he'd eventually walk away?"

Daria grimaced. Lenore's tone warned of a coming storm. She was about to blast Daria with both barrels.

I'm a full-grown woman. I no longer have to cower at Aunt Lenore's diatribes. Daria snorted. *Yeah. Right. Girl, you're shakin' in your boots!*

She flicked Lenore a nervous glance. "No..." Daria squirmed in her seat.

"Did he tell you he had a problem with your taking on the responsibility of raising Nicki?"

"Uh...no."

A sinking feeling started in the pit of Daria's stomach. Had she made a mistake? Had she been too hasty?

"You know the Lord knows Michael better than anyone else possibly could. Did you pray about this? Did you ask the Lord what His will was in this situation?"

"No." Daria's one-word answer was weighted down with a whole lot of guilt. *What have I done?!*

"Daria Alexis Simpson, I could turn you over my knee!" Lenore's sharp reply hit Daria like a slap. "I still might. How could you do such a thoughtless thing? Girl, where was your head at when you came up with this nonsense?"

If her skin wasn't so dark, Daria knew she'd be beet-red right about now. "Um—"

"No. You listen to me. You're still reeling from Peaches' death. Just yesterday, you found out that you're an instant mother. You're not thinking clearly—you can't be. You know better than to make such a life-altering decision while you're in this state of mind.

"I like Michael," Lenore continued. "He's a good, solid man. I don't believe for a minute he would've walked away from you because of Nicki." Lenore paused and shook her head. "Mmm-mmm-mmm, girl, good men don't grow on trees, and you just threw this one away like yesterday's garbage."

Oh, no! You, big goof! You've done it now. You've ruined what you had with Michael. How could you have been so stupid!

"You're right. I've messed up." Daria's anguish almost choked out her words. "How in the world am I going to fix this? How am I going to get him back?"

"You're going to give Michael some time to deal with whatever he may be feeling right now. And while you're waiting, you're going to do what you should've done in the first place—pray!"

Daria nodded. "Okay."

Lenore grunted and patted Daria on the arm. "We all make a mess of things when we leave God out of our decisions. Give this situation to Him, and let Him work it out. I truly believe that Michael will forgive you and come back. If he doesn't, I'll have to seriously question my ability to read people."

From your lips to God's ears.

Later that week, on Saturday night, Daria sat in her living room having a pity party. She hadn't seen or spoken to Michael since the night of their break-up. They lived so close to each other, she thought she would've at least seen him entering and leaving his home. Evidently, he'd chosen to stay as far away from her as possible. Who could blame him?

She'd repented, prayed, waited, hoped, and prayed some more. Yet, Michael still hadn't returned to her.

Oh, how she missed that man! She missed his smile, his laugh, his conversation, his warm embraces, and his kisses—definitely his kisses. She missed his very essence.

"Lord, please send him back to me!"

Go to her. Tomorrow.

The following Tuesday evening, Michael's heart sang when he heard those words. He recognized the voice of the Lord. He understood the Lord was telling him he could go to Daria.

He'd been patient, but it had taken everything he had in him to stay away from Daria this past week. He'd worked long hours. He'd hung out with his family. He'd stayed away from their complex until he'd known it would be too late for a visit.

That modern convenience called the telephone was another hurdle he'd had to master. He'd lost count of the number of times he'd picked up the receiver to call Daria and then put it down again without making the call.

His heart raced with anticipation. "Daria!" Her name trembled on his lips as a thrill jigged down his spine.

Tomorrow, this drought would be over. Tomorrow, he'd renew his relationship with Daria. Tomorrow, he'd hold her in his arms once again. Tomorrow…

Chapter Twenty-One

The next morning, Michael rang Daria's doorbell. His heartbeat raced at a gallop as he waited, not so patiently, for her to answer the door.

Last night, he'd been so anxious for this moment he hadn't gotten a wink of sleep.

Daria opened the door with Nicki in her arms. "Hi, Michael." Her voice was noncommittal. Her eyes—filled with uncertainty and apprehension—roamed over his face.

The confidence he'd felt last night after receiving a green light from the Lord had diminished with every step he'd taken toward her door.

Okay, this is good. We're off to a good start. She didn't slam the door in my face.

"Hello, Daria." Michael's heart thumped wildly as he devoured her with his eyes.

"Would you like to come in?"

"Yes! Uh…yes, thank you." Michael quickly moved through the door, not giving her a chance to change her mind.

They moved into the living room where Daria placed Nicki in her seat. She gestured for Michael to take a seat on the couch. She sat down beside him.

He decided to get right to the point. "Daria, this past week has been the longest and darkest week of my life. Why? Because I couldn't be with you." He captured her hand in his.

His confidence level ratcheted up a bit when she didn't snatch it away. "Don't you know you're everything to me? I could never just walk away from you." Gazing into her eyes, he placed a butterfly-soft kiss on her hand. "How can I walk away from my heart?"

"Can't we reason together and work this out? Daria, I love you. I *need* you."

With tears streaming down her face, she threw her arms around his neck. "Oh, Michael, I love you, too. I am so sorry. I was wrong. Would you please, please forgive me? I thought I'd lost you forever. This week has been difficult for me as well. I've missed you so much."

He kissed her. All of the anguish and longing he'd been feeling for the past week was conveyed in that kiss. None of the kisses they'd shared in the past were anything like this one. The passion was almost palpable.

He broke the kiss first and put some space between them. "Whoa, I'm definitely getting a Monster Alert! No more of that."

"Mmm-hmm." Daria giggled.

"I'm going with you to Peaches' memorial service. That's why I'm dressed in my finery." Michael gestured at his suit. "I'll watch Nicki. You go and get dressed."

"Are you sure you don't mind?"

"No, not at all. I know how to handle babies. I got a lot of practice with Brandon when he was an infant. Don't worry," Michael said with a smile and a wink. "Go on and get changed."

He lifted Nicki from her seat and moved back to the couch. "Now, little lady, it's time for us to come to an understanding. You're not going to have Daria all to yourself for much longer," he said softly. "I want you to take a good look at me. Very soon, you're going to be seeing a lot more of this face. What do you think about that?"

Nicki's hazel eyes penetrated into his, and he felt a jolt of awareness and some other indefinable feeling. A germ of knowledge hovered around the periphery of his mind.

He stared back at Nicki, trying to figure out what had prompted the craziness he was feeling.

Her eyes! His mind screamed, and his heart took off like a jet. Those were Fruit Lady's eyes. He didn't remember much about how she'd looked, but he did remember those eyes and her light skin—skin the same tone as Nicki's.

Peaches had been Fruit Lady!

Michael took several deep breaths to slow his heart rate. It didn't work. He felt like he was caught up in a rip current—tumbling and rolling without any control.

Why hadn't he noticed Nicki's eye color before? He'd been zoomed in on Daria, trying to read the negative vibes that had been rolling off her. He honestly hadn't paid much attention to Nicki.

Don't flip over this. You're just jumping to conclusions. There's no way Nicki is your daughter. Think, man! Think!

Daria had said Nicki was three months old. He quickly counted back to that long ago night he'd shared with Fruit Lady—Peaches. The one-and-only night he'd ever been stinkin' drunk and hadn't taken care of business.

The band around his chest loosened a bit after he'd finished counting. By his calculations, if he had fathered Nicki, she'd be two-months-old now. *Whew!* He mimed flinging sweat from his brow.

There was one more thing he could check for that would completely put the maybes to rest—the Greer Diamond. He gently inspected Nicki's arms and legs looking for the diamond-shaped birthmark that was passed down to the offspring of every Greer male. *She didn't have it!* He exhaled a gust of relief and smiled hugely into Nicki's face.

He guessed it really didn't make much sense for him to panic the way he had over the possibility that Nicki was his daughter. After all, she *would* be his daughter when he and Daria married. But the very idea that a child was created on that night he so desperately wanted to forget gave him the willies.

Nicki beamed a grin at him and reached for his face with her hands.

Now that he was no longer panicking, he basked in her smile. It reached all the way to his heart and filled his chest.

He lifted her a little and placed a kiss on her tiny, soft cheek.

When he lowered her, Nicki looked into his eyes and smiled. "Goo."

"Oh, yeah, I'm going to have to beat them off with a stick because you're going to be a heartbreaker."

Five minutes later, Lenore arrived. Michael and Nicki opened the door to let her in.

"So, you're here. If you hadn't been, Clifford and I would've paid you a visit," Lenore said with a serious note.

Michael knew exactly what she meant.

He cast his voice low, so Daria wouldn't overhear their conversation. "Lenore, I'm not going anywhere. I told you I love Daria. That hasn't changed."

Lenore lowered her volume to match his. "So, you're telling me Nicki's sudden appearance hasn't made a difference?"

"No, I'm not going to say that because it has made a difference. It's changed things. There are more responsibilities involved. I'll gladly embrace whatever I have to, to have Daria in my life." He paused and then winked at her. "Besides, now instead of having one lady to love, I have two."

"Hmm-mmm." Lenore smirked and rolled her eyes. "All right. I was just beginning to wonder if I was wrong about you."

"No. You're not getting rid of me that easily, old lady."

"Old lady! Boy, I've got your old lady. I'll take you down."

Michael laughed. "I believe you can do it, too."

After Peaches' memorial service and burial, everybody returned to Daria's home.

When they arrived, they found Amelia and Euvinia in the kitchen surrounded by many containers of food.

Daria's eyes rounded in wonder. "Where did all of this food come from?"

"I asked Amelia and Euvinia to fix a little something," Lenore explained. "I allowed them to use my key to get in while we were at the service."

Daria gave Amelia and Euvinia each a big hug. "Thank you. I hadn't even thought about what needed to be done after we got back here."

"That's okay, baby." Amelia kissed Daria's cheek and patted her on the back. "You've had a lot on your mind. We're glad that we can help."

"She's right. You're family, and family takes care of each other," Euvinia added. "Now, I've smelled this food long enough. Let's eat!"

Daria kept a watchful eye on Nicki as she was fussed over and passed from arm to arm. The baby seemed to enjoy all of the attention.

After everyone had eaten their fill, Daria and Otis went into the den to read the will. It was really a formality because they'd already discussed everything contained in the document last Wednesday.

"Do you have any questions?" Otis asked.

"Not about the will, but my aunt and I went to Peaches' house to take a look at the nursery. I wanted to see if there was anything I could bring over here for Nicki. Peaches had almost finished the nursery. I'd like to get Nicki settled as soon as possible. Do you have any idea yet how long it'll be before I can get her settled in Peaches' home?"

"I've called in a few favors and pulled some strings since I last saw you. I believe we can get the house situation settled in two weeks. Will you be okay until then?"

"Yes. I'm not having any hardships taking care of Nicki. I just want to get her settled."

"I understand. Do you have any other questions?"

"Not right now, but I'll call you if anything comes up."

By the time Daria and Otis exited the den, most of the people had already left.

"I'm going to have to get going," Otis said.

"Okay. Thank you for everything, Otis," Daria said with sincere gratitude.

Michael and Calyssa had just finished clearing up the kitchen, and the Greers were preparing to leave.

"We're going to leave now, baby, but you call us if you need anything." Amelia gave Daria a warm hug.

"Thanks again for everything," Daria said.

"Bye, Ms. Daria," Brandon said, "I'll babysit for you when Nicki gets old enough to play. She can't do anything fun right now." The adults chuckled.

"I'm going to head out, too, Daria." Lenore gathered her things. "Now, you get some rest."

Daria closed the door after her departing guests and turned to Michael. "Well, everybody left at the same time. Are you planning to leave, too?"

Michael smiled. "The only way you're going to get rid of me is to kick me out."

Daria returned his smile. "I think I'll let you stay."

He walked over to Nicki's seat and lifted her out. After shifting her to one arm, he stepped over to Daria, and caught her hand with his free hand.

"It's time for you to relax." He sat on the couch and pulled Daria down beside him.

"Princess Nicki will be demanding her food shortly."

"Would you do something for me? Would you take a nap and let me take care of Nicki for you while you sleep?"

"You want to babysit Nicki?" Disbelief was written all over her face.

Michael chuckled. "I want you to get some rest. Nicki and I have come to an understanding. I think she'll go easy on me."

"You've got a deal. Before I lie down, I'll get her bottle ready and bring you some diapers."

"Don't worry about us. We're going to have fun," Michael said after Daria brought him the things he would need.

Daria went into her room and closed the door.

"It's just you and me, princess," Michael said to Nicki as Daria's door swung shut.

He entertained Nicki with "talking" stuffed animals and Bible stories.

When she started to fret, he popped her bottle into her mouth before her cries could gather steam. "Can't have that, now can we? Daria needs her sleep."

After Nicki finished her bottle, Michael changed her diaper.

"You little people sure require a lot of energy. You wore me out. It's time for us to get a little shut eye."

He laid her on a blanket on the floor in front of the couch and then stretched out beside her.

After a few minutes, she fell asleep.

His mind migrated back to the panic attack he'd had earlier that morning. He rolled his eyes and shook his head at his own foolishness.

He was dozing off when Lenore's advice surfaced in his mind. *"Don't ever lie to Daria—deliberately or by omission."*

His eyes popped open. Now why'd he think about that? He hadn't lied to Daria, nor did he plan to. He squirmed on the floor a little and reluctantly admitted to himself that he hadn't been exactly forth coming about the "panic" moments he'd had concerning Peaches and Nicki since he and Daria had been dating. But was it really necessary to share those moments with Daria?

As far as he was concerned, his one night with Peaches was history and was best left buried in the past. Peaches was dead and could tell no tales. He'd already determined that Nicki wasn't his biological child. Why borrow trouble?

Michael yawned and stretched, releasing the troubling thoughts from his mind. *Ah, all is finally right with my world.*

Chapter Twenty-Two

Three weeks after Peaches' memorial service, Daria answered the phone and jiggled Nicki in the curve of her arm. "Hello."

Nicki burped and spit up.

A pot boiled over on the stove.

Daria clenched the phone to her ear with her shoulder, then reached for a cloth diaper.

The timer on the dryer pinged, signaling the end of its drying cycle.

"Hi, Daria, this is Calyssa. How are you?"

Daria wiped Nicki's mouth and moved to the stove. "Frazzled, girl." Daria blew out a breath that puckered her lips and expanded her cheeks. "I don't have enough hands. I need at least two more." She removed the pot and turned the burner off.

Calyssa chuckled. "Oh, I do remember those days. It'll get better...once you get past the terrible two's."

Nicki blew bubbles and flexed her fingers.

Daria lifted her eyes to the ceiling. "Are you trying to cheer me up or bring me down?"

Calyssa laughed softly. "Actually, I called to give you a break. I'd like to take care of Nicki for you today."

Daria strapped Nicki in her seat. "Calyssa, that's sweet of you to offer," she said with a smile, "but you don't have to do that."

Daria appreciated Calyssa's offer. Calyssa would take good care of Nicki, but Daria wasn't exactly comfortable leaving Nicki with anyone else.

"I *really* want to, Daria," Calyssa coaxed. "My baby is seven years old. I can't pick him up and cuddle him any more." Calyssa let out a pitiful sigh. "Come on, take pity on me. Let me watch Nicki for a couple of hours."

I could use the time to run some errands.

Daria wavered. "Well…"

"Don't you have some things to take care of today?" Calyssa asked. "Think about it. You'll be able to move around a lot easier and faster without Nicki and all of her gear."

Daria's last errand-run with Nicki had not been fun. In fact, it had been exhausting.

Calyssa continued. "I'll even babysit Nicki at your house, so she'll be in familiar surroundings."

"All right. All right," Daria's wide grin spilled over into her voice, "you can stop the sales pitch. You'll get your baby fix today."

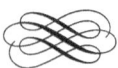

Two hours later, Nicki's squeals filled the living room as Calyssa blew raspberries on her tummy.

"We're going to get you a bath and surprise Mommy Daria when she returns. Let's go find your things." Calyssa found the items she needed and headed for the bathroom.

She prepared Nicki's bath and then returned to the bedroom to undress her. She leaned Nicki forward to better remove her jumper. She freed Nicki's arms, and the jumper pooled around the baby's tiny hips. Calyssa gasped and froze.

After several seconds, Nicki screeched her displeasure at the inactivity, setting Calyssa into motion once again.

She placed Nicki across her lap with her back exposed. She ran her hand gently over the diamond-shaped mark that sat nestled between Nicki's shoulder blades. "Oh, little brother, what have you done?"

Nicki's squirming prompted Calyssa to finish undressing her and complete her bath.

Shell-shocked, Calyssa finished her ministrations. Many questions swam in her mind. When? Where? Had he lost his mind?! She knew without a doubt that Nicki was Michael's child. The Greer Diamond was proof positive of that.

She sat Nicki in her seat and cleaned up the mess they'd made in the bathroom. When Calyssa finished, she sat on the couch. She rolled up her shirtsleeve, exposing her upper-right arm. There it was. A replica of the mark that graced Nicki's back.

She groaned. *This is going to turn everything on its head.*

She shuddered just thinking about Daria's possible reaction. If she was in Daria's shoes, she'd be very, very upset. *Shoot! I'm the idiot's sister, and I want to brain him.*

The doorbell rang, startling her out of her reverie.

Calyssa peeked through the security hole and opened the door. Before Michael could clear the doorway, she went on the attack. "Boy, what have you done?! How could you be so irresponsible and stupid?"

Michael lowered his brow. "Sis, what are you going on about?" His eyes roamed over the room. "Where's Daria?"

She sucked her teeth and huffed, "You better thank the Good Lord that Daria is out." She planted her hands on her hips. "And don't try to change the subject. You know what I'm talking about. Don't try to play the innocent with me. I know you, little brother."

He threw his hands up in surrender. "Look, I don't know what you're talking about. Whatever it is you *think* I've done, I'm sorry."

Her foot tapped at a steady and fast beat. "Not good enough!"

He shook his head, and his voice took on a pleading note. "Sis, look, I'm tired, hungry, and I don't have a clue what you're talking about. You're going to have to help me out here."

She flung her arm in Nicki's direction. "I'm talking about her. How could you bring a child into this world and abandon her?"

Michael's eyes rounded, and he took a step back. "Whoa! Just slow your roll. I'm not Nicki's father."

"Yes, you are!" Calyssa snapped.

"No. I'm not!"

"Are too!"

He exhaled in exasperation. "Sis, I think I'd know better than you whether I've fathered a child."

"Humph!" Calyssa marched over to Nicki and lifted her out of the seat. She unbuttoned the row of buttons that climbed up the back of Nicki's shirt. When she'd bared Nicki's back, she turned her so Michael would have an unimpeded view. "If she's not yours, then how do you explain this?!"

Michael's eyes bugged out, his jaw dropped, and he collapsed into the nearest chair.

"This mark is only passed down through the males in our family. Daddy's only brother, Uncle John, didn't have any sons. You are the only Greer left who could have passed on this mark."

Michael absently rubbed the diamond-shaped birthmark that sat high on his left thigh.

"But she's three months old. By my calculations, she should be two months old." Michael's voice sounded hollow.

Nicki squirmed.

Calyssa tightened her hold on Nicki and watched Michael, looking for the slightest indication that he had known he was Nicki's father. What she saw was a man who'd been totally flattened by her discovery.

"She was born a month prematurely." A little of the harshness drained from her voice. "You didn't know about Nicki, did you?"

"No." He shook his head slowly. "It was just one night. One…night. I didn't even know the girl was Peaches until a few weeks ago. She didn't know my name either. I never saw her again." Shame filled his voice.

Nicki sucked nosily on her fist and wriggled.

Calyssa caressed Nicki's back and made a sound of disgust. "That's pathetic. You know that, don't you?"

"It was in the past, Cal." He ran his hands over his face.

"Yeah, well your past has come back to haunt you—for the rest of your life." Sarcasm, as thick as molasses, clung to her words.

He pulled his ear lobe, then let out a clipped, self-deriding laugh. "I know it's no excuse, but I was wasted that night."

"You're right. It's not an excuse for your recklessness," she said without an ounce of sympathy.

He leaned forward and rested his head in his hands.

Nicki kicked her legs and let out a protesting squeal.

"What are you going to do now that you know Nicki's your daughter?" Calyssa refastened Nicki's buttons and sat her upright.

He shrugged his shoulders. "I don't know."

"You don't know?!" Calyssa's tone was as hard as flint. "What do you mean, you don't know? It's obvious to me. You're going to step up to the bat and take responsibility for your child."

"I know that, Cal. It's just that I need time to…" Michael made a gesture of helplessness with his hands.

Calyssa's eyes swung to the door because she heard a key being inserted into the lock. "Your time just ran out, little brother. You better tell Daria about this—tonight. I'm going to give you a little bit of time…" she held up her thumb and forefinger, leaving a few centimeters of space between them, "…to get your act together, and then, if you haven't done so, I'm telling Mom that she has another grandchild."

Michael glowered. "Just keep your mouth shut!" He whispered hotly.

Calyssa walked over to him, placed Nicki in his lap, and smirked nastily. "Here's your daughter, Papa. Maybe one day you can order her around, but you can't tell me what to do!"

Daria had pulled into the parking lot of her complex with anticipation. She'd been running late returning, so she'd known Michael would be at her place waiting for her when she got home.

She marveled and thanked the Lord that everything was falling into place so smoothly. Her request for parental leave had been approved when she'd explained her situation to her supervisor.

She'd finally been able to relax and enjoy motherhood. She and Nicki had established a pattern that worked for them. Daria had learned that she could get more rest if she slept whenever Nicki did.

Daria had met with the pediatrician recommended by Beatrice and had requested all of Nicki's medical records from Georgia. She was thankful Otis and Beatrice had gotten the doctor's address from the Joneses when they'd brought Nicki to Florida.

The thing that really had her heart shining bright was that she and Nicki had been spending a lot of time with Michael. They'd become a sort of family. They'd met him for lunch in the park during the week, and he'd had dinner with them almost every evening.

As far as the monster alerts, they'd finally decided to limit their kisses to pecks or smooches on the cheek to keep the monsters at bay.

Daria smiled. Nicki had also proven herself to be an able chaperone. Nothing puts a damper on "the mood" like spit up or a dirty diaper.

It was taking longer than Otis had anticipated for the transfer of the ownership of Peaches' home. Daria knew things would be finalized soon, so she'd started packing. Michael had helped her in the evenings.

Life is good! Thank God my spark of insanity hadn't caused me to lose him forever!

She unlocked the door and pushed it open.

"...you can't tell me what to do!" Calyssa was saying—rather yelling—when Daria stepped into her living room.

The hostility radiating from Calyssa and Michael halted Daria in her tracks. *What in the world is going on here?*

Michael and Calyssa didn't acknowledge her entrance. They were too busy staring each other down.

She'd seen the two of them go at it before, but she could always sense the deep caring and respect they had for each other. This was different. They looked like they might come to blows.

She glanced at Nicki, lying in Michael's arms. Nicki was bicycling her legs and looking up at Michael, totally oblivious to the undercurrents in the room.

Daria cleared her throat. "Hey, you guys. What's up?"

Michael's eyes swung to hers with a deer-caught-in-the-headlights look in them. Calyssa's eyes darted to Daria, and then back to Michael.

"Hi." Michael cleared his throat. "Hi, Daria."

"Hey, Daria. I was just leaving." Calyssa moved around the living room, in what seemed to Daria to be inordinate haste, gathering her things. "Nicki and I had a blast. She's had her bath. She's ready for her dinner and her bed."

This is too strange. Daria looked at both of them like they had lost their wits. "Uh...thank you for watching her for me."

Calyssa zipped past Daria to the front door. "Any time. Any time." Calyssa turned back and looked at Michael. "Remember what I said, Michael. You'll be hearing from me."

Daria could see the rigidity of Michael's posture from where she was standing. At Calyssa's words, he tensed up even more if that were possible.

Nicki squeaked her displeasure at being held so tightly.

Daria frowned and removed Nicki from Michael's arms. She looked back at the door in time to see Calyssa pull it closed softly behind her.

Chapter Twenty-Three

Daria turned to Michael with drawn brows. "What was that all about?"

Nicki blew bubbles from the cradle of Daria's arm.

Michael ran his hand over his face. *This is bad. Real bad.*

He rubbed the back of his neck and took a circuit around Daria's coffee table. He wasn't ready to talk to Daria about this tonight. He was still reeling, trying to find his footing.

I have a kid! With Fruit Lady…Peaches. There was no easy way to tell Daria. He rubbed his temples with his fingertips.

He should have told her about his encounter with Peaches when he'd first realized the truth. If he had, Nicki's parentage would be easier for her to swallow. *Man, you're going to be in the doghouse—big time.*

He'd done exactly what Lenore had warned him not to do—lie by omission. He groaned to himself. His actions had made a difficult situation almost impossible. *Lord, please throw a little mercy and grace my way.*

"Michael?"

He'd run out of time. He walked over to Daria and guided her to the couch. Once they were seated, he sat and stared at her. Would she end their relationship? Or would she allow him to remain a part of her life? *Lord, please don't let me lose her.*

He cleared his throat and reached for her free hand. "I want you to remember that I love you. I'd never do anything, *anything* to hurt you. Okay?" Nervousness and fear wrestled in his belly.

"Okaaay. You're scaring me, Michael. Get to the point." Worry filled her voice.

"All right." Michael pulled on his ear lobe. "Nicki's my child." He felt Daria tense.

"Nicki's your child. What do you mean?" Confusion masked her face.

"I'm Nicki's biological father." Michael searched her face, trying to read the slightest change in her expression.

Daria's eyes rounded to enormous proportions. "You're what?!"

Nicki startled at her outburst. Daria absently jiggled the baby.

Michael felt like his skin was two sizes too small. "She's my child."

"How? When? I thought you and Peaches had never met before."

"We met one night in Atlanta last year. After that, we never saw each other again."

Suspicion and accusation crowded into Daria's eyes. "Why didn't you tell me you'd met? Why did you hide that from me?"

Michael swallowed. "I didn't know Peaches and the lady I met that night were the same person until recently."

"Look, Michael." Anger tinged Daria's voice. "I'm not going to sit here and play twenty-questions to get the whole story out of you. Just tell me everything I need to know about this situation." She narrowed her eyes. "I'm advising you ahead of time that now is *not* a good time to be selective with your information."

Oh, man! Michael ran his hand over his head.

"See, it's like this. We met at a bar. Peaches was high. I was drunk." Michael paused because Daria seemed to draw into herself. The hand that wasn't holding Nicki started clutching her stomach.

"Are you okay?"

"Just tell the story," Daria snapped through gritted teeth.

Michael frowned, took a big fortifying breath, and then continued his story with heated embarrassment flushing through him. "Well…uh, we didn't exchange names. She told me to call her Fruit Lady."

The corners of Daria's lips turned down. "You slept with her and didn't even know her name?" Disgust and disbelief filled her voice.

Michael winced. "Yeah. I'd never done anything like that before. I'm not proud of what happened that night."

"You shouldn't be." Her zinging reply cracked like a whip.

This is not going well—at all. Desperation crawled up his spine.

"I never saw her again after that night." His ending sounded lame to his own ears.

"Oh, I beg to differ." Indignation radiated from Daria. "You've seen her. You saw her picture that day you barged in here." Her neck snaked, but her eyes never left his face. "You also saw her lying on her kitchen floor."

Oh, no. Not the neck movement. I'm toast.

His voice took on a pleading note. "Daria, the only thing I remember about Peaches from that night was her light skin and her eyes. The eyes in the picture on your mantle are shadowed." He gestured toward the picture. "When we found her on the floor, her eyes were closed."

Daria looked at him like he was either being deliberately dense, or he was a total doofus.

Okay. I admit the clues were there if I'd wanted to see them. I didn't.

"Wait a minute." Daria's hand left her stomach and planted itself firmly on her hip. "You said you didn't know Peaches was the lady you'd met in the bar until recently. When did you come to this realization?" Anger sparked in her eyes and steel ran through her words. "And you'd better tell me it was while you were talking to Calyssa this evening."

Michael's heart seeped out through his toes. *I'm sunk.* "On the day of Peaches' funeral," he mumbled.

She heard him. "That was three weeks ago! Three…whole…weeks ago. When exactly were you planning to share this epiphany with me?"

How does she do that thing with her neck?

"Uh…" *Would it make things better or worse if I admit that I wasn't going to tell her? Tough call.*

Daria's eyes bore into him. "You weren't, were you?"

Michael cringed. *I plead the fifth.*

Daria drew in a hissing breath. "I thought you were different. You're just like my…" She stilled. "How are you so sure that Nicki is your child anyway?" Her tone demanded an honest answer.

"Because of the Greer Diamond."

"The what?" Daria's tone reflected that she thought his senses had gone begging.

"The birthmark between her shoulder blades. Calyssa and I both have the same mark in different places on our bodies. The mark is only passed through the males in my family. We can have a DNA test done if you'd like, but I'm one hundred percent sure that Nicki is my daughter."

Incredulity was written all over her face. "So, you were tripped up by a tiny mark? How long have you known that Nicki has this 'Greer Diamond'?" Her eyes dared him to be dishonest.

"Calyssa discovered it this evening and showed it to me. We were 'discussing' it when you came home."

Daria puffed. "That was some discussion."

She lifted Nicki from her lap and turned her so that she could see her face. After staring at the baby for a few minutes, she said, "The nose. She has your nose." She returned Nicki to her lap.

Michael glanced at Nicki's nose. Now that Daria had pointed it out, he could see the resemblance.

He reached for Daria's hand. Her eyes froze him in mid-reach. He cleared his throat. "Daria, I don't know what to say except I'm sorry you had to find out this way."

"You're kiddin' me. I didn't *have* to find out this way. You could have told me about you and Peaches weeks ago. You *chose* not to. I find that very disturbing, Michael. What else have you neglected to tell me? How do I know I can trust you?" Her voice choked on a sob. "I *can't* trust you."

Nicki began to fret. Daria stood and walked into the kitchen where she fixed Nicki a bottle.

Michael followed them. He felt so low an ant couldn't crawl under him. "Daria, I'm sorry. I love you and wouldn't hurt you for anything."

"Guess what, Michael? You just did," she snapped with a sniff.

"I'm sorry." Michael held out his hand in supplication. It didn't do him a bit of good.

Daria shot him a you've-got-to-be-kidding look and moved past him back into the living room where she sat in an armchair.

Nicki sucked noisily on her bottle.

How am I going to make this right?

"I want to know what you're planning to do about Nicki," Daria said.

"I don't know. The more immediate question for me is what's going to happen to us?" Michael searched her face looking for something—anything—that would give him hope.

Daria zapped him with a paralyzing look. "What us?" Her neck rolled emphasizing the question. "There *is* no us." Another neck roll cemented her statement.

Michael felt the bottom drop out of his world.

"Daria, c'mon, baby. Don't be like that."

Her eyes turned chilly, her face expressionless. "Get out."

"Daria—"

"When you're ready to talk about Nicki, give me a holla. Until then, get out."

Michael got out.

He walked in a dazed fog to his door.

They'd just mended the rift that had torn them apart when Nicki had come onto the scene. This was *not* supposed to happen.

Lord, what's going on here? I thought You were in my corner!

The minute the door closed behind Michael, Daria released the dams and let the tears run in rivulets down her face.

Unbelievable! She'd started the day looking forward to this evening with eager anticipation. Then it arrived and brought utter devastation.

Michael was Nicki's father. He and Peaches had…She shook her head to dislodge the tentacles of jealousy she felt for her dead friend. *I'm not even going to go there.*

The disappointments of her youth, caused by her father's enumerable lies, crowded in on her. She shivered. She couldn't have a relationship with a man she couldn't trust.

When Michael said he and Peaches had met in a bar, Daria thought she would be sick. Just like her father, Michael had frequented bars and drunk irresponsibly. Her father's lying and drinking had taken her mother away from her.

She wiped at the tears running down her cheeks with the back of her hand. No. She'd rather have a little heartbreak now instead of a lifetime of it.

"Oh, Nicki. It hurts." Her anguished voice bounced back at her off the walls.

Nicki! What if he tried to take Nicki away from her? *Don't borrow trouble, Daria!*

She had more immediate things to concentrate on right now—like getting through the night with a shattered heart.

Chapter Twenty-Four

Early the next morning, Daria sat in her living room in quiet agony. As they'd been doing off and on all night, tears coursed down her face. Her head pounded in time to the beating of her heart. Exhaustion shrouded her like a thick mist.

Thankfully, Nicki slept in blissful peace in the bedroom.

Daria inhaled a shaky breath and exhaled a prayer. "Lord, I need You. Please lift this weight from my spirit and heal my battered heart!" She swiped at her tears with a tissue and drew in a shuddering breath.

The telephone rang. She knew who it was before she lifted the receiver—Aunt Lenore. They were supposed to have a crab boil. She groaned. *I can't do that today.*

"Hello." Her voice was heavy and congested. She sniffed.

"Daria?"

She sniffed again. "Yeah." Her one-word reply swam in tears.

"Girl, what's wrong with you? What's going on over there?" Lenore's worry and concern embraced Daria.

She struggled to push words past her sobs. "Michael and Peaches…Last night, he…hit me with…He…He…hurt me so badly!" Daria ended on a wail.

"Oh, he did, did he?" Lenore's anger vibrated over the phone lines. "He hurt you?! I told him…We'll see about that! I'm on my way over there." Lenore disconnected the call.

The dial tone buzzing in Daria's ear mocked her. She grimaced. She'd badly mangled her explanation. She reached for the phone to call Lenore back, but pulled her hand back. *I'll do it when she gets here. Right now, I just want to be left alone.*

Michael lounged on his couch, flipping from one sports channel to the next. He didn't care what sport was showing. He just needed to "hear" the game. It helped him think.

He'd been in the same spot since he'd dragged himself home last night. He was in the same clothes and in the same frame of mind— stunned disbelief.

He, Michael Greer, was a father. How did he feel about that?

He'd lost the only woman who'd ever made his heart sing. How could he get her back?

Lord, the Bible promises that You'll never leave me or forsake me, but I feel like You've kicked me to the curb. Lord, where are You?

He'd never felt so alone in his life. He felt like he'd left a crucial part of himself with Daria.

He grunted. He was honest enough to admit that he was partly— well, okay, totally—responsible for the current mess. He'd attempted to deceive Daria. Therefore, he'd lied to her. Not verbally, but by his deeds—actions. Lying is a sin. Sin brings death. In this case, it brought death to his relationship with Daria. He ran his hands over his face and exhaled a loud gust of air.

In the back of his mind, he heard the fans roaring on the TV. He let out a derisive chuckle. Okay, he'd finally taken ownership of his actions. *Give the man a trophy!*

He earnestly repented and inexplicably, he felt God's presence with him again. His mind traveled back to a statement he'd heard a few Sundays ago. Pastor Wicham had said sin separates us from God. Genuine repentance removes the partition and restores the relationship. He'd heard the message with his natural ears, but his spiritual ears had missed it.

The fans on the TV roared again as their team scored.

What was he going to do about Nicki? It was a given that he was going to take care of her. She was his child. What form that caring was going to take was the question.

How was he going to get his woman back? How could he repair the damage that he'd done?

Lord, I'm at Your mercy. I'm clueless about what I need to do.

His ringing doorbell startled him, yanking his runaway thoughts to a halt.

He shot a dark look at the door. *Go away!* His next thought had him scrambling up off the couch. *It might be Daria!*

He snatched the door open and was rewarded for his haste by a baseball bat being poked in his stomach.

"Oof! Lenore!"...*and Clifford!*

"I told you we'd be visiting if you hurt my baby." Clifford connected with Michael's stomach again. "Did you listen? No!" Clifford jabbed Michael again. Lenore's eyes shot fire.

Michael backed up from the door with his hands raised. "Uh...Lenore, I can explain." He was embarrassed at the slight quaver in his voice. *This woman is crazy!*

Lenore closed the door behind her with her foot. She and Clifford were relentless in their pursuit.

"My baby told me you hit her. There's no acceptable explanation for that, so you can save your breath for your screams." Lenore bobbed her head.

"Hit her? I *hit* her?" Michael's eyes bugged with shock. "Lenore, I promise you. I've never struck a woman in my life."

Lenore narrowed her eyes at him.

Clifford stopped jabbing.

Lenore nodded her head once. She held Clifford in one hand and lightly slammed his "head" into the other. She repeated this movement for a few minutes.

"All right. Get to talkin', and it had better be good." Her tone told Michael his reprieve was a very short one.

"Would you care to sit down?" Michael gestured toward an armchair. *If she's sitting down, I'll have a head start if she comes after me again.*

"No!" Lenore snapped. "You just lost a minute."

Michael cleared his throat. "Um…what exactly did Daria tell you?" He took a few steps away from Lenore's immediate vicinity.

"She said something about you and Peaches. Then she said you'd hit her with something and hurt her." Lenore's face took on a thoughtful look. "Mind you, she was blubbering something fierce at the time."

Michael let out a gush of air. "I didn't *physically* hit her. I had to tell her some things last night that left her—both of us—reeling."

Lenore cocked a brow. "And those things would be?"

Michael moved a little further away from her, and his eyes darted to the door. *I wonder if I could get through the door before she could stop me.*

As though Lenore had read his mind, she shifted her position, and put herself between him and the door.

Clifford slammed into her hand.

Michael took a deep breath. "I found out last night that Nicki is my biological daughter."

Lenore's forehead snapped into angry lines. "You what?! What kind of foolishness is this?"

Michael told her everything that had transpired last night. How many times would he have to recite the tale of his stupidity?

When he'd finished, Lenore walked over to the before-offered armchair and sat down. She propped Clifford up against the arm of the chair—well within reach. "You young folk can sure do some *dumb* things." She shook her head in disgust.

Michael made a non-committal sound. He thought about some of the foolish antics he'd seen on the news lately involving the "aged" and snorted to himself. No way was he going to point that phenomenon out to her. He may be stupid, but he wasn't that brand of stupid.

Lenore, thankfully oblivious to the detour his thoughts had taken, said, "I told you!" Her hand sliced through the air. "Now, didn't I?" Her index finger pointed at him, emphasizing her question. "I told you not to lie to Daria. And what did you do? You lied to her. I thought you were smarter than that."

"Yeah…" Michael pulled on his earlobe. "Do you have any advice about how I can fix things with Daria?"

Lenore shook her head and rose from her seat.

Michael tracked her movements carefully. If she reached for Clifford in an aggressive manner, he was outta there.

Lenore picked up Clifford and walked toward the door. "Honey, all I can tell you to do is pray." When she was almost at the door, she turned to him. "What are you going to do about Nicki?"

"Beyond knowing that I'm going to take care of her, I don't know."

Lenore shook her head again. "Oh, what a mess! For Nicki's sake, I hope you and Daria get your acts together quickly."

Daria greeted Lenore at the door with a red-eyed, despondent stare. "Hi, Auntie." She didn't wait for Lenore to return her greeting. She turned and went back into the living room, where she plopped down onto the couch in an untidy heap.

Nicki sat in her seat, drooling and playing with her toes.

Lenore followed Daria into the living room. She leaned Clifford against the arm of the couch and stood looking down at Daria. "You're a mess." After making her pronouncement, Lenore sat in an armchair adjacent to the couch. "Have you showered and eaten?"

Daria sniffed. "No."

Lenore's brows climbed up her forehead. "Do you plan to?"

"I don't know." Daria sniffed again.

Lenore made an irritated sound. "Look here, Daria Alexis Simpson. You *cannot* let yourself go like this. You've got this baby to think about."

"I know, but it just hurts so badly," Daria whined.

Lenore rolled her eyes. "Yeah, I know. He hurt you. I went over there this morning ready to give Clifford some exercise on his head."

Daria sprang forward in her seat. "Oh, no, Auntie. Please tell me you didn't."

"Yeah, I did too. What did you expect to happen when you told me he'd hit you? You know I don't play that."

A frowned crinkled Daria's forehead. "But he didn't hit me. *I* wouldn't stand for that!"

"Well, I know that now. You were crying and going on so on the phone that I couldn't make out everything you were saying. And you know me, I protect my own."

She actually went after Michael with a baseball bat. This situation is going from bad to worse.

"Besides, from the sound of things, I'd say he could've used a little shakin' up." A smile played at the corners of Lenore's mouth.

Daria gave her a watery chuckle.

"Michael told me everything," Lenore continued after a moment. "This situation is something straight off the soaps." She pinched her lips together.

"Yeah, I guess you're right. But the pain feels very, very real."

Lenore pinned Daria with her eyes. "Daria, I've sorely regretted the damage Ralph did to you—now, more than ever."

What is she talkin' about now? Daria sent her a cautious look.

"Don't look at me like you don't know what I'm talking about. My brother lied at the drop of a hat if he felt it would help him to get what he wanted. You and your mother were disappointed repeatedly. The last lie he told Evelyn resulted in their deaths. You never got over that. Now it's coloring your reaction to this situation with Michael."

Daria's anger sparked and kindled. "Auntie, I have every right to be angry with Michael. He deliberately kept something very important from me." She sucked her teeth. "Humph, if it had happened to you, you'd be angry, too."

"All right. Watch yourself." Steel ran through Lenore's words. "Don't make me shake you up, too."

Daria exhaled. "I'm sorry."

"Child, why are you so angry? Because he had relations with Peaches? Because he didn't tell you about it? Or because he and Peaches had a child together? Just make sure that you're angry for the right reasons."

"I'm angry because he didn't tell me about it. He deliberately kept that from me." Daria made a slicing motion with her hand. "He deceived me."

"Honey, Michael is not your daddy. It's not fair to him for you to paint him with the same brush. First of all, Michael is a Christian. Your daddy didn't even pretend to be one. You need to ask yourself why Michael did what he did. What was his *intent*? Was he trying to hurt you? Was he trying to protect you in some way? Did he gain anything by keeping that information from you? If so, what?

"Frankly, I believe he was embarrassed by what had happened between him and Peaches and wanted to keep it buried. Think about it. Why would he tell you something about himself that would make him look bad in your eyes or hurt you in some way? If Peaches was still living, I don't doubt that this would have played out differently. He would have told you right away what had happened. Daria, he *is* an honorable man."

Daria shifted on the couch. "Maybe."

Lenore grunted. "Make sure you don't get yourself in trouble with the Lord by being bull-headed."

Daria gave Lenore a sullen look. "What's that supposed to mean?"

Lenore placed her hand on her hip. "It means, young lady, that you *have* to forgive Michael. You can't harbor unforgiveness in your heart and expect to keep your relationship with Christ intact."

"Maybe I'll be able to forgive him someday, but today is *not* the day."

"Mmm-hmm, just remember that tomorrow is not promised to you. And while you're trying to decide whether Michael deserves your forgiveness, think about all of the times you've needed somebody to forgive you."

Lord, You know I believe in keeping it real with You. You know where I'm at right now. I can't see past the pain Michael has caused me.

"Well, pray for me," Daria's said with a dismissive wave of her hand.

Lenore sucked in air through her teeth and narrowed her eyes. "You'd better get yourself together before I knock your teeth down your throat. Gather up Nicki's things. I'm taking her with me for the rest of the day. Depending on how our day goes, I may keep her overnight."

Daria was instantly contrite. *Ooh, I so don't like myself very much right now! I'm being ugly! Aunt Lenore doesn't deserve my ugliness. She's just trying to help.*

She expelled a huge sigh and dropped her shoulders. "I'm sorry, Auntie. Please, please forgive me."

Lenore cocked a brow at her. "Sure I will, honey. We *all* make mistakes sometimes."

Touché.

Daria dragged herself up off the couch and started to gather the things Lenore would need for Nicki. Lenore's words about forgiveness hounded her every step. She knew her aunt was right, but she couldn't—wouldn't?—let Michael get away with what he'd done.

Lord, please pull me up out of this dark place and help me to obey Your word!

Chapter Twenty-Five

B y noon, Michael had managed to find enough energy to shower, put on clean clothes, and get something to eat.

Thank God today's Saturday! He wouldn't have been worth a plastic penny to Kytech if he'd had to work today. He settled into his recliner and picked up the remote. He mindlessly flipped through the channels as his situation raced through his mind. Daria—how to win her back. Nicki—what to do about her.

His doorbell rang and momentarily halted the race. His eyes swung to the door. After this morning's visit from Lenore and Clifford, he was hesitant to answer it.

The doorbell rang again.

He frowned his displeasure at being bothered as he rose from his chair. This time, he looked through the security hole before opening the door.

"Hey, Auntie. Come on in." Michael eyed her warily. She could have any number of valid reasons for being there. But the grin on her face and something he couldn't quite define dancing in her eyes, told him that it had something to do with his present predicament.

He closed the door after Euvinia had moved through it.

"Come here and give me a hug. What kind of greeting is that for your favorite auntie?"

"I'm sorry. No disrespect intended." Michael gave her a half-hearted smile and a hug.

Whack!

Michael jerked back and grabbed the back of his head. "Hey! Why'd you do that?"

"Because you've earned it." Euvinia nodded her head once. "What's this I hear about you makin' babies when you ain't married?"

Michael groaned and lifted his eyes to the ceiling. "Calyssa's been running her mouth."

"Calyssa ain't told me nothin'. So, it's true? Nephew, I expected more from you. You were out there playing in the devil's playground. Didn't you know how to take care of business?"

Michael flushed with embarrassment. *We are not having this discussion!*

He was tired of explaining himself, but he knew his aunt wouldn't relent until he'd given her some kind of explanation for his behavior.

"Have a seat, Auntie." He pointed to the armchair Lenore had vacated earlier that morning. When she'd settled into the chair, he summed up the situation in a few succinct sentences.

"So, Daria broke up with you. I don't blame her one bit." Euvinia gave him a fierce frown. The twinkle in her eyes negated its ferociousness.

"Hey! Whose side are you on?"

Euvinia pointed her thumb in the direction of Daria's home. "Hers."

Michael shot her a disgruntled look, and she dissolved into knee-slapping laughter.

"C'mon, Nephew. You've got to admit that you made a big boo-boo. You messed up—big time."

Michael sent up a prayer for patience. "What about blood being thicker than water and all that?"

"You've got me there." Euvinia collapsed into another round of laughter.

"By the way, if Calyssa didn't tell you about my situation, who did?" Michael knew what her answer would be before he'd finished voicing the question.

"Lenore. She called me this morning after she left Daria's place." Euvinia shot him a sly look. "Lenore also told me you had a visit from Clifford this morning." Euvinia howled with laughter and slapped her knees.

After she'd calmed down, Michael said, "Auntie, you are enjoying my discomfort too much. I thought I was your favorite nephew."

Euvinia wiped her eyes with her hand. "You are my favorite nephew. I just don't think you've been very bright." She chuckled and wagged her head.

"Uh…does Moms know about this?"

Glee beamed from her eyes. "Not yet." She shot him a wink. "Give me about an hour."

Dread clawed its way up his spine. *The wrath of Amelia!*

"Would you consider *not* telling Moms about this?" Pleading filled his voice, and he begged her with his eyes.

Euvinia gave him a huge smile. "Not a chance." She rose to take her leave.

Michael trailed dejectedly after her to the door.

When she reached the door, she turned and held open her arms. "C'mon, give me a hug. I still love ya'. I won't hold your past against you."

Michael complied, but his thoughts were not charitable. *Humph. If you loved me, you wouldn't feed me to the lion—lioness.*

Whack!

Michael jerked upright and grabbed the back of his head. He knew he hadn't voiced his thoughts. He scowled. "Why'd you hit me this time?"

Euvinia's shoulders shook with suppressed laughter. "I just felt like it."

Sometimes I wonder whether she's all there.

He couldn't disrespect his aunt and tell her to get out. But, oh, how he wanted to. Instead, he opened the door and gently ushered her—shaking shoulders and all—out the door.

The ringing telephone jarred Michael awake. He woke up feeling disoriented. How he'd managed to fall asleep with his mind in such turmoil, he'd never know. He guessed his body had taken a siesta to get some much-needed rest.

He stared at the ringing phone, lying on the floor next to the couch. He gave his head a shake to clear it, but before he could get his act together and answer the phone, the answering machine picked up the call.

"Michael Allen Greer!"

His heart leaped into his throat. *Moms!*

"You had better be on my doorstep within the hour, or I'll be on yours." Amelia's voice said she'd brook no disobedience and promised dire retribution if she had to come looking for him. The click of her receiver reverberated around the room like a shouted Amen!

He screwed up his eyes and rubbed his forehead. *Lord, save me from the women in my life!*

His phone rang again. Just in case it was his mother calling back, he decided to let the answering machine pick up the call. He'd have to talk to her soon enough. He'd rather postpone that event as long as possible.

"Uh…Michael. This is Cal. Mom knows. Before you go jumpin' to conclusions, I want to let you know that I didn't tell her. She just called me and blistered my ears for keeping something this important from her. Little brother, you'd better get on over there and calm her down." Calyssa ended the call.

"Calm her down?" Michael grimaced. "Not without divine intervention."

After gathering his wallet and keys, he exited his home. He paused briefly and stared at Daria's door. He longed for just a glimpse of her. He let out a gusty sigh, then proceeded on his way to what felt like his execution.

He pulled into his mother's driveway with two minutes to spare. Before he could knock on the door, Amelia swung it open.

Her eyes, filled with anger and disappointment, pierced him like a dagger. Her disappointment flayed him way more than her anger.

"Get in here." Amelia gestured with a slight movement of her head and turned away.

Michael followed, his steps laden with dread.

She sat at the kitchen table and gestured for him to do the same. Before his bottom hit the seat, she began. "Tell me everything. Start at the beginning, and you'd better not leave anything out." Her voice dared him to disobey her.

Michael obeyed. He told her every humiliating detail.

Amelia shook her head. Disgust was written all over her face. "You played Russian Roulette with your life. You could've contracted a fatal disease. I know I taught you better than that! How could you do something so asinine?"

"But—"

"Boy, don't you talk back to me. You may be grown, but you're not *that* grown. I'll knock you up from this table!" Her eyes seemed to beg him to do or say something stupid, so she could follow through with the threat.

Michael sat as still and as mute as a statue.

"What are you going to do about my grandbaby?"

He stared at her in indecision. *Is she expecting an answer, or was that another rhetorical question?*

Amelia's hand slapped down on the table. "Answer me when I ask you a question!"

She'd expected an answer! "I don't know." From the tightened lines on her face, he knew he'd given her the *wrong* answer. He groaned.

"You don't know." She threw her head back and lifted her hands. "He doesn't know." She rose from her seat, placed her hands flat on the table, and leaned forward. The movement brought her closer to him—too close as far as he was concerned, given her threats to do him bodily harm. "You...don't...know?"

Amelia continued with narrowed eyes, "I'll tell you what you're going to do. You're going to fix this mess because Nicki *will* be raised as my grandchild." Her neck undulated with every sentence, adding power and strength to her words. "You'll do whatever you have to do to make that happen—pray, fast, beg, crawl, *whatever*. I...don't...care. But fix it you will! You got that?"

Despite the seriousness of their conversation, Michael was fascinated. *How do they do that?*

"Don't sit there looking at me like you've lost your mind. Answer me!" Amelia's eyes snapped.

"Uh...um...yes, ma'am." At her emphatic nod, he released the breath he'd been holding.

"Right answer! Now go and handle your business."

He sprang up out of the chair like somebody had lit a fire under him. He couldn't remember a time when he'd ever been so glad to get away from his mother. He walked to his car feeling like he'd gone ten rounds in the ring with a heavyweight champ.

He drove back to his place trying to find an answer to a burning question—how to get away from the women in his life. They wouldn't leave him alone. Why couldn't they understand that he needed time to wrap his mind around this situation? He didn't want to talk it to death. He just wanted to think.

The solution popped into his head as he pulled into the parking lot of his complex. He smiled. *I'm gettin' out of Dodge.*

He'd take the next available flight to Atlanta. Whether he wanted one or not, David was about to have a houseguest.

Chapter Twenty-Six

Sunday morning, Daria's rebellious eyes scanned the congregation for what seemed like the thousandth time. Once again, she brought them to attention and focused on the worship leaders singing on the platform.

I don't care one bit that he hasn't arrived yet. It means nothing to me. Humph. Right. She scoffed silently. *Keep thinking that, my girl, and it just might become true.*

At least she didn't have to worry about Lenore picking up on her inattention. After taking Nicki to the nursery, Daria had slipped into the back of the sanctuary and sat as close to the back as possible. She didn't have the heart to sit with Lenore and the Greers today. She wasn't ready to deal with their questioning and pitying looks.

The sanctuary doors swung open, drawing her eyes in that direction like a magnet. Her shoulders drooped in disappointment when the entrant wasn't Michael.

Daria, Ms. There is no us, you ain't nothin' but a fraud. You're sitting here about to give yourself whiplash looking for that man.

Daria grimaced when the worship leaders walked off the platform. She'd been so lost in herself that she'd missed the entire worship service. *Lord, forgive me.*

Pastor Wicham laid his Bible on the pulpit and then looked out over the congregation. "Today, I feel led by the Spirit to address a topic that is the Achilles heel of Christians everywhere—unforgiveness."

Daria squirmed in her seat. *Ooh, I should have stayed home.*

"We are careful to obey every command of God except that one. I Corinthians 5:6 asks a question that I want to put to you today: 'Do you not know that a little leaven leavens the whole lump?'"

Daria flushed with discomfort.

"There are no little sins and big sins with God. Sin is sin. Unforgiveness is sin, and it separates us from God. For many of you, it has halted the fullness of God's blessings in your lives. Brothers and sisters, the Bible tells us that if we don't forgive others, God will not forgive us." The pastor's earnest plea rang out over the congregation and hammered at Daria's heart.

"Unforgiveness is like a slow poison. It spreads through you, corroding and contaminating your soul, leaving bitterness and hatred in its wake." His compassionate eyes moved over the congregation and then seemed to rest on Daria, divining her innermost thoughts.

Now why is he looking at me? I wonder if the 'family' has been telling tales. Daria was immediately contrite for the unworthy thought. She knew they wouldn't discuss her and Michael and their situation with anyone outside of the family.

"I implore you to let it go," the pastor continued, "You are only hurting yourself. Release *yourself* today. Release God's blessings in your life."

Daria flushed with shame. Or was it irritation? Indignation? Conviction? She couldn't pinpoint the prevailing emotion. A war raged inside of her. She knew she should—had to—forgive Michael, but, at the same time, she wanted to punish him for his actions. If she forgave him, she felt like he'd be getting off scot-free.

"I know forgiveness is not an easy thing," the pastor said, "It's human nature to want to punish others for their offenses. We have to remember we've taken on a new nature. We live by a different set of rules. The Bible says vengeance belongs to God. Brothers and sisters, we are not God." He chuckled. "We'd be zapping people with lightening left and right if we were." The congregation emitted answering amens and chuckles.

Daria sat stock still, her emotions raw and exposed.

The pastor sobered and continued. "Some of you have held on to your unforgiveness so long that you don't know when it began. Yet it controls and shapes you." He paused and skimmed his eyes over the congregation as though trying to bore the truth into their spirits. "I want every head bowed and all eyes closed. Dig deep and reflect on what started you on the journey to the place where you are right now. Is it a childhood hurt, an abusive relationship, a cheating spouse, false accusations, or have you been mistreated? Whatever it is, lock in on it."

Daria trembled as her father's image formed behind her eyelids. The anger, disappointment, and hurt he'd caused her and her mother squeezed her heart like a vise.

"Mentally take everything you're feeling right now and place it in your hands." Tears and strong emotion filled the pastor's voice. "Now, I want you to lift your hands toward heaven and repeat after me. Lord, I lay my pain, heartache, and disappointments at Your feet. Heal me and fill those empty places in my soul with Your love. I forgive…say the name of the person or persons who have offended you. Forgive me for sinning against You and holding unforgiveness in my heart. Amen."

An earthquake shook Daria's foundations. Something momentous began to happen inside of her. She sat with tears streaming down her face.

The pastor continued. "Those of you who want help breaking through, come quickly to the altar, and I will pray with you."

Before he'd finished the invitation, Daria ran down the aisle. It's a wonder she didn't fall flat on her face because her tears blinded her. When she reached the altar, she fell to her knees, threw her head back, and lifted her hands to heaven in surrender.

As the pastor prayed with her, the negative emotions seeped out of her, and the band gripping her heart broke. Freedom and lightness filled her as her soul was renewed. "Ah, God, thank You!"

When she stood and turned to go back to her seat, she found that her family—Aunt Lenore, Aunt Euvinia, and the Greers—had surrounded her. They enveloped her in a group hug that was filled with overwhelming love and acceptance. She sobbed uncontrollably in their arms.

After church, the family stood in the parking lot talking. Nicki rested in the cushioned cradle of Amelia's arms.

Amelia touched Daria's arm and motioned for her to walk with her. "Daria, we all know that Nicki is Michael's daughter. Regardless of what happens between you and him, we want you and Nicki to remain a part of our lives. We love you. Not because of Nicki, or because you and Michael are…were dating, but because of who you are. You're a lovely person."

Daria flushed with pleasure at her words. "Thank you. I hope Michael and I can work this out." She paused, struggling to find the right words. "It's my fault that things have deteriorated between us. I wouldn't listen to his explanations, or forgive him." She exhaled. "I know it's no excuse, but the baggage I've carried around since my childhood was responsible for my actions. By God's grace, I believe I'm free from that now." She laid a hand on Amelia's arm. "With the Lord's help, Michael and I will work this out."

Amelia beamed at her and then kissed her on the cheek. "It will work out. I feel it in my bones. It will all work out."

"Is Michael okay? I haven't seen him since we quarreled on Friday."

"Pshhhh. Yeah, he's all right. He's run off to Atlanta 'to get away from the women in his life.'" Amelia chuckled. "We did come down on him pretty hard. He had to carry the weight of the blame by himself because Peaches is not available to share it with him. I mean, we can rail about her part in this—she was just as irresponsible as Michael—but what good will that do? The child is dead."

Amelia waved her free hand in the air. "Well, anyway, he'll be gone for a week. Let's see what happens when he returns. I know he'll do the right thing." She nodded her head once. "We'll just have to pray that the Lord gives him clarity while he's away."

Euvinia opened the car door. "Hey, Amelia, let's go." She placed one leg inside of the car. "You can call Daria after you get home. I'm ready to eat."

The group laughed.

Amelia rolled her eyes and chuckled. "I tell you, as much as that woman eats, she should be as big as a house. It's not fair. Just look at her. She's as slender as a teenager." Amelia waved at Euvinia, acknowledging her summons. She turned back to Daria. "Baby, just stay prayerful. The Lord will work it out. We'll all be praying with you."

Late Sunday afternoon, Michael navigated toward the baggage claim area of Hartsfield International Airport, keeping an eye out for David. They were supposed to rendezvous there after Michael's plane had landed.

He had just pulled his duffle bag off the conveyer belt when David approached. "Michael, my man, how are you?" David cuffed him on the shoulder.

Michael dropped his duffle bag, and they hugged each other with one hand clasped between them and the other draped across each other's shoulders. "Good to see you, man." Michael slapped David heartily on the back.

David stepped back, his black eyes demanding an explanation.

Michael knew he'd have to give David a reason for his impulsive visit sooner or later. Telling David that he needed to hole up in Atlanta for a few days was woefully inadequate, but he wasn't ready to talk about his situation yet. "Later."

David looked at Michael a moment longer and then nodded. "Okay. How long will you be staying?"

Michael exhaled his relief at the reprieve. "I've got a week. My boss was working this weekend, so I was able to clear everything with her before I left. I've worked a lot of overtime lately and knew I wouldn't have any problems getting the time off."

David grunted.

A smile stretched across Michael's face. "I see you're into the dome look." He took in David's bald head and neatly trimmed goatee.

David chuckled and rubbed his head. "Yeah. It was not by choice. I'd promised some of the kids I work with down at the community center that I'd shave my head if they got at least two A's on their report card." He stroked his goatee. "I grew this to add some contrast to my face. Man, it was strange looking at nothing but miles of brown skin every time I looked in the mirror." David hesitated and then asked, "I don't look too scary, do I?"

Michael slapped him on the back and gave a shout of laughter. "Nah, man. You're okay. That is, I don't believe you'll scare any small children."

Since his arrival five days ago, Michael had done a lot of thinking and praying, trying to come up with a plan of action.

David had had to work, so Michael had the place to himself. The most blessed thing of all was he didn't have to worry about being harassed by his women-folk. He could stew over his problem without being badgered for answers he didn't have.

He had two clear goals in mind: To be a big part of his daughter's life and to get Daria back. The million-dollar question was how to make them happen.

Daria's face flashed before his eyes. *Ah, I miss my woman!*

By day five of Michael's great escape, he was still no closer to a solution.

When David walked in the door that evening, Michael lifted his head from his sprawled position on the couch.

David lifted his eyes to the ceiling in exasperation and shook his head. "It's time, man."

A corner of Michael's mouth kicked up in a sheepish half-smile. "I know." Michael got up from the couch and ordered some pizza while David changed out of his suit.

After the pizza had been delivered and they'd started eating, Michael cleared his throat. "Do you remember Fruit Lady?"

"Of course. We've talked about her. Why?"

"Well…um…she was Daria's best friend. You know. The one that died." Michael swallowed hard.

David's brows snapped together, and he lowered the slice of pizza he'd been eating from his mouth. "Really?" Michael could imagine wheels turning in David's brain as he tried to connect the pieces of information.

"Yeah. See…uh…the thing is…I'm her baby's daddy."

The following silence was thick enough to cut with a knife. David looked at Michael like he'd sprouted two heads. "Please tell me you're jokin'."

Michael let loose a snort. "I wish. I know it's not true, but sometimes I feel like the Lord is jerking me around for His entertainment. When Daria and I broke up the first time, I prayed, and He told me to go back to her. Okay, I obeyed, and we patched things up. He is in control, David. He knows everything. He *knew* that all of this drama was coming. Just when I thought Daria and I had it all together…" Michael made the motion of jerking hard on a chain.

David chuckled softly. "Man, that's weak. You set this stuff into motion. You made your own choices. All of this is a result of the choices *you* made. But God *can* turn this around for your good."

Michael exhaled. "Man, you ain't telling me nothin' I don't already know. I'm just keepin' it real. Right or wrong, that's how I've felt at times. The way I see it…" Michael shrugged his shoulders, "…I might as well fess up. God knows about it anyway."

"True that," David said, then lifted the neglected slice of pizza to his mouth. "Let me guess, the night we met Fruit Lady, your brain took a siesta."

Michael's face burned with shame. "Yeah. That's it in a nutshell."

"That's why you refused to tell me what happened after I'd left that night." David shook his head and gave Michael a humorless chuckle. "That's messed up, man."

"You're telling me."

"How did you find out?"

Michael told him the details of his enlightenment and everything that had happened afterwards.

David guffawed at the activities of Lenore and Michael's family. He laughed so hard at Lenore's—and Clifford's—antics that Michael thought he'd tumble to the floor.

David dug the heels of his hands into his eyes and wiped away the tears. "Oh, man. I'd rather you than me."

"Yeah. Well, thanks." Michael's affront came through loud and clear in his voice. Okay, it was a little comical, but it wasn't *that* funny.

"I'm sorry." David held up his hands, trying to stifle his chuckles. "What can I do to help?"

"Pray," Michael responded earnestly.

David sobered. "That's a given."

"Other than that. I don't know what to do. I've been racking my brain, trying to find a way to fix this mess."

David gave him a commiserating grunt.

They ate in silence. The silence didn't bother Michael. He knew David had already started petitioning the Lord about the situation.

Suddenly, David's eyes—lit up from within—seemed to focus on something Michael couldn't see. "I feel compelled to tell you something," he said.

A shiver ran down Michael's spine. "Yes?"

"You are still in God's will. The Lord brought you and Daria together, but He's still preparing you for each other. Think about it." David's demeanor became intent. "Think about the changes that have occurred in you since you met her. You renewed your relationship with Him. You hooked up with her and then you broke up. How did you grow spiritually and as a person during that time? Okay, you guys got back together. You knew God brought you back together. And now you've broken up again. What have you learned about yourself this time? How has this experience changed you for the better?" David leaned forward, his elbows resting on the table. It seemed like he was trying to drill understanding into Michael with the forcefulness of his presence.

David continued. "I'm sure Daria has been shucking old baggage, too. I believe He's been dealing with her as well as you. When He finishes molding and stripping the two of you, you'll better fit together as a whole." David blinked several times, and his eyes sharpened on Michael. "Am I making sense?"

Michael's mind traveled back over the past months. He saw a journey of self-discovery, remorse, repentance, and renewal. David was right! Michael couldn't explain it, but everything in him embraced David's words as truth.

"Yeah! Man, I'm *feeling* what you're saying. That's it. That's the answer I've been looking for: Let go—be still—and let God. He's still in control. I've been searching for a course of action when the best course is no action at all."

David chuckled. "Good. Now you remember that speech so you can give it back to me when I find my lady."

Michael laughed, jumped up from the table, and pumped his fist in the air. "Ah, God is good!"

David's laughter joined Michael's. "That He is, my brother. That He is."

Michael looked at David. "It's time for me to go home."

Chapter Twenty-Seven

Saturday morning, Calyssa's excitement traveled over the phone lines into Daria's ear. "He's coming home today."

Daria's heart skipped a beat. "When did you hear from him? How did he sound? When will he be arriving?"

Calyssa laughed. "Slow your roll, Daria. He just called me. He was on his way to the airport. He sounded like he always does. Sorry, I can't help you there. Mmm, then again, his voice did sound a little lighter. He'll be arriving at three o'clock this afternoon." She paused. "So, what are you going to do about it?"

Daria frowned. "What do you mean? I'm hoping he'll be willing to talk to me when he gets here, but I don't have any specific plans."

"If I were you, and I wanted to see my man as badly as you do, I'd meet him at the airport."

Daria could just imagine Calyssa examining her nails as she threw out that little nugget.

"What if he's decided that he doesn't want to have anything further to do with me? What if he ignores me? We are talkin' big-time embarrassment here, Calyssa."

"Girl, you know that man loves you. Ain't no way my brother is going to dis you at that airport. Pshhhh, if anything, he'll start doing cartwheels at the sight of you." Calyssa's voice took on a cajoling tone. "C'mon, Daria. Go meet him and knock his socks off. If you do, it'll pay off, girl."

Daria hesitated. If she met Michael at the airport, she'd be laying all of her cards on the table. Her presence would shout, "I want you back!" Did she want to risk public humiliation? Then again, her being there might shock him so much that he wouldn't react negatively. *Oh, what to do? What to do? What to do?* The answer came to her in a flash. It was simple—whatever it took.

A smile spread across Daria's face. "I'll do it." Newfound confidence blossomed in her.

"Good." There was no mistaking Calyssa's satisfaction. "He drove himself to the airport when he left, so he doesn't need a ride home. I'll drive you out there, and you can ride back with him."

"Sounds like a plan."

Daria hung up the phone and stood with a big cheesy grin on her face. "I can't believe I'm going to do this. I've never taken this kind of initiative with a man before in my life." She turned and walked toward her bedroom. "But then again, Michael is not just any man. He's *my* man, and I'm going to get him."

She could almost hear Peaches in the background saying, "You go, girl!"

As his airplane approached the Orlando International Airport for landing, Michael wondered for the umpteenth time what turn his life would take next. Would Daria be ready to resume their relationship, or should he expect another round of visits from Lenore and his family? He quivered at the thought of receiving another visit from Clifford.

When bid to do so, Michael filed off the plane with the other pas-sengers. As always, the airport was crowded. He was glad he hadn't checked his duffle bag in Atlanta. At least he wouldn't have to wade through bodies to reach the baggage claims area.

He walked the long trek toward the exit with his head down, lost in thought. He inhaled deeply, then jerked his head up. *Daria?* He chuckled softly to himself. *Man, you've got it bad. You want to see her so bad that you're conjuring up the smell of her perfume.*

He started to lower his head again, and then he saw her. Every beautiful inch of her, standing just a few feet away from him. His steps slowed. The closer he got to her, the faster his heart raced. When he got a good look at her eyes, he thought his heart would pop right out of his chest. Her eyes were shining with tears and…love. Yes! Love!

He stopped in his tracks and dropped his duffle bag. Holding her gaze, he slowly opened his arms.

Daria quickly crossed the distance that separated them and launched herself into his arms. A mixture of laughter and sobs tore from her as she clutched him tightly.

Michael didn't think he could hold her close enough. "Daria. Daria. Daria." He felt a lone tear trail down his cheek. He put just enough space between them to allow him to look into her face. "Baby, I've missed you." He wiped at her tears with his hand.

"Oh, Michael, I'm so, *so* sorry. I was wrong. Please forgive me. I love you! I've missed you so much!" Fresh tears fell from her eyes.

"I love you, too, baby. Yes, I forgive you. Will you—can you—forgive me?" He searched her face intently.

Daria gave him a watery smile. "Yes. I can. I have."

Michael couldn't stand it any longer. He had to kiss her. Just one light, little kiss, he promised himself.

When his lips touched hers, a thick fog of heated pleasure enveloped him. He stepped back and searched her face. The same heat that he felt radiated from her eyes. *Lord, I'm in trouble.* He picked up his bag, grabbed her hand, and headed for the exit.

When they reached his SUV, he unlocked the door and stored his bag in the back. He walked Daria around to the passenger door. Instead of opening the door for her, he backed her up against it. He stared at her, drinking in her features. He cradled her face in his hands and kissed her. Daria returned his kiss with matching enthusiasm and intensity.

Michael groaned and broke the kiss. He removed his hands from her face and placed them on the truck on either side of her. He pushed himself back to put some space between them. Daria dropped her head to his chest, but left her arms around his waist. He looked off into the distance, trying to pull himself together. Monster alerts were clanging, but he felt powerless to heed them. Daria seemed to be in the same shape. Michael squeezed his eyes shut. *God, help us!*

"Daria?" His voice sounded heavy to his own ears.

"Hmm?" She didn't raise her head from his chest.

Michael moaned silently as her voice vibrated through him. "Where's Nicki?"

"With Calyssa." Daria's voice sounded dreamy. "She's staying there tonight."

Michael groaned. They didn't even have Nicki as a deterrent. "Uh, Daria, I need your help here."

Daria raised her head and looked at him. Her eyes scorched him. "I can't." His heart nose-dived to his toes.

Michael groaned again. "Let's go home." He moved back, maneuvered her out of the way, and opened the door.

After he climbed into the driver's seat, he placed the key in the ignition and sat staring off into the distance. Indecision tore at him. Finally, he put the truck into gear and started for home.

He'd arrived at a place with Daria where he'd never wanted to be while they were dating. The old Michael would've been elated. The new Michael was torn. On the one hand, if he allowed this day to take its natural course, he'd be putting their relationship with Christ in jeopardy. On the other hand, he loved this woman in a powerful way and wanted to express it.

He glanced over at Daria. She hadn't said anything since they'd left the airport. She was probably fighting the same battle.

It was imperative that they talk and clear the air. But he couldn't focus his mind on that right now. He needed to work this other unforeseen problem out…and *fast*. When he'd left Atlanta this morning, he'd had no inkling he'd be waging this kind of battle when he reached Florida. *Lord, help me to do the right thing.*

Snippets of his conversation with David popped into his mind. *You set this stuff into motion. You made your own choices. How did you grow spiritually and as a person during that time? How has this experience changed you for the better? When he finishes molding and stripping the two of you, you'll fit better together as a whole.*

Michael knew there was a message in there somewhere, but he was in no frame of mind to puzzle it out. *Lord, if You're trying to tell me something, You're going to have to hit me over the head with it. All I can see clearly right now is that I'm supposed to deny myself something that I want real bad. Not only that, but within the next five minutes or so, I'm expected to find a way to lead…us…out…of this temptation.*

He—Michael—could make the choice to move them past these treacherous waters. He could take on the mantle of being the spiritual leader in their relationship and lead them out of this situation. He had every intention of marrying Daria. He also intended to fill the role that God had established for him and be the spiritual leader in their home when that day came. The time to take on that responsibility was now—not later. If he messed this up, there might not *be* a later.

After they arrived at their complex, Michael retrieved his bag from the back, captured Daria's hand, and walked to her door.

She inserted her key into the lock and opened the door. She turned to face him with questions in her eyes. He knew she wanted to know where this was going.

He placed his bag at his feet and lightly touched her arm. "I can't go in there, Daria. If I do…I just can't. Do you understand what I'm trying to say?"

The corner of her mouth kicked up in a smile that he had to strain to see. "Yeah." A contrast of relief and disappointment filled her voice and played on her face.

"We need to talk, but not right now. I could call you, but I'd rather not do it that way. Are you okay with that?" Michael searched her face.

She nodded and exhaled. "It's for the best. It's the *right* thing to do."

Michael picked up his bag. Instead of moving away as he'd intended, his hand took on a life of its own and slowly caressed her face. A car door slammed in the parking lot, shattering the moment. He yanked his rebellious hand down to his side and took a step back.

Daria grabbed him by the front of his shirt and pulled him to her. She planted a swift, hard kiss on his lips and then released him. She stepped inside of her doorway, and, before closing the door, shot him a smile and a saucy wink that he felt all the way down to his toes.

Michael laid his palm on the closed door. After taking several deep breaths, he moved away from the door, then turned for home. "Lord, if You're going to be giving out crowns for sacrifices in heaven, I deserve one of the biggest crowns You've got for this."

Daria woke up the next morning with a smile on her face. Michael was back!

Her smile dimmed a few watts when she thought about their reunion. She'd never experienced anything like that before. The intensity. The passion. What she had felt overrode everything. Everything else diminished in significance. If Michael hadn't taken on the leadership role yesterday, she knew she would've been lost. *Now,* she understood why Christians failed so often in this area. She'd stood on the precipice herself.

Her respect for Michael had increased a few notches yesterday. She wanted a man who could take care of her. She didn't mean monetarily—of course, that's *not* a bad thing,—but emotionally, physically, and spiritually. It had to have been very hard for him to walk away from her, but he'd done it, saving the both of them from making a disastrous mistake.

The phone rang, interrupting her thoughts.

"Well?"

Daria laughed at Calyssa's disgruntled one-worded question. "I can't get a thing out of my brother. I think he's getting a lot of enjoyment out of keeping me in suspense."

"It's all good, Calyssa. It's all good."

"I knew it!" Calyssa's genuine delight zipped into Daria's ear. "I'm happy for you guys. That's all I wanted to know. When do you want me to bring Ms. Nicki home?"

"Can you keep her until this evening? Michael and I haven't really had a chance to talk yet."

"Ya'll haven't talked yet? What *did* ya'll do all evening and last night?" Curiosity laced Calyssa's words.

"Um…we didn't spend that time together. We…couldn't." Embarrassment heated Daria's face.

"Why?…Oh." Calyssa giggled. "Girl, I've been there. It's a tough row to hoe, ain't it?"

Daria chuckled. "Mmm-hmm."

"Just call me when you're ready for Nicki. We'll probably be hangin' out at Mom's today."

"Okay. Thanks, Calyssa."

After Daria ended the call, she decided to get dressed. She had no idea what time Michael was going to show up, but she wanted to look her best whenever he did.

She had just finished her breakfast when Michael arrived. When she opened the door, he greeted her with a kiss on the cheek. *So, we're back to that are we?* She was disappointed, but common sense told her that it was *definitely* for the best.

Once they got past the "how are you's," he suggested that they go to the park and have their talk there.

Daria agreed, and Michael drove them to Jay Blanchard Park. Fortunately, they were able to find a vacant bench in a sparsely populated area.

"Michael, I want to go first." When he nodded, she continued, "On Sunday, Pastor Wicham preached a message on unforgiveness. I *heard* the message and realized that I had severe problems in this area because of my experiences with my father. I'd never forgiven my father for his lies, for disappointing me, and more importantly, my mother's death. The seeds of that unforgiveness sprouted in my relationship with you and almost destroyed it."

She stopped and placed her hand on his face. "I've been set free. Free to experience the joy of the Lord's blessings." She smiled into his eyes. "You and Nicki are the blessings He's placed in my life."

Michael leaned in close, gave her a quick, butterfly-soft kiss on her lips, then moved away. "When you told me we were over, I was devastated. Daria, I don't ever want to feel that way again. I spent almost every waking moment trying to figure out how I was going to get you back." He squeezed her shoulders. "I know I hurt you, and I deeply regret that. I can't promise you I'll never hurt you again. But I can promise with a certainty that I'll never, *ever* intentionally hurt you. I love you, Daria. You're everything to me." He raised her hands to his lips and placed a soft kiss upon each of them.

A wave of pleasure washed over her. *Oh, yeah, the park was the right place to have this talk.*

"About Nicki," he went on, "Peaches wanted you to raise Nicki, and I respect that. I don't think she could've chosen a better mother for my child. I want to be a big part of Nicki's life. I don't want to just wear the title of father. I plan to *be* a father to her."

Is he about to do what I think he's about to do? Daria's heart felt like it was going to hammer its way out of her chest. "Yes!" trembled on her lips.

Michael shifted a little on the bench, moving closer to her. He cleared his throat. *Oh, be still my heart. Here it comes!*

Michael squeezed her hands, then released them with a soft caress. "Daria, will you…"

Her hands flew to her chest to keep her heart from bursting through.

"Will you be comfortable with that?"

Talking about a letdown! This is the queen of all letdowns! She deflated like a balloon that had sprung a leak.

"Yes," she said around the lump of disappointment lodged in her throat. "I'd be upset if you'd decided to do less."

"Good!" Michael said with satisfaction. "It's been a while since Peaches' memorial service. Have you heard anything more from Otis about Peaches' estate?"

Daria tried to switch gears, so she could give him an intelligent answer. Her mind was still stuck back on that marriage proposal that didn't happen. "Um…he called last Tuesday to tell me that everything had finally fallen into place. I'll be meeting with him on Friday to sign the final papers." She turned and looked into his face. "I want to get Nicki settled into the nursery Peaches prepared for her—as soon as possible."

"How soon are you planning to move?"

"I was thinking maybe next Saturday."

"Will you be ready by then?"

"Yes. Peaches' home is already furnished, so I'm not taking any furniture."

"Have you decided what you're going to do with your place?"

They had kicked around a couple of ideas before their breakup, but Daria hadn't come to a solid decision on what she was going to do with her home.

"I've decided to rent it. If I leave the furniture, I can rent it furnished."

"That'll work. What do you want me to do?"

"I know you'd move us over there, but I don't want you to spend your entire weekend moving us into Peaches' house. I'm going to hire a moving company."

"Are you sure you want to do that? I'm more than willing to move your things over there."

"Positive. Peaches has already purchased Nicki a baby crib, but it's not assembled. I'd really appreciate it, if you'd put that together for me."

Michael smiled. "Yeah? How much?"

Daria returned his smile. "More than you can imagine."

"Hmm, sounds promising." He leaned in close and kissed her on the cheek. He moved back a little, searched her face, and then brushed his lips lightly over hers. The banked fire in his eyes roared to life, and he groaned. "Let's go and get our little chaperone."

Daria's giggles floated in the air as they walked hand-in-hand to his truck.

Chapter Twenty-Eight

The movers were scheduled to be at Daria's place at seven o'clock Saturday morning. Fifteen minutes before they arrived, Michael was standing at her door.

Daria opened the door with a smile. "Good morning." She and Michael exchanged cheek-kisses. "I believe Nicki and I are ready."

"Great. I have something for you and Nicki." He handed her a large shopping bag.

"Ooh, a present. We love presents, don't we, Nicki?"

Nicki sat in her seat with her foot in her hand, watching them.

Daria reached into the bag and pulled out a baby pouch. She'd seen parents with these contraptions strapped to their waists and had thought they were the coolest things.

"This is fantastic! Now I can carry Nicki around and still have the use of both hands. Thank you, Michael." Daria rewarded him for his thoughtfulness with another kiss on the cheek.

He smiled and winked. "Anything for my two ladies."

Ooh, I love this man!

"How are you this morning, princess?" Michael lifted Nicki from her seat and bussed her on her tiny cheek. She cooed in response.

Surprisingly, the movers showed up on time. After they'd finished loading the truck, Daria looked around one more time to make sure she hadn't forgotten anything.

When she was satisfied that she had everything she intended to take with her, they left for her new home. With Nicki strapped in her car seat in the backseat, Daria led the procession. The movers followed them, and Michael brought up the rear in his SUV.

Daria arrived at the house and found Lenore, the Greers, and Craig Adams—a close friend of the Greers and member of Prayer Tabernacle—standing outside waiting for them.

"Nicki, we've got plenty of help," she said. "It's not going to take long to get moved in." Daria parked on the street, so the movers could back into the driveway.

"Good morning," Calyssa greeted Daria, then opened the rear door of the car and removed Nicki from her car seat.

"Hi! I didn't expect you guys to be here."

"Now you know better than that," Calyssa gently chided. "There's no way we'd leave you to undertake this move by yourself."

"Thank you." Daria gave her a hug. The perpetual worry in Calyssa's eyes seemed more pronounced. "Are you okay? How's Alex?"

Calyssa blew out a deep sigh. "His condition hasn't changed. Sometimes it weighs heavier on me than others." She twisted her lips. "But Brandon and I are okay." She blinked away unshed tears. "Thanks to Craig's financial advice, we don't have any money worries. And Alex's health insurance has been paying cash benefits since he lost earning power."

Daria squeezed her hand. "You know I'm here for you if you ever need anything or just want to talk."

Calyssa returned the squeeze. "I know."

They turned and walked toward the rest of the group. "Where's Brandon?" Daria asked.

"I let him sleep over at Stefan's last night. He'll be spending the day there as well, so I can help you without him being underfoot."

Daria's eyes scanned the group and came to rest on Craig. "I'm surprised to see Craig today. When did he get back in town?"

"Last night." Calyssa made a face. "That man works too hard. His computer-software consulting business is doing very well. I keep telling him he needs to shift more responsibility to his staff." Calyssa breathed out a loud sigh. "He won't listen." Her brow crinkled. "It's almost like he's…driven."

After Daria greeted the group in general and thanked them for coming to assist her, she turned to Craig, clasped her hands together under her chin, and batted her eyelashes at him. "I am truly blessed to have such a personage as yourself, Mr. Mel Jackson, take time out of your busy schedule to help little ol' me."

Craig's caramel-colored skin did nothing to hide the glowing tips of his ears. "Now, see, why'd you have to go there? Don't start that Mel Jackson stuff. I don't look like that dude. I look like myself." His dark-chocolate eyes begged her to drop the subject.

Standing close enough to overhear Daria, Calyssa chuckled. "You're a dead ringer for him. For the last three months, you've been in Chicago, Texas, and Hawaii. Tell the truth. How many times were you asked for an autograph?"

Craig shot her a disgruntled look. His lips curved up in a slight smile, and he stroked his neatly trimmed goatee. "I'd rather not say."

Daria chuckled and lightly touched his arm. "It's really good to see you. I appreciate your coming to help me."

"I called Calyssa to ask about Alex, and she brought me up-to-date. There's been a lot going on. I'm sorry for your loss."

"Thanks—"

"Hey, get away from my woman!" Michael yelled as he crossed the yard toward them.

Craig pitched his voice so that it would carry to Michael. "Daria, I've always liked and respected you. But for taming him…" He gestured in Michael's direction with his thumb. "…you have my undying gratitude."

Michael placed his arm across Daria's shoulders and laughed. "All right. Your day will come. One day, some lady's going to send you into a tailspin, and you won't know what hit you."

Something flashed in Craig's eyes before he chuckled and extended his hand to Michael. "Seriously, I'm happy you two found each other."

Michael grasped Craig's hand and gave it a firm shake. "Thanks, man."

A teasing light twinkled in Craig's eyes. "Daria, if he steps out of line, just let me know, and I'll set him straight for you."

Daria grinned. "I don't think I have to worry about that because I believe he's afraid of Aunt Lenore."

Michael grunted. "You've got that right. That old lady and her sidekick, Clifford, are formidable foes."

Craig sent Michael a commiserating look. "I don't blame you, man. I'm a little afraid of her myself."

Lenore stood at the front door with her hands on her hips. "Look, y'all can talk later. Daria, come and open the door, so I can sit down."

Daria gave her an indulgent smile. "Sit down? Auntie, I thought you came over here to help me move."

"I did. Every job needs a supervisor." Lenore pointed her thumb at her chest and nodded her head once. "I'm the supervisor."

The group laughed and moved into the house.

"No. Man, that's the wrong way. It goes this way." Michael repositioned a section of crib to demonstrate. For the last hour, he and Craig had been trying—without much success—to assemble Nicki's crib.

"No, this is right. The screw goes here." Craig pointed with his screwdriver to a hole in the wood.

Calyssa walked into the room. "Do you two know what you're doing? You should have that thing together by now."

"We've got this. Just go on back in there and let a man do a man's job." Michael waved her away.

Calyssa picked up the discarded assembly instructions from the floor. She looked back and forth between the instructions and what Craig and Michael had done so far. "If you two would bother to read the instructions, you'd see you're not doing that right." She sucked her teeth in disgust. "Men! What's so difficult about reading the instructions?"

Craig held out is hand. "Give me that." When she complied, he pointed toward the door. "Bye, Cal. See you later. We'll call you, if we need you."

"Get out," Michael added bluntly.

Calyssa chortled and left the room.

Michael and Craig looked at each other and started laughing.

"She's right, you know," Craig said.

"Yeah, but we don't have to tell her that."

"So Michael, just how serious are things between you and Daria?"

"Very, why do you ask? Are you interested in her? If so, back off."

Craig smiled. "No, it's nothing like that. Can't a brother ask a question?"

Michael returned his smile. "I just wanted to make sure you understood the lay of the land."

"All I ask is that you give me enough time to air my tux before the wedding."

Michael shot him a speaking look. "Stop fishin'."

"Just a word of advice: If you love her, tell her. Don't put it off. Never take it for granted that she'll always be there. You may wake up one day and find that she's no longer available. It's a devastating thing to watch the lady you love marry someone else." Craig's voice held undertones of sadness.

"You sound like you're speaking from experience. I've known you since we were kids, and I don't remember you having a serious relationship with anybody. Have you been keeping secrets? Who is she?"

Craig laughed. "Now who's fishin'?"

Michael knew he wouldn't get any answers out of Craig about his mystery lady, so he dropped the subject.

It took them another hour, but they finally finished assembling the crib. They were clearing away the boxes and tools when Daria popped her head in the door. "Nice. You guys did a good job. I've ordered some pizza, and it's just arrived. Come into the kitchen and get something to eat."

When Michael entered the kitchen, Euvinia asked, "Have you finished putting that crib together yet?"

Michael gave her a sideways look. "We just finished."

"Humph, well, it's about time. Did you and Craig have to go out and cut down trees to make the frame?" Euvinia laughed at her own sally.

"Give us a break, Auntie. That was hard work."

"Yeah, give us a break," Craig said, helping himself to a slice of pizza. "That bed has a very intricate design. It was very complicated to put together."

His comments earned him a snort from Lenore. "Yeah, right."

Michael looked over at Daria. She was standing at the counter feeding Nicki. He could tell something was bothering her. She was laughing along with them, but her eyes were sad.

He went over to her and asked softy, "Are you okay?"

"I was just thinking about Peaches. I'll always remember that she died in this kitchen."

He draped his arm around her shoulders. "I know you will, but you can create some happy memories for Nicki in her mother's kitchen."

Daria gave him a half-cast smile. "You're right. I'll be okay."

Michael kissed her and then Nicki on the cheek.

He looked at the others sitting around the kitchen table with a sense of contentment. *My family.*

Craig reached for another slice of pizza, and Michael said, "Man, don't take all of it. Save some for the rest of us." The laughter in Michael's voice nullified the seriousness of the rebuke.

"Hey," Craig replied with a shrug. "You snooze, you lose."

By five o'clock that evening, the group had finished placing everything where Daria wanted it.

They helped her pack up Peaches' clothing and personal items. Daria decided to donate the clothing to the church, so they could be sold at the next church bazaar.

She'd go through Peaches' personal items later and choose some things to keep for Nicki.

It had been a long day, and everybody was starting to leave. Daria and Nicki walked out to the driveway to see them off.

"Whew, I'm tired." Lenore opened her car door and threw her purse into the passenger seat.

Michael cocked a brow at Daria and said with a teasing note, "I don't know why she's so tired. She didn't do nothin' today, but criticize and give orders—'You're doing that wrong. What's taking you so long? Put that over there. Pick that up.' You'd think she was a drill sergeant."

Daria giggled.

Lenore narrowed her eyes at him. "Watch your mouth and save your teeth, young man. I may be tired, but I'm not too tired to show you a thing or two."

Craig let loose a loud guffaw. "Man, you'd better leave her alone. I'd hate to have to take you to the hospital and explain to the doctors that a lady beat you up."

Euvinia cackled and slapped her thigh. "Lenore, cut him some slack. He must have fried his brain trying to figure out how to put Nicki's bed together; else he wouldn't have said that—at least not within your hearing anyway."

Amelia looked on with an indulgent smile.

Calyssa chuckled and opened the front passenger door of her car. She pulled out a bag and handed it to Daria. "I almost forgot to give these baby monitors to you. You can put one in Nicki's room and keep the other one with you. They'll help to alleviate some of the worries you may have about her sleeping alone in a separate room."

"Thanks. We have been sleeping in the same room, and I'm concerned about her sleeping in the nursery by herself."

After the others had left, Michael walked back into the house with Daria and Nicki. "I'm going to leave as well. Are you sure you have everything you need?"

"Yes. We'll be fine."

"Bye, Nicki." He kissed Nicki's cheek.

He looked into Daria's eyes. "I'm going to miss having you close by." He kissed her on the cheek, and then pulled her close.

She smiled. "I'm going to miss you, too."

Nicki tolerated being squashed between the grown-ups for about a minute. Then she squirmed and bicycled her legs.

Michael moved back from Daria and looked down at Nicki. Nicki gave him a big gummy grin.

Michael chuckled. "Our little chaperone."

Chapter Twenty-Nine

Two months later, Michael stood in Daria's foyer waiting for her to finish getting ready for their date.

He flicked a glance at his watch. "Daria, we need to get going."

"Okay. Okay. I'm ready." Daria pulled on a light jacket over her knit top. She didn't know where Michael was taking her. He'd just told her to dress comfortably. She was dying of curiosity, but she was trying to play this by his rules and not pester him for details. "We're leaving," she called to Calyssa who was giving six-month-old Nicki a bath.

Brandon barreled out of the den at full speed. "Bye. See ya later. Bring me somethin' back, Uncle Michael."

Michael rubbed Brandon on the head.

Quickly losing interest, Brandon returned to the den where cartoons could be heard blaring on the TV.

Michael had volunteered Calyssa for babysitting duty, so he could give Daria this night out. Calyssa stepped out of the bathroom with a towel-wrapped, giggling Nicki in her arms. "Bye. Have fun you guys."

Nicki flapped her arm. "Ba." Her attempt to mimic Calyssa earned her beaming smiles of approval from the doting grown-ups.

Daria rewarded Nicki with a kiss on her cheek. Michael blew a raspberry on her tummy, causing her to squirm and shriek with delighted laughter.

Michael drove them to Lake Eola Park in downtown Orlando where some sort of festivities were taking place. A half hour later, he pulled into a parking space and turned to Daria with his arm resting across the steering wheel. "There's a Festival of Nations this evening in the park. It features several countries and some of the products and foods of those countries. I know how much you want to go to Europe, so I thought you'd enjoy this."

Daria smiled and grabbed Michael's hand. "This is great! Of course I'll enjoy it."

Each country represented was assigned an area of the park. The names of the countries were prominently displayed. If food was being offered, they had a small sitting area set up as well.

The first "country" Michael and Daria came across was England. They took their time smelling the different English perfumes and soaps. Daria really loved the lavender and rose-water fragrances.

In France, they enjoyed the antics of three mimes. The sitting area resembled a quaint, outdoor café.

They stopped in Germany and marveled at the beautiful hand-painted eggs. They were both hungry, so they decided to sit for a while and eat schnitzel.

After they left Germany, they went to Italy and sampled the Italian chocolates. By the time they left there, it was eight o'clock.

The final event of the festival was a fireworks display. The show was scheduled to begin in half an hour. Michael found them a bench located some distance away from the crowds, so they could watch the fireworks comfortably.

Music played by a live orchestra accompanied the fireworks. When the show ended, Daria turned to Michael. "Absolutely fascinating. The way the pyrotechnics and music worked together was awesome." She started to stand, thinking they would join the general exodus leaving the park.

Michael caught her hand to stop her. "Let's wait until the crowd disperses before we leave." When she sat down, Michael put his arm around her shoulders.

She snuggled into his side. "This has been wonderful, Michael. I've really had a good time."

"I'm glad you enjoyed it. I did, too, but what I enjoyed most was being with you."

"Oh, Michael, you say the sweetest things." She kissed him on the cheek and looked into his eyes.

A small flame flickered in their depths and ignited. "I know you want to go to Europe someday," he said. "That's been put on hold for now, but I tried to give you a little taste of it today." He placed a light kiss on her temple. "Daria, I love you so much. I can't imagine life without you."

Overwhelming joy and happiness swept through her. Tears filled her eyes. "I love you, too, Michael."

Michael cleared his throat. "Daria, would you…"

Her heart took off like a runaway train. *Is he about to…Nah, uh-uh, I'm not setting myself up for another major letdown.*

He reached into his pants pocket and pulled out a small, black velvet box.

Th-Thunk!

Her heart pounded and butterflies took flight in her stomach. *Girl, calm down. That doesn't mean a thing. A small, black box does not equate to a marriage proposal. Anything could be in that box—earrings, a brooch. Don't do this to yourself.*

He flipped the lid open, and she almost fainted. A heart-shaped, solitaire diamond mounted on a platinum band winked at her. She blinked several times to make sure she wasn't seeing things.

"Daria, would you marry me? I'll love and cherish you for the rest of my days."

"Yes! Yes, I'll marry you!" She couldn't get the words out fast enough.

"Ah, baby. I promise you won't regret it." He slipped the ring onto her finger, pulled her close, and kissed her deeply.

When they came up for air, she gazed into his eyes and said, "A lot has happened since the Lord brought you into my life. Some of it has been very painful. Some of it has been joyous. But I have to say, having you in my life has brought me many unexpected pleasures."

Epilogue

One year later, Michael and Daria sat on the same bench they'd sat on that special night when he'd asked her to marry him. She basked in contentment and in his love, as she thought about their wedding and family.

After receiving the long-awaited proposal, she'd put together the fastest and classiest wedding she could plan in two months. She hadn't wasted any time before marching her man down the aisle.

Of course, Michael hadn't minded the speed of the preparations one bit. As far as he'd been concerned, "The sooner the better." Marriage meant no more monster alerts.

It had been a beautiful wedding. Michael had stood at the altar and watched her walk toward him with love and anticipation shining in his eyes. She'd felt like a queen that day—*his* queen. *Still do.*

Sculpted by adversity, their relationship was very fulfilling. It was grounded in friendship, love, honesty, and trust. She trusted him in a way that she never *ever* thought she'd be able to trust a man. *Thank God for His liberating power!*

David had been Michael's best man. He seemed to enjoy getting to know the family. The aunties, Lenore and Euvinia, kept him in stitches.

He'd had a few dicey moments that put a haunted look in his eyes at the wedding reception. When Michael had asked him what was wrong, he'd responded, "Man, I don't know how you could stand it. These sisters are looking at me like I'm a choice cut of prime rib. Look at their eyes. I tell you, I've seen a few of them licking their lips. Man, I've got to get back to A-town. At least there, I'll be on my home turf and can safely navigate around the danger zones."

Peaches' legacy and Michael's hefty income allows Daria be an at-home-mom, free of money worries. She'd initially thought she'd have difficulties adjusting to being unemployed. Not so. Her familial obligations keep her hopping.

Little Nicki is flourishing under her parents' nurturing love. She has her daddy wrapped securely around her pinky. Mom isn't quite so indulgent, though. Her grandmother, Amelia, is perfectly content to spoil her rotten, and then send her home with her parents.

Although Peaches has been dead for over a year, she has in no way been forgotten. She lives on in Daria's heart. The memories they created together through the years are vivid in her mind, periodically eliciting feelings of deep sadness.

The aunties are still bosom buddies. They haven't taken their European vacation yet. They're in a perpetual planning stage. Michael frequently teases them about that, saying the reason they haven't gone on the vacation is because they're afraid something is going to happen while they're gone, and they'll miss it. Of late, they seem to have taken a keen interest in Sonja Grey, one of the singles at Prayer Tabernacle. There's no telling what prompted this new interest, but knowing those two, it'll be revealed soon enough.

Aunt Lenore still has her sidekick, Clifford. Every now and then, she trots him out to remind Michael of his existence. Her reason: "Just in case he gets stupid."

Aunt Euvinia hasn't stopped sporting elaborate hairdos and neon-colored tracksuits. Her laughter is as ready as ever. Well, except for the time Michael suggested she might want to hook up with a deacon at their church who'd been giving her the eye. That day, her laughter turned into an imposing scowl. She told him, "Boy, have you lost your mind?! Humph, when he walks on water or turns it into wine, give me a holla. Then, I *might* consider it for 'bout a minute."

There is one dark spot—Alex is still in a coma. The family's still hoping for the day when he'll wake up and praying it'll be soon. It's painful to watch Calyssa struggle to stay upbeat for Brandon day after disappointing day. The only time her worries seem to lighten is when Craig is in town. His presence seems to bring her a measure of peace and comfort.

Craig. That good-looking brother is *still* single. His company's prospering, and, despite Calyssa's nags to slow down, the amount of time he spends out of town on business trips hasn't decreased. But when he is in town, he's either at Alex's bedside, holding a spot at Amelia's dining room table, sitting with the family during church, or just being a rock for Calyssa and Brandon.

What does the future hold for this family? Daria didn't know, but she was confident that come what may, their faith, friendship, and love would see them safely through.

www.ingramcontent.com/pod-product-compliance
Lightning Source LLC
Chambersburg PA
CBHW020405120726
47904CB00002B/710